Pieces
OF
Perfect

# Pieces

OF

# Perfect

LOVE LESSONS BOOK ONE

# ELIZABETH
# HAYLEY

WATERHOUSE PRESS

*For our husbands, who provide us with a constant source of inspiration.*

# chapter one

"Do you have your boarding pass printed, ma'am?"

Ma'am? *Ugh, when did I become a ma'am? I'm only twenty-seven for Christ's sake.* "Yes, it's here somewhere." Placing my Vera Bradley carry-on on top of my suitcase, I fumbled through my purse. "Give me a minute." I heard the agitation in my voice.

*Breathe, Lily. It's not this woman's fault that you lose everything.*

"Sorry. Rough night." It had been rough, all right. My parents had practically begged me to come out to Colorado to spend Christmas break with them at their home in the mountains. Well, at least my mom had. But as soon as they picked me up from the airport, they both went off on a tirade about my career. I just wanted to shout at them, "I get it. I'm a huge fucking disappointment. Can we move on now?" But they wouldn't. Of course they wouldn't. They're lawyers. Reasoning with them was useless.

"Would you like me to print you another boarding pass?" The line behind me increased, and I could feel the intense stare of the weary woman behind the counter, who was about as impressed with me as my parents were.

"No, I swear I have it right here." Though I clearly *didn't* have it right there. I pulled my purse onto my shoulder as I stooped to look inside my carry-on, ignoring the exasperated sigh of the woman before me.

I grabbed my bag off the top of my suitcase, unzipping it simultaneously. But when I went to plop it onto the ground, I quickly morphed from well-dressed professional to sideshow attraction. As I lowered my carry-on, my bracelet snagged on the zipper of my suitcase, wrenching it open and causing it to slam to the floor and eject my clothing in every direction.

I shook my head slightly as I looked up to heaven, sarcastically thanking God for making me his own personal comedy sketch show. As I bent down quickly to pick up my clothes, along with my dignity, I felt my face flush. I surveyed the wreckage I'd caused, when I noticed that some of my clothing had landed on the feet of the man behind me. Too humiliated, I hadn't bothered to look up at him yet. Seeing my boarding pass, I pulled it out and frantically began shoving everything that had fallen out into every available compartment, including inside my carry-on.

"Oh, fuck me," I muttered under my breath. *Could this day possibly get any worse?*

"Well, that's pretty presumptuous. I usually insist on a drink first." A deep voice coughed back a subtle laugh and extended a strong hand for me to grab. "Did you find what you were looking for?"

"Yes, I . . ." Finally glancing up at him as I finished collecting my belongings, I found possibly the bluest eyes I had ever seen were flashing back at me. "I . . . I found what I was looking for," I stumbled over my words. Fuck, did I ever? This man was gorgeous. So gorgeous that I was willing to overlook his sexually charged response.

He pushed his dark, wavy hair away from his square-jawed face as he looked down at me, the left corner of his smooth pink lips revealing an amused smirk that he made no effort to conceal.

*Why is he smiling at me like that?* Then, realization hit me. *Because you're still on the ground, asshole.*

I managed to compose myself as he grasped the side of my arm firmly, helping me to my feet. Maybe *lifting* me to my feet would be more accurate. *Damn, he's strong.* The skin on his hands was soft, but I took note of his muscular fingers. *What does he do for a living?* His strong forearms and hands screamed blue-collar worker, but his skin was much too soft for that. As his flesh made contact with mine, I couldn't ignore the energy between us. My skin grew warm at his solid touch, and I suddenly longed to have his powerful fingers exploring my entire body. I willed myself to brush the thought from my mind as I handed my boarding pass to the woman at the counter, who was sadly not as amused with my display as the handsome stranger had been.

"You look a little stressed," he said, laughing as he lifted up my suitcase and placed it on the scale for me.

Gee, what gave it away? He was a real genius, this one. *No shit I'm stressed! My parents think I am wasting my life because I decided to become a teacher, I have a four-hour flight ahead of me that doesn't get in to Philly until two thirty in the morning, and this bitch at the counter thinks I'm a complete fucking moron. Not to mention that I'm pretty sure my thong fell onto your foot a few seconds ago. Was it even clean? Jesus, fuck!* "I'm fine," I managed, turning my attention to the counter again.

"You sure are," he whispered in my ear before he leaned back to take his place in line.

His warm breath tickled my neck, causing goose bumps to break out all over my body. I shuddered slightly at his forwardness as irritation bloomed. What a creep. Who the hell did this guy think he was? I mean, really. Does he say things like that to any woman he thinks might be an easy lay?

Though I had to admit, as I felt a fluttering low in my abdomen, my mind was giving serious thought to becoming an easy lay. Could this ruggedly handsome man really find me as attractive as I found him? The possibility turned that subtle fluttering into a steady, full-fledged throb between my legs. *What am I thinking? I gotta get out of here. Now!*

I finished checking in, grabbed hold of my purse and carry-on tightly, and left to make my way to security without looking back.

❤

The line at security was longer than I would have expected for a Monday evening. I placed the hand sanitizer and lotion from my purse into a clear plastic bag and put them into the gray container, along with my shoes.

I popped open my compact, suddenly feeling the need to assess my appearance. My usual pale face was still partially flushed an embarrassing shade of crimson. *Oh well, at least I had a little color.* I pressed some powder on the darkness below my clear hazel eyes and applied some tinted gloss to bring out a little color in my muted lips.

I was definitely regretting not getting changed after dinner. Heels and a pencil skirt were not the best choice of attire for a late-night flight, but I had left in such a hurry after my parents' hurtful remarks about how I was wasting my life.

Changing had been an afterthought. Instead, I had grabbed my luggage out of their car and opted to call a cab, heading straight to the airport while my parents were still waiting for dessert.

A part of me thought that at least one of them would come after me, try to smooth things over after I had announced that I had endured enough and was leaving. But heaven forbid they end their meal early on my account. My disappointment was still palpable as I placed the container on the conveyer belt and walked through the metal detector when the portly, balding security officer motioned me through.

"Ma'am, please step into the area to the right for a full-body scan."

*Here they go with that "ma'am" shit again.* And what was all of this crap about? Was getting one break tonight asking too much?

"The detector didn't even beep. Why do I need to be scanned?"

"It's just protocol. Completely random."

*Random, my ass*, I thought. *Those pervs in the back room probably get off on watching women go through body scans.* I had no choice but to comply, so I stepped into the clear box and spread my legs slightly in order to place my feet in the painted outlines on the ground.

As I turned impatiently toward the officer at my right to give him a look of disdain through the glass barricade, my eyes widened as they locked in on the "gentleman" from check-in. He was a few people back in line. His head was pointed toward the ground, but his eyes were tilted up toward me, staring at me intently, clearly amused by my perpetual inconvenience. What an asshole!

A smoking-hot asshole, though. He removed his zip-up

black Nike hoodie and lifted up his fitted white T-shirt at the waist slightly to allow me a peek at his hardened abs. He took off his belt with his other hand and placed it in the container, never once taking his clear blue eyes off me as he made his way through the security area easily.

My eyes followed him to my left as he slid on his shoes, bending down for a few moments to fix the bottoms of his faded jeans before pulling the waist up slightly and putting on his belt. Damn, he had a nice ass! Now I was the voyeur, raking my eyes over him as he stood there completely oblivious. Or did he know that I was watching? Maybe he was doing this intentionally—putting on a show for me to enjoy while I was stuck in this cage, helpless. Tossing his black backpack over one shoulder, he ran his hand through his hair and strolled away, his gait unhurried and confident. This time, it was his turn to not look back.

❤

I knew two things for certain. I desperately needed a drink, and I needed to forget about everything that had happened during the past seventy-two hours. By the time I left security, I still had about forty-five minutes before my flight boarded, so I found an open bar and took a seat near the door, at the corner of the U-shaped counter.

I organized my belongings—I'll be damned if I was going to lose my boarding pass again—and hung my purse on the hook under the bar as I sank down onto the red cushioned stool. I looked up to get the bartender's attention when my periphery registered movement. *Oh, you have got to be kidding me.*

My eyes darted to the right while my head stayed stationary. I felt like a deer in headlights, silently hoping that if I just didn't move, he wouldn't see me. My brain scolded itself for not noticing him when I arrived. How the hell had I missed him? He was only three stools away from me, and with the shape of the bar, I was nearly facing him. Not to mention the fact that he was freaking massive, over six feet tall and pumped full of hard muscle. I could kick myself for not being more observant. There was no way I would have stayed here if I had noticed him. *I don't think.*

I quickly assessed whether or not I could make an inconspicuous getaway without looking like a psycho. With a few other patrons at the bar, most middle-aged men in varying degrees of inebriation, my exit would probably go unnoticed. But for some reason, I couldn't bring myself to stand. I told myself that I didn't want to give him the satisfaction of seeing me leave. Good thing I was well versed in delusional tendencies.

Without looking my way or saying a word, he slid a drink toward me. He must have noticed me immediately and ordered the drink while I was preoccupied with my bags. The red liquid splashed a bit when I went to grab it, and I licked a little of the cool liquor off my finger.

"Well, how can I pretend not to look at you when you're licking your finger like that?" he asked playfully, his tongue running across the corner of his upper lip involuntarily. I think I saw a small scar just above his mouth. I had to resist craning my neck toward him to get a better look.

I needed a witty retort to shut this cocky son of a bitch down. "Let's not pretend," I said huskily, leaning forward slightly to allow some of my ample cleavage to sink into his line of view. "You stop pretending that you're not watching me"—I quickly sat up, dropping the seduction from my voice—"and I'll try to pretend I don't think you're a total douchebag. Thanks for the drink." I put the glass to my lips, silently praying that it wasn't loaded with roofies. It tasted sweet, but I wasn't sure what it was.

"Wow, such harsh words coming from such a beautiful mouth." The sound of his words was like velvet: rough with just the right amount of smoothness. He had clearly spent a lot of time perfecting his panty-dropping voice.

I paused for a moment at his directness and furrowed my brow a bit. "What is that? A pick-up line? You can't be serious."

"Oh, I am serious. Beautiful creamy skin. Silky brown hair I'd like to run my fingers through. An ass...well, we'll leave that comment for later. What's not to like?" he said, taking a sip of his drink. "And I did enjoy your little show back in security, by the way."

A chill ran down my spine, and I shifted uncomfortably in my seat before silently cursing myself for letting him see that he had affected me. As I shifted, I felt the wetness that had been created by his words. *Is he seriously turning me on?*

I studied him more closely, becoming distinctly aware of his appearance for the first time. I didn't have men who looked like him coming on to me like this every day. He couldn't have been older than his late twenties and had that brooding, bad-boy look to him that I'd always been silently attracted to. His posture was assured, relaxed even. The smoothness of his skin contrasted with the scruff around his delicate lips. He couldn't even be bothered to shave every day.

Suddenly I took note of his long dark lashes. *When did eyelashes become sexy?* And speaking of hair... His was just the right length to yank on while he moved his head back and forth between my legs. *Jesus Christ, Lily. Get back to reality.* "Show? Um, it wasn't me who was putting on the show. You, lifting up your shirt, taking off your belt, and staring at me? Any of that ring a bell?"

He slid a few seats closer to me, closing the space between us. I could feel my heartbeat quicken as the warm throb in my lower abdomen returned. I swallowed hard. Facing me and raising his left eyebrow, he lowered his voice and cleared his throat. "Well, I'm glad to see I wasn't the only one enjoying a show."

"I didn't say I enjoyed it!" I snapped back. Yes, I needed to be clear I wasn't interested . . . even if that wasn't entirely true.

"You didn't say you *didn't* enjoy it either. Tell me your name," he said as he turned his attention back to his drink.

*Tell me your name?* I didn't take orders. Plus, I was taught as a young child never to tell my name to strangers, and I damn sure wasn't going to break that rule for this guy. "Why would I want you to know my name?" As eager as I was to keep myself anonymous, I couldn't help but wonder what was really behind his deep-blue eyes, chiseled jaw, and hard exterior. I wanted to know more about this man who was such a mystery, while revealing nothing about myself. It was difficult for me to ignore the irony.

"Suit yourself, doll. But I thought you might be interested to know *mine* since I'm fairly certain you'll be screaming it later." He rubbed his hand across his face, and I found myself daydreaming again about how the coarse hairs on his face would feel brushing against the insides of my thighs.

"Wow, you've got a big head, don't you?" I asked, rolling my eyes at his forwardness.

This must have amused him, because he cocked his head to the side a bit like a confused puppy, obviously entertained by my comment. Lowering his voice, he ran two cool fingers lightly down the side of my left arm, sending chills running all the way up to my neck. "Oh, honey, you have no idea."

"Aaand . . . that's my cue to go," I said, raising my glass in the air and taking a final gulp. As I began to lower it, a mischievous thought crept into my mind, along with the memory of his words during our first encounter of the night. "Looks like I'm the one who got the drink. But I have absolutely no interest in fucking you. Have a nice flight," I said with a wink. I then turned, grabbed my bag, and stalked out of the bar, satisfied. Two could play at that game. I made it to the door before my brain registered a noise from behind me. *Did that prick just call me a liar?*

I started off toward my gate. I couldn't believe that guy. Who did he think he was, saying things like that to someone he just met? But, more pressingly, who was I to like it? He was right. I was a liar. Thank God I got out of there before I did something I might regret.

Although, if his "head" was as big as he claimed, there might not be much reason to regret anything. *Stop thinking about him, Lily. He's a sleazy asshole who's probably just looking for a quick fuck before he hops on a long flight home to his wife.* I breathed in deeply to calm my nerves before heading to the terminal. *You're better than this.*

# *chapter two*

I practically ran to my gate, stopping only to grab a bottle of water and a *Cosmo* magazine to take with me. I looked forward to finally relaxing a bit, and I hoped that the late flight would mean that the plane might be somewhat empty. Between my parents and that irritating man from the bar, I had dealt with enough arrogant assholes for one day and was hoping not to be stuck next to one for the next four hours.

I found a seat at the gate facing the window and gazed out into the night sky, trying to clear my mind. Seeing my reflection staring back at me, I *was* pretty—extremely pretty, actually. And why should I be offended by that? I was five-foot-five, with wavy brown hair that fell about three inches past my shoulders, voluptuous breasts, and a flat tummy. I could definitely pull off a sexy outfit, and yet I hadn't really thought of myself as attractive in a sexual way until now. Was it *him* who made me feel that way?

I'd never lacked male attention and had had my fair share of romances. I even thought I would eventually marry Chris, my college boyfriend of a little over two years. I always felt special and beautiful with him, mostly because he called me those things on a daily basis.

I giggled fondly at the memories of Chris: his leaving me little notes in the morning when he'd leave my apartment to get to class while I was still asleep, the times he ransacked his apartment for change so he could buy me dinner, and the way he would always have his arm around me, showing everyone that I was his girl.

After our graduation, he had moved to Chicago to pursue a Master's Degree at Northwestern. Of all the places he needed to enroll in grad school, he had to choose my hometown. Despite how much I loved him, I just couldn't bring myself to move back there after I had decided, against my parents' wishes, to become a teacher and not a lawyer—a cardinal sin in the Hamilton household.

When Chris and I parted, I felt so much pain that I almost gave in and returned to Chicago to be with him. But I just couldn't. I needed to be my own person, and I wouldn't be able to do that in Chicago. I would always be Howard and Lynn Hamilton's daughter there. I'd never get to just be Lily.

And while our relationship wasn't lacking in passion, I never felt *hot* with him. Never felt so irresistibly desirable in the way that I had in that bar several minutes ago. But if I learned nothing else from my pretentious parents, it was how to act properly. A good girl didn't just screw some guy she met in an airport—even if she wanted to.

Despite that fact that my mother and I disagreed on many topics, we shared the same viewpoint as far as this subject was concerned. Acting on my body's desires would draw me too far out of character. They did not mesh with the person I had tried so desperately to become. So what if that jerk made my body clench with just the sound of his voice? I would never see him again, and if I did, I could never pursue it. Clearly, he was a top-notch prick.

I was ready to get on that plane to get home and back

into my routine already. So far they had boarded first class, passengers with small children, followed by children flying alone, and I found myself contemplating stealing someone's newborn just so that I could board earlier.

I had nearly dozed off when I was jolted back to full consciousness. "Now boarding all remaining passengers," blared the muffled announcement.

I shoved my magazine and water into my purse, took a sigh of relief that this bullshit trip to my parents' vacation house was finally over, and walked through the narrow hallway and onto the plane.

I had barely turned the corner to proceed down the aisle, when I stopped dead in my tracks, causing the person behind me to barrel into my back. But I remained stock still as I glared at the all-too-familiar piercing blue eyes.

"Oh, you've gotta be shittin' me," I muttered under my breath as I started to inch a few paces closer to him. The line paused to let some passengers place their bags in the overhead compartments before taking their seats, and I found myself stopped nearly in front of him in first class, my pelvis almost directly in front of his face. Despite my best efforts, I couldn't resist glancing down once as I daydreamed about burying his face between my legs right here in aisle three.

He looked up at me. "It's Max," he said with a cocky wink.

*What an arrogant bastard.* I thought back to his advances at the bar, and I knew exactly why he had told me his name. *Un-fucking-believable.* Did he know what I was just thinking about? Did something on my face give it away? If this motherfucker thought he had an actual chance with me, he was sorely mistaken.

I could definitely control my baser urges, especially now

that he had intentionally made me feel uncomfortable. He clearly knew how to read people, and he was pushing all my buttons. As the line started to move again, I shifted the bag to my other shoulder, intentionally knocking him in the side of the head in the process.

*Thank God*, I thought as I eyed up row nineteen. I placed my carry-on in the overhead compartment above my row and took my seat by the window. I had never been so happy to be sitting next to an old guy who smelled like cough drops in all my life. Sure, he'd probably snore and pass gas intermittently throughout the flight, but there were about sixteen rows of distance between me and Mr. First Class, and this ancient fellow next to me seemed relatively innocuous. For once in my adult life, I was happy to be flying coach.

Coming from a wealthy family, I had flown many times, but it always made me slightly uneasy. Maybe it was knowing you were doing something that goes so directly against nature. Or the feeling that, despite your better judgment, you have to give up all control to someone you don't even know. The risk was strange and unnerving, but at the same time, it had a certain allure to it.

I asked the flight attendant for a blanket and took a few deep breaths to calm myself before taking out my book, hoping that it would tire me enough so I could get a little sleep.

❤

I must have dozed off at some point, because I awoke a while later and glanced down at my watch, which I had set to East Coast time before leaving Colorado. Almost two o'clock. Not much longer before I'd be home and able to relax for a couple of days before heading back to work. I pushed up the shade on the window to look into the darkness, took a deep breath, and yawned. It was then that I noticed the conspicuous presence of a fresh, clean scent.

"Did anyone ever tell you that you sleep with your mouth open?"

*Oh, fuck!*

"Your head bobs around a little too. It was pretty entertaining to watch, actually. And also a bit of a turn-on, I might add." Out of my periphery, I could see that his arms were folded across his chiseled chest as he stared straight ahead at the seat in front of him, not even glancing my way.

"You've got some fucking nerve sitting here," I snapped. *Good, pretend you're angry—and not at all intrigued—that he's sitting only inches from you.* "When that old guy comes back from the bathroom, you'll have to get up and leave. You know that, right?"

"Oh, he won't be returning. He's up front, happily crossing 'flying first class' off his bucket list, courtesy of me. It's just us, sweetheart." The words sounded menacing and enticing leaving his full, pink lips. He paused momentarily, assessing his surroundings. "Well, just us and the gorgeous creature sitting to my left." He threw a slight head nod in the direction of the round, gray-haired old woman to the other side of him. "She's been sleeping for a while too." He suddenly turned his attention back to me, flashing a mischievous smile. "Though watching her doesn't exactly give me the same thrill as staring at you with your head back and your mouth open," he said playfully as he leaned toward me, imitating my sleeping pose.

*Fuck. He'd been watching me sleep. For how long?*

I felt my cheeks flush with embarrassment. "What the

hell do you think you're doing back here?" I asked quietly through my tightened jaw. Though I hated to admit it, seeing him lean into me with his mouth open and eyes closed had the same effect on me as it had on him.

He unfolded his arms and dropped one to the armrest between us, bringing him close enough to me that his fingers could caress my arm. He lowered his mouth to my ear, invading my personal space and clearly enjoying it. And though I hated to admit it, I was enjoying it a little too.

"Well, I've been sitting in first class with my cock pressed up against my jeans for three excruciating hours. It was either take care of things myself in an airplane bathroom or take my chances here with you. So here I am. Sitting next to you. Still fucking hard. You can probably guess which one I would prefer, given the two choices." His words grew huskier as he talked, reflecting the same strain that existed beneath the fly of his jeans.

I couldn't help but look down to his lap at the mention of the word "cock." I sucked in a breath quickly and reached up to turn on the air above me before slowing my breathing and allowing myself to exhale. *Jesus Christ, it was hot on this fucking plane suddenly.* I couldn't bring myself to look at him, but I didn't have to. My body felt him. There was something primitively erotic about him that couldn't be denied. I just had to try to ignore it for the next half hour or so.

I deliberately looked over my shoulder at the bathroom door. "Bathroom's vacant. Guess you'll have to settle for your plan B," I said, pointing over my shoulder with my thumb.

But he wasn't fooled. "Oh, don't act like you don't love every dirty word coming out of my mouth when you're sitting here reading porn," he said with a wicked grin as he withdrew from me slightly so that he could hold up the book that had been on my lap when I'd fallen asleep. He opened to a passage. Beyond embarrassed, I tried to tune him out as he read aloud a paragraph about moaning and throbbing ecstasy against someone's ass. He raised an eyebrow, clearly pleased with his comeback.

"*Lolita* is a classic tale about a man's obsessive passion for the girl he loves," I explained defensively.

He smiled. "Classy porn is still porn, doll." He raised both hands up with open palms. "Not judging. Just saying. And I'll also have you note that reading your 'classy porn' did nothing to help alleviate my pesky erection problem." Pausing for a moment, seemingly to gauge my reaction, he leaned back in and softened his voice seductively. His breath smelled of sweet mint mixed with alcohol. All I could think about while he talked was feeling that tongue colliding with my own and letting him devour me. "Listen, girl who won't tell me her name, I am a tenacious, arrogant, and skilled man who always gets what he wants. And right now, what I want is you. Your long, lean legs wrapped around my waist as I thrust myself into you without regret or apology. And I can tell by the way your body is tensing in all the right places that you want exactly the same thing." He lifted up the armrest that separated us, moving his smooth, solid hand toward me with controlled slowness, allowing me time to stop him if I so desired. I didn't.

As his hand reached under the blanket I had strewn across my lap and began to draw soft, lazy circles on my knee, my nipples hardened instantly. The tingling sensation from the bar returned as he made his way slowly up my thigh, his eyes staying steadily on mine, reading me as he had my book.

*Oh, shit! Is he actually going to do what I think he's going to do?*

"What the hell do you think you're doing?" I whispered, trying to resist my primal desires. But I knew as I heard myself speak that my pleading was much too weak to convince him that I didn't want this. Or even to convince *me* for that matter.

"I'm only doing what we both want me to, doll," he whispered, again searching my eyes to make sure he wasn't forcing me to do something I didn't want to do. My mind was flooded with conflicting opinions of this man. He was domineering and firm, yet he took great care to ensure that he wasn't pushing me further than I was willing to go. His touch short-circuited my entire body. The more he touched, the more I *wanted* to be touched. And he damn well knew it.

Just then, a flight attendant appeared beside us. "Excuse me," Max beckoned. "Can my friend get a white zinfandel? Thank you." He quickly turned his attention back to me, his hand creeping up toward the juncture between my thighs.

This jackass may be controlling my body's response to him, but he wasn't going to control what I drank. "Um," I said, stifling a moan as his fingers traveled delicately over my lace thong. "I'm sorry, miss, but I'll actually have a gin and tonic instead." *Yeah, that'll show this dominant bastard who's boss.* I wasn't about to drink some fucking girly drink that *he* had ordered *for* me.

"Gin and tonic, huh?" he said, smirking. "Whatever will, ahem, loosen you up a little."

I became acutely aware of his deliberate choice in words. *Loosen me up a little?* The acknowledgment of his intentions sent a shiver up my spine. Could I let him do this? And here?

The attendant smiled pleasantly. "I apologize, ma'am, but drink service for this flight has just been suspended. We will be touching down shortly," she said with an apologetic smile.

He turned his head to gaze at her—and obviously her name tag. "Kristen, is it?" And I could see the hint of a genuine smile emerge from the corner of his eye as he clasped her hand gently in his free one. "Just one last drink, please? I'd be very grateful. She's not really a fan of flying," he said, nodding his head in my direction while sliding two fingers forcefully inside me.

I inhaled sharply, staring straight ahead. The blissful feeling that radiated throughout my body contrasted with my sour mood. I couldn't believe this asshole. I mean, really? Did he seriously think that now was an appropriate time to be flirting with the flight attendant? Holding her hand with his left while he fingered me with his right?

"I'll see what I can do," she replied with a white grin as she turned to leave. But she only made it a step before she found a reason to turn back to Max. "Could I also bring you a drink, sir?" *What a slick little temptress.*

Max smiled sweetly. "Oh, that would be great, Kristen. I'll take a Scotch. Neat." Christ, this son of a bitch was charming. There was no denying that. His sexually magnetic pull clearly could not be denied by any woman, including me. Though I wasn't sure if that revelation was supposed to make me feel better or worse about being finger fucked by a stranger in coach.

His thumb began to circle my clit, and he slipped a third finger inside me, moving slowly and discretely. *Oh fuck, this feels good.* I held my breath and bit my lip as he stroked me gently with his thumb and pushed powerfully into me with his fingers.

*Yup, this is really happening.*

I wanted to push against his hand to create some more

resistance, but I didn't want to seem too eager. Although something told me it was a little late to care about appearances. The flight attendant returned a few minutes later, lowering each drink carefully to the tray in front of Max, when he motioned for her to do so. "Just put it on my card, please, Kristen."

"Certainly, sir. I *will* have to ask you to hold the drinks, though. Your tray tables will need to remain in the upright position for the rest of the flight. We should be landing shortly."

"Thank you," he replied dismissively without moving the tray.

*Oh, for the love of God, Karen, Kristen, whatever the hell your name is, just leave already! Don't you have to go make sure people's seats are up or some shit?*

I gripped the armrest tightly and tried to control my racing heartbeat, which was causing my breath to quicken. With *Karen/Kristen* gone, I squirmed in my seat and moved my skirt up to give him better access, finally accepting what I had probably known all along. I was going to give him exactly what he wanted, because I wanted it too.

He leaned into my neck and breathed heavily against it. "Do you have any idea how fucking hard I am right now?" he asked as he began to pump his fingers more roughly, swirling them inside me. "Listen to how wet you are when I move inside you." I could feel the soft hairs on his face graze my ear as he spoke.

With his left hand, he picked up my drink, and I urgently tilted my head back. "Now swallow," he insisted, placing the cool glass to my lips.

I did as I was told, drinking quickly as the alcohol burned my throat. In my urgency, a little dribbled down my chin, and he wasted no time leaning in to suck it off my skin before dragging his tongue up to let it graze my mouth. I parted my lips, inviting his tongue to invade. When it didn't, disappointment washed over me briefly, but the feeling was quickly replaced by need.

He was right about one thing though. I needed to loosen up. Mentally. The nagging part of my subconscious was yelling at me to stop this behavior. That this wasn't how a respectable young lady would act. *Wow, my subconscious sounds a lot like Mom.* But the rest of me, for reasons I couldn't even have begun to explain, trusted Max. He was introducing me to a part of myself I had never even met before. And he wasn't doing it in a skeevy, dirty way. It felt liberating.

I felt my orgasm building steadily inside me as he put the glass down gently. "Now where were we?" he whispered. "Oh, that's right, I was bringing you so close to climaxing, and you were about to beg me not to stop. You remember my name, right, doll?"

*Stop? What was this talk of stopping?*

I hoped he wouldn't really leave me wanting, because there was no way I was going to *beg* him for anything, and I was definitely not about to say his name. That would give his inflated ego way too much satisfaction.

When I said nothing, he pulled out a little, leaving just the tip of one finger barely inside me. *Oh, he really knew how to be a fucking tease!* I couldn't let him stop now. We were about to land any minute. *I'll let him see how it feels, so to speak.* I moved the blanket to cover his lap too and began to palm him through his jeans with my left hand. He wasn't kidding either. He was as hard as stone.

I began to move my hand back and forth quickly over the fly of his jeans, and he responded as I'd hoped. "Fuck, that feels good," he groaned into my neck. His fingers again plunged deep inside me, and his palm pressed against my clit, rubbing me vigorously as my impending orgasm approached. As the landing gear touched down and the plane braked, his palm pushed harder against me and the vibrations of the plane nearly pushed me over the edge. I quickly loosened his belt, frantically shoving my hand into his pants. My mind flashed back to the "big head" comment, and from what I could feel, he seemed right on target with that observation.

Suddenly, he pulled my hand out and held on to my wrist roughly as he fought to regain his self-control. At least one of us had some. He then suddenly released my hand and reached across my chest to grab my hair and pull my face gently toward the window as his body pushed against me.

*You've gotta be fucking kidding me!*

I was so close that I was beginning to second-guess the "not begging" promise I had made to myself only moments earlier.

"Oh, no, darling. There is no way I'm gonna come in my pants after all this, and if you touch me any more, I promise I'll have no choice in the matter," he whispered amusedly as his mouth pressed against my ear. "And you're not gonna come here either. That isn't how this is gonna end. I *will* take what I want when we get off this plane. And this time you *will* say my name and beg me not to stop. And you'll do all of that because, deep down, you want exactly the same things." He released me and withdrew his fingers completely as the plane came to a halt.

I sat back in my seat, silently seething. This guy had some fucking nerve.

"Welcome to Philadelphia," the pilot announced. "Current

time is two thirty-two a.m. And the current temperature is twenty-three degrees. We hope you had an enjoyable flight. Please take a look around your seating area and take note of any trash you may have left behind before getting off."

The pilot's words hit home as I watched this stranger fix his belt, hand me his drink, and stand up as if nothing had happened. I grabbed what was left of his drink and downed it. I was a fucking mess. I took a brush out of my purse and combed my disheveled hair while I waited to stand up and get my bag.

*What the fuck just happened? And more importantly, what is about to happen?*

I had never let any man have this much power over me, sexually or otherwise. But he was so commanding, so strong, and—dear God—so fucking sexy. I couldn't help but stare at his sculpted stomach as he reached up to grab a bag and hand it to the old woman who was still unaware that she had nearly been part of a threesome only a few moments before. As he placed my bag on the aisle seat, I became instantly mortified. He unzipped it and carefully slid in the rest of my blue lace thong that must have been sticking out of the side compartment ever since it had fallen on his foot during my check-in fiasco.

Grabbing my bag off the seat, I scooted out to stand in front of him without saying a word. I was tired, annoyed, and desperately in need of an orgasm. He had left me hollowed and needy, and I was pissed. As the line began to move, I walked quickly to the front of the plane to increase the distance between us. I was about to turn and exit when I felt a forceful arm reach around my waist and pull me against him. I couldn't ignore his erection pressing up against my lower back.

"You ready to get off?" he asked loudly enough for the people nearby to hear. I felt his smile on the back of my neck.

He was clearly impressed with his play on words.

I ignored his attempt at humor and exited the gate as fast as I could. When I realized I still hadn't lost him, I was determined to find the most serious voice I could conjure up in the middle of the night when I was slightly drunk and so horny that I was nearly delirious. "I can't do this," I insisted. "I can't just fuck some stranger in the Philadelphia airport at two forty-five in the morning." Had that convinced him? It certainly sounded more persuasive than my half-assed attempt on the plane.

I didn't wait for him to respond. I turned to leave toward baggage claim when he grabbed ahold of my bicep and pulled me around a nearby corner and into a narrow, dimly lit hallway. I quickly took in my surroundings. The walls were a muted gray, and an ugly blue carpet was beneath our feet. To my left was a doorway marked "Staff Only."

He leaned his hips into my stomach, pinning me against the wall with his hardness and lowering his voice. "The way I see it," he said, "you have two options. You can go home and touch yourself while you think about my thick cock plunging into you over and over again while I make you come. Or"—he paused, eyeing me with a playful grin—"you can actually let me do it."

*Well, the persuasive fucker does make an excellent point.*

# chapter three

There was something erotically thrilling about his proposal. Then again, it could have been that there was just something erotically thrilling about *him*. Our sexual connection was indescribable. Like nothing I'd ever felt before. And I'd be damned if I was going to let him leave without exploring it. *I'm doing this for me,* I told myself. *It has nothing to do with the fact that this is what* he *wants.*

I drew in a quick breath. And as I put my arms around Max's neck, signaling my intention, I prayed that no one would come bursting out of that "Staff Only" door. Though, I suppose some aroused part of me kind of hoped someone *would*.

I pulled his mouth to mine, demanding the kiss I hungered for. His lips spread into a smile before they enveloped mine, his tongue probing my mouth savagely. In an instant, his hands found my skirt, roughly hoisting it above my hips. Then, in one deft and experienced movement, he tore my thong away from my body. I internally praised myself for wearing panties—since I normally didn't with this skirt—so that I got to experience the thrill of having them shredded from my body.

My hands flew to his pants, undoing them with a dexterity I didn't know I had and pushing them to the floor. Jesus Christ! The man was completely nude beneath them! During my urgency on the plane, I somehow hadn't noticed. The realization made my body flood with desire. I withdrew from him for just a moment to take in the full sight of his body, naked from the waist down. He wasn't kidding; his cock was thick. And long. I had serious doubt that I would be able to sheath him, but I was damn sure going to enjoy trying. I continued to watch in awe as he tore open a foil condom wrapper he had been palming and spread the latex over his firmness.

As my eyes continued to devour the sight of him, he reached around the nape of my neck and gathered my hair with a firm pull, tilting my head up to him. Every one of his movements was commanding, forceful with just the right amount of compassion. I could tell he was tempering the control he exerted over me. He brought his lips to mine and growled needily against them, "Don't forget the magic word."

Before I had time to respond, he had me off the ground. He dug his hands animalistically into the backs of my thighs as he pressed me into the wall and roughly slid me farther down the hall, pinning me in place. That's when he became the man I'd envisioned. The one who took what he wanted without permission. I instinctively wrapped my legs around him. He paused only briefly, allowing me this bit of suspense as I felt his dick at my opening. Then, he thrust forcefully into me. As I stretched to accommodate him, I felt an arousing mixture of pain and euphoria that radiated down my thighs and up to my swollen breasts.

"How does that feel?" he whispered. "Can you take more?"

*God, this isn't even all of him.* I was already so full. His physical size and his arousing words filled me completely, creating a need that increasingly ached low in my abdomen. I realized that I would beg this man not to stop if it came to that. I would give him almost anything to bring me to a climax this time. The only thing I would not do was say his name. "Please," I whimpered.

Then, with a sudden, punishing jerk of his hips, he gave me the rest of him. As he pumped wildly into me, I nearly got lost in him, in this feeling of uninhibited desire and raw passion. I had never experienced this kind of need and intensity all wrapped up in one beautifully sculpted man. I clawed at his back through his shirt as I bit into his shoulder blade, needing to inflict my urgency onto him in every way available to me.

"You like that, baby?" he growled into my ear.

"Oh, yes. Yes" was all I had in me as a reply, the words expelled in heaving breaths. My brain was too busy sending pleasure waves to every part of my body to elaborate further.

"Mmm, you feel so tight. It's a good thing you're so wet for me. Though maybe it'd be better if you weren't. Then you'd be reminded of me tomorrow. Every time you moved, you'd remember what I did to you. I could keep this up for hours. Is that what you want?"

I had a feeling I wouldn't forget this anytime soon, regardless of how wet I was. "Hmmm, you know what I want," I moaned in reply.

"Then you're going to have to beg for it. Beg me to end this and give you what you want. Beg me to fuck you harder."

"Please. Oh my... Please."

"Mmm," he scolded playfully, "Not good enough. Say the magic word. Say it, and I'll finish you right here in this hallway. I'll make you come so hard you'll feel the reverberating quake in your knees for days. Just say it, baby. Who are you coming for? Say my fucking name."

But he had underestimated his sexiness, because I wasn't going to last long enough to say it, even if I had wanted to. His thickness and the power of each thrust had dangled me at the edge, but it was his words that finally pushed me over. I convulsed around him, orgasming so violently I thought I would never come down from this high.

He thrust into me twice more, both rough and deep. His breath halted, and he stifled a deep groan into my neck as he experienced the same release I had, before pulling back to look into my eyes. There was something unsettling about his expression, like he was looking into me, seeing what I hid beneath the surface. Suddenly, I felt naked and exposed. My legs released their hold from him and dropped toward the floor. He let them fall as he pulled out of me, but he didn't look away. His blue eyes were hypnotic, and I could see how women fell prey to him. Much like I had.

Needing to break his hold on me both physically and mentally, I gently pushed him back, my hands open on his chest. Then, I reached down and lowered my skirt. He gruffly stepped back, reaching down for his jeans and pulling them up, shielding the instrument that had provided me with the most mind-blowing, earth-shattering orgasm I had ever experienced.

Then he looked up at me, his eyes blazing and set in purpose. "So," he said, his voice hoarse and raw, "are you going to tell me your name?"

I couldn't think of the right thing to say, so I allowed a simple gesture to say it for me. I shook my head slowly, not giving him my eyes.

"If you don't tell me your name, you won't have the pleasure of me getting you off again." He smirked. But I heard something behind his words, a pleading almost.

My voice got lost in my throat. I didn't think I wanted him again. Or maybe I was just too afraid I'd never want anyone else. I could see how sex with this man could become like an addiction, a desire that I would need to satisfy above all else. My insides already throbbed for him, missing his cock like it belonged in me. I was already itching for him to fill me again. I had to get out of there.

"No names," I finally managed. I looked up at him, peeking out just under my eyelids. I thought I saw his face fall briefly at my response. But in a flash, his cocky grin was plastered back onto his face, so I was sure I had imagined it.

"Suit yourself," he whispered as he leaned in to kiss my cheek. "But remember what I said, doll. I *do* always get what I want. And what I want is your name. Actually," he said, cocking his head to the side playfully, seductively even, "what I *really* want is *you*. Over and over and over again."

Then, he bent next to me and retrieved his backpack and my tattered thong. He slipped the latter into his jeans pocket slyly and winked. Then he walked confidently down the hallway and around the corner as he ran a strong hand through his tousled hair before disappearing from my view.

I leaned my head back against the wall. A smile crept over my lips as I replayed the evening's escapades in my mind. Max was a man who found a way to take what he desired. And what he desired was me. His promise of having me again and again made me a little uneasy. *How would he ever find me?* But what scared me even more was the thought of him *not* finding me. I took a deep breath, letting it escape from me slowly as I leaned the back of my head against the wall and whispered the only thought that came to mind.

"*Max.*"

# chapter four

It took me a few days to come down from the high I had experienced on the plane ride home and to finally feel as though I had been thoroughly cleansed of Max, both physically and emotionally. And it wasn't long before I was able to get back into my old routine. The next few weeks were a blur. Between focusing on work, taking an online grad class at Widener, and trying to find time to get to the gym here and there, I could barely enjoy the finer things in life.

And by finer things I mean taking advantage of the after-Christmas sales at the King of Prussia Mall with my roommate, Amanda, and playing Quizzo on Monday nights at the bar within walking distance of my apartment.

But thankfully my busy schedule kept me from thinking about him. Well, almost. I couldn't help that from time to time I allowed myself to close my eyes and play back the memory of his long length ceaselessly pounding into me until I begged him to let me finish. And I still felt an empty ache between my legs when I wore the thong that he had tucked back into my bag after our flight.

I took comfort in the fact that my fantasy was simply that: a fantasy. An erotic image that could allow me a little pleasure when I needed it but not something I could ever act on again.

I mean, a girl was entitled to a harmless fantasy every now and again, right?

♥

I hated rain. Almost as much as I hated having to wake up early. And the cold. And birds. God, I hated birds. I pulled my blue Hyundai Elantra into the coffeehouse down the street from my apartment. I desperately needed a caffeine jolt, and since I always slept as late as possible, I never had time to brew any myself. Maybe that was why I was always broke. Oh, well. It's not like I could do anything about it. A girl needs her beauty sleep.

I swung into the only open parking space, which also doubled as a moat. I opened my door and assessed how I was going to get out of my car without completely soaking the lower half of my legs. When I finally realized that my options were wet shoes or no coffee, I pulled my ass out of the car.

It was seven forty-five. I had fifteen minutes to get to work, which ordinarily wouldn't have been a problem since I only lived eight minutes from the school. But clearly the coffeehouse had chosen this day to hand out Wonka Bars wrapped in golden tickets, because the line was ridiculously long. A better person may have considered leaving, being punctual their top priority. I was not one of those people. If I didn't get some coffee in my system, I was going to kill someone's child. And not a simple murder, like a stabbing or a chair to the back of the head. That little fucker was going to suffer.

Okay, only two more people in front of me. I glanced at my watch. Seven fifty-five. I started tapping my foot impatiently, as if this would make the surly baristas suddenly realize that

I was in a hurry and begin to give a shit about their minimum-wage jobs and speed things up.

"Next," said a small woman who looked like she could be sitting in one of my classes waiting for me to teach her the difference between a verb and a noun for the eight hundredth time.

"Yes, I will have a tall caramel macchiato and a blueberry muffin." May as well eat, too. She meandered over to the coffee machines and poured. Then she walked like a hunchback toward the muffin display. If only she had decided to drag one of her legs behind her, the image would have been complete.

"Ten eighty-nine, please."

*Fucking inflation.* I handed her thirteen dollars and told her to keep the change. I figured a little tip might keep her from spitting in my drink the next time I had the pleasure of her service. I turned away from the counter and took a sip of my macchiato.

Oh, no, a bitch didn't. This was not a macchiato. I didn't know what it was, and it wasn't half bad, but if I was going to be late for work, I was damn well going to get what I ordered.

"Excuse me, sorry. I'm not cutting. I was already here," I said as I pushed some guy away from the counter mid-order so I could take his place in line. "I'm sorry, but this isn't a caramel macchiato. Could I please get what I ordered?" The elven creature simply nodded, took my cup, and plodded back to the brewers. I felt like I needed to say something so that the stranger I had nearly assaulted to regain my place in line understood that it wasn't my fault he was no longer being waited on. It was merely a case of bad luck all around.

"Why does this stuff always happen to me?" I asked rhetorically but loud enough for him to hear, and therefore pity me. When the woman returned with my order, I sipped it at the counter to let her know that I didn't trust her. Not one bit. Then I turned to the stranger I had interrupted and said, "Sorry, sir. Need my caffeine fix before heading to the zoo." I didn't wait for a reply but quickly left and sped toward Swift Middle School—an ironic name this morning since the coffee joint had been anything but swift.

I strolled into the building just as the kids were being released from the cafeteria. I quickly signed in, avoiding eye contact with our secretaries who had eyes laced with judgment, and raced toward my classroom to begin the day.

# chapter five

I couldn't for the life of me figure out why these parents insisted on parent conferences just weeks before the regularly scheduled ones. Every parent would get a set time to meet with each of their child's teachers at the end of February. But, here we were, at the end of January, and we were being dragged into the guidance office for a coup d'état.

"Good morning, Mrs. Jenkins," I directed at the guidance secretary. The only acknowledgment I received was an eyebrow raise, and even that was difficult to detect since she was looking down at her desk, filing her nails. *Cocksucker.*

I was clearly destined to make an awesome impression since I was about ten minutes late for the meeting. I had stopped to intervene in an escalating battle between two students about who made better comic books: Marvel or DC. Friggin' dorks.

I walked down the narrow, gray-carpeted hallway to the conference room. As I turned the corner, I had already begun to apologize for my lateness, when I spotted him.

*Fuck!*

I stopped short as all the air drained from my lungs. Please tell me this was not Eva Carter's father. Please. But of course it was, because this was my life—which clearly was some huge cosmic joke. There, sitting at the head of the giant conference table, was the guy from the coffeehouse yesterday morning—the one I had made the zoo comment to. Note to self, start looking for a new job, for I was soon to be canned from this one.

I suddenly remembered that I should still be moving. God, why did I have to be late? Now everyone was looking at me, including him. Did he recognize me? No familiarity showed on his face. I regained my composure and sat in the nearest open chair, which was thankfully three seats away from Mr. Carter.

"This is Miss Hamilton, Eva's English teacher," Mrs. Kline, the guidance counselor, said. I got a nod of acknowledgment from him, to which I nodded back.

"As I was saying," Mr. Dees, Eva's math teacher, grumbled as he eyed me wearily. *What a dick.* "Eva is a bright girl, but she hasn't been applying herself as she needs to in order to . . ." *Blah blah blah.*

I began to tune out, too wrapped up in my own internal conundrum. There hadn't been any sign that Mr. Carter recognized me. I was actually surprised that I recognized him so easily. Our encounter in the coffeehouse had been brief and indirect. But he did have a memorable quality to him. I just hoped that I was as easy to forget as he was easy to remember.

Besides, what's the worst that could happen to me? I mean, seriously, could I even be fired for my comment? I hadn't mentioned any specific names. So I had said I worked in a zoo. So what? Maybe I could play dumb and act like he was a raving lunatic. *I would never say that!* I could argue. Or maybe I could claim that he had just misheard me. *What rhymes with zoo? Boo, shoe, coo, doo, flu. Maybe I could play it off like I was going on a field trip to the zoo. Was the zoo open in January?*

I was yanked from my thoughts at the saying of my name. I glanced around to see eight pairs of eyes looking at me expectantly. Shit. Well, clearly we're here to discuss Eva, so . . .

"Eva is a great girl, but I have noticed a decline in the quality of her work. Ever since our return from winter break, it has been very difficult to keep her on task and focused. Her mind just seems to be perpetually wandering." Boy, could I relate to that. "She was a B student before break but has been barely pulling Cs since."

Mr. Carter had his hands crossed in front of him, resting on the table. He listened intently, and I was suddenly mad at myself for being annoyed that he had called this meeting. The truth was, I had noticed a shift in Eva's behavior, and he was right to ask for this conference. She could be failing miserably by the end of February. I could tell that he was a good father, not just because he had gone to the trouble of coming in here and meeting with all of us but because he wore it on his face— the concern for his daughter, his love for her.

Mr. Carter cleared his throat. "Eva had a tough winter recess. I'm a single father, so my parents offered to take Eva for a few days to give me a break. Without going into too much detail, Eva overheard my parents discussing her mother, and she's been having a rough time of things since. This isn't an excuse for her academic decline, but it is the explanation for it. I just want us all to be on the same page going forward so that Eva can have the best shot at finishing the year as strong as she began it."

Fucking parents. They ruin everything. I suddenly had the urge to shout *Amen* and emphatically nod my head like he was a minister and I was an avid member of his congregation. Preaching to the choir, my brother!

"I've sought counseling for Eva, to give her an impartial third party to speak to about what she's feeling. Your comments have been very helpful, and I will share them with her counselor so that she may get deeper insight into Eva's school self."

"Okay," Mrs. Kline added. "So, maybe it would be helpful if we could all stay in contact with Mr. Carter and provide him with periodic updates about Eva's progress in each of your classes. I will email each of you Mr. Carter's contact information right after this meeting. Any more questions, Mr. Carter?"

"No, I think that will do it."

*Thank you, Lord!* I was going to escape unscathed.

"Oh, wait, I'm sorry. I did have one more question. Eva's counselor thought it may be helpful to equate Eva's personality in more tangible terms. Uh, Miss Hamilton."

*Shit.*

"If my daughter were say, a zoo animal, which would you say she was?"

And there you had it. I couldn't have felt more exposed if my face had been plastered on *Wanted* posters and tacked to every tree in town.

"I, umm, I don't..." I fumbled. How was I supposed to answer that?

Thankfully, Miss Flower Child, aka Miss Mason, our school's art teacher, interrupted. "A giraffe. She would definitely be a giraffe."

*For fuck's sake.*

# chapter six

I couldn't get the hell out of that room fast enough. After Mason's "giraffe" comment, Mrs. Kline had clearly had enough. I had never been more appreciative of a crotchety old hag who should have retired ten years ago. She said that the teachers needed to get back to class before the next period began. As I walked out of the office and started down the brightly painted hall, mortified thoroughly, I heard my name from behind me.

"Excuse me, Miss Hamilton, could I have just one more moment of your time, please?"

I closed my eyes and breathed in slowly. I knew who had said it. I must have been a real bitch in a past life to deserve this.

I turned, plastered a bright smile on my face and, through nearly gritted teeth, replied, "Certainly, Mr. Carter."

He stopped in front of me, and as I took in his face, I became acutely aware that he was trying to suppress a smirk. Whew! Maybe he wasn't going to hold my comment against me. Maybe I wasn't staring the end of my career directly in the face.

"So, I was just wondering how you like it?"

"Umm, I'm sorry. I don't understand what you're referring to."

"Being a zookeeper. How do you like it?"

*Oh, shit.* The only thing left to do was beg for mercy.

"Mr. Carter, I apologize for the completely inappropriate and distasteful comment I made. I don't know what I ..."

When I finally got the courage to lift my eyes and look at him, I felt relief mixed with definite annoyance. Mr. Carter's head was bowed so that his chin rested on his chest. I could see the slight shaking of his shoulders. The bastard was laughing at me! Just what I fucking needed. *What was it with men?*

He looked up when I stopped talking, put his hand to his chest, and choked out, "I'm sorry."

I stood there, giving him time to regain his composure.

"I'm sorry," he started again. "I couldn't resist."

"Glad I could give you a laugh. Nice to meet you, Mr. Carter. Enjoy the rest of your day," I said politely before turning to leave. I had already suffered enough during the meeting; I wasn't up for any more humiliation.

As I began to walk away, I felt a strong hand on my arm. It was not an unkind, rough hand. Just a sure, confident one.

"Miss Hamilton, I really am sorry. That was wrong of me. I wasn't trying to make you uncomfortable."

He looked down at his hand and quickly withdrew it, like he suddenly realized it probably wasn't appropriate to be manhandling his daughter's teacher. Not that I minded. I'd come around to manhandling a few weeks back—literally.

It was then that I really looked at him. He was incredibly attractive, with bright-green eyes, dirty-blond hair, and a genuine, pearly white smile. And his lips were perfectly pink. My eyes were drawn to them as he bit his lower one, waiting for me to reply.

But all I could think about was how much I'd like to sit on

those gorgeous lips. I shuddered slightly at the thought, which effectively brought me back into this tortuous moment with Mr. Carter. What was my deal? A single one-flight stand had morphed me into a complete nymphomaniac. Had he noticed my involuntary shudder?

"It's a little cold in here," I stammered as I drew my arms across my chest. *Nice save, Lily, you horse's ass.* "How about this: I'll forget about your oh-so-witty practical joke if you please, please, for the love of God, not hold my zoo comment against me. Deal?"

Mr. Carter smiled broadly, and his eyes crinkled slightly. Sweet Christ, he was hot.

"Deal," he agreed as he held out his hand. "Under one condition..."

Apprehension rushed through me again. I'd had enough of these men and their conditions. I stared expectantly at him.

"Call me Adam," he said with a smile.

Relief flooded through me as I took his hand gratefully and offered my own megawatt smile, compliments of the nightly headgear Dr. Schiffer made me wear.

As we shook hands, I noticed that he was holding my hand longer than was typically acceptable. His green eyes were gazing at me. Curiously? Mischievously? I couldn't quite be sure.

I withdrew my hand as I said, "Goodbye, Adam."

"Miss Hamilton," he replied with a firm nod of his head. He then walked around me and strode out of the school, oozing success and sex appeal. Just then, the bell rang, preventing me from any more X-rated daydreams.

*Awesome,* I thought. Thank God I had already taught that man's daughter today. I grinned as I pictured myself contemplating, during a discussion about our current novel *The Outsiders*, if Eva's father was as good in bed as he looked. The thought almost caused me to laugh out loud as I scampered down the hall to beat the late bell to class and ensure that the animals didn't claw each other to death.

# chapter seven

Thankfully, the rest of the day had been smooth. I guess I had made enough of an ass of myself for one day. My students were engrossed in *The Outsiders* and completed their reading assignments without complaint. Or at least without much complaint.

As I sat at my desk, scanning the empty desks, I smiled. I recalled the heated discussion in third period over whether or not the Socs and Greasers were really all that different. Fourth period willingly delved into the significance of having a gentle, forthright character like Johnny present in the book. Sixth period uncovered the crux of the novel—that gentleness and violence often existed side by side, and that perhaps, without one, the other would also cease to be.

Highlights like those reminded me why I chose this profession instead of entering law school after graduating with an English degree from Penn. Law school had been all my parents could talk about since I was able to walk. My father was a defense attorney, and my mother had been a prosecutor until she got pregnant with me and my dad convinced her that motherhood would allow her to have a far greater influence on the world than working for the Chicago DA's office. You'd think an assistant district attorney would have been able to see right through that line of bullshit.

I had never disappointed my parents until the day I told them that, not only would I not be returning to Illinois, but I was also accepting a teaching position at a public—for shame!—middle school twenty-five minutes outside of Philadelphia. They hadn't known that I had taken on a minor in education my sophomore year. I had done it simply to keep my options open, but as graduation approached, I knew that all I could really envision myself doing was teaching a subject I adored to the precocious young minds of our future generations. That last bit ended up being a hot pile of dog shit, but I still do adore the subject and I still get lost in the hope that I may make a true impact on a child's life.

Okay, time to end my trance of bliss and get the hell out of here. I still had thirty minutes before I could actually leave, but I would damn sure be ready when the clock hit three fifteen. Just as I was closing out all of the open programs on my computer, I heard our PA system click on and our principal's voice bellow, "Attention staff: there will be a mandatory meeting in the auditorium immediately following this announcement. See you there."

Jesus Christ! I had already done my job for the day. Couldn't they just leave us alone? I was shaking my head at the injustice of it all when my friend Tina walked in. "This had better be good," she declared. "I was in the middle of a very important game of solitaire."

We walked to the auditorium, loudly voicing our dissatisfaction with the administration. They had no respect for our after-school time, time we needed to make sure our lessons were in order. Sure, some teachers may be using this time to sit around, shoot the shit, and play on their cell phones.

But no need for subtle hair splitting.

Tina and I walked in and took seats in the middle of the auditorium. We had learned the hard way that sitting in the back would only get you asked to move forward and that only ass kissers sat in the front. I kept my eyes cast down, examining my cuticles, refusing to give the principal my focus and therefore making it clear what my priorities were. Surely he would notice how I refused to look at him. I mean, there were only seventy-five of us, after all.

Tina interrupted my examination of my nail beds. "Holy shit, look at that hot piece of ass."

"Who?" I asked as my head shot up. I strained to see over the heads of the people in front of me. *Duck, damn you. I have a hot guy to ogle.*

I lifted myself slightly out of my seat as my eyes scanned everyone at the front of the auditorium before they came to a screeching halt. *Ho-ly fuck*! I immediately slammed myself back into my seat. This couldn't be happening again. This couldn't happen twice in a lifetime, let alone in one day. I lifted my head slightly to get another look. It couldn't be him, could it?

It sure as shit could be.

I would have recognized him anywhere, for obvious reasons. What was he doing here? I never thought I'd see him again, especially not at my work. My mind was reeling so fast, it was making me dizzy. I was utterly shocked, and not in a good way.

As I looked up again, my gaze met his. The fucker saw me. Why had I been so overly zealous to see who Tina was talking about? By practically standing up to get a better view, I had drawn attention to myself. His eyes were boring into mine, and his mouth turned up into a smile. *Cocky son of a bitch.*

Tina eyed me nervously as Principal Murdock began speaking. How could he speak so calmly at a time like this? I wished I was sitting closer to a fire alarm. Where was my cell phone? I could call in a bomb threat. Why was he still staring at me? Principal Murdock was saying something about some guy named Max Samson... hockey... volunteering his time at our school. Then my brain started working.

My fuck buddy from the plane was a hockey player? A professional one? Holy shit, go me! The words the principal was saying started to morph from fragments of information to a coherent lump I could process. Max was going to be the new ice hockey coach. Wait, we had an ice hockey team?

"Mr. Samson will be donating all of the funds necessary to start up a youth hockey club and will take on the role as head coach. Please join me in welcoming Max to our team." Our principal began to clap, prompting all of us to join in. But he didn't realize that he was a day late and a dollar short. I had done enough welcoming for the entire staff two weeks ago.

"Mr. Samson, any words for the faculty?" Please, Mr. Murdock, don't ask him to speak! God only knows what is going to come out of that perfectly vulgar mouth of his. Max hadn't dropped my gaze since he picked it up. And, for some reason I couldn't even begin to explain, I couldn't look away. I sat motionless as he began to speak. As soon as the first gruff syllable escaped his lips, I was catapulted back to our flight from Aspen to Philly. I instantly became wet and my nipples hardened. Damn you, body. Judas!

"Thank you, everyone. I'm excited to get to know all of you better and get this hockey program off the ground." Maybe it was just me, but he seemed to overly enunciate "excited," so that I immediately pictured his penis. And "off the ground" conjured up a host of images: the literal flying in the plane, his helping me up after I decided to dump the contents of my suitcase all over the airport floor, and, oh yeah, his hoisting me off the ground so that I could wrap my legs around that gorgeous ass as he savagely and euphorically thrust into me.

I was so lost in my thoughts and in Max's eyes that I didn't realize people were filing out of the auditorium. The meeting was over? When did that happen?

"Hey, you okay?" Tina questioned.

"Uh, yeah, I'm fine," I said as I shook my head, finally dropping Max's gaze and pushing myself out of the chair. Tina eyed me curiously, opened her mouth, and then quickly shut it, as if she wanted to say something but thought better of it.

I turned to head up the aisle toward the exit as I heard "Miss Hamilton" being called from behind me. I had never experienced déjà vu before. It sucked. The voice was coming from Principal Murdock. He motioned for me to come toward them. I inhaled loudly as I trudged toward the front of the auditorium. My eyes again found Max, but this time I didn't hold his gaze. I was already turning beet red; if I continued looking at him, I would burst into flames. My day had been going so well. I had resolved that pesky zoo issue, my kids had actually learned something, and now it was all shot to shit.

I smiled expectantly at Mr. Murdock when I reached them, not trusting myself to actually form words.

"Oh, yes. Miss Lily Hamilton, I'd like you to meet Max Samson."

Max reached out his hand to me. The bastard kept his lips closed, but his eyes were cackling hysterically.

I shook his hand limply. "How do you do, Mr. Samson," I managed dryly.

"Nice to meet you, Lily," he replied, with a discreet wink. "And please, call me Max."

What a sly prick. His thumb briefly massaged mine before he released my hand. I had to resist the urge to yank it back like he had burned me. But that seemed dramatic, especially since he had touched far more intimate parts of my anatomy than my hand.

"Lily, I was hoping you would show Mr. Samson around tomorrow morning. He wanted to come in at nine and re-familiarize himself with the building, and when I looked through teacher schedules, I noticed that you were one of the few who had a prep period at that time. I'd show him around myself, but I'll be out of the building for a conference."

*Of course you will be. Because why would the universe want me to miss out on this thoroughly mortifying and awkward experience?*

"Sure," I replied with a chipperness I didn't feel. "I'll meet you at the front of the building at nine."

"Are you sure?" Max asked. "I could meet you in your classroom."

*Oh no you don't, buddy. I know your game, and I am not playing it. Again, that is.*

"No, it's no problem. I'll meet you in front. See you tomorrow. It's been a pleasure meeting you." The last sentence had slipped out before I could catch it. This had been far from pleasurable for me.

I balled my hands into fists at my side as I tried to regain my composure for the long, lonely walk up the aisle.

About midway through my journey, I heard his deep tone behind me, "The pleasure's all mine."

My mind immediately homed in on the word *pleasure*.

My body quaked, but I didn't dare a look back until I reached the doors. With my escape imminent, I couldn't resist a glance back. And there he was, speaking to Mr. Murdock, but his eyes were still locked on me.

Tomorrow was really going to blow.

# chapter eight

The night had passed with excruciating slowness. I had drifted through intermittent bouts of restless sleep and terrified alertness. I ran scenarios over and over in my mind of what this day could bring: horror, tragedy, mortification? The only thing I was able to guarantee myself was that it was going to be a long day.

As I walked bleary eyed into school the next morning, I had wound myself so tight that I had nearly convinced myself that quitting was a better option than actually going through with this tour. I plodded down the hall toward my classroom, thinking what a damn inconvenience it was to have to deal with these kids all the time.

I pulled my copy of *The Outsiders* from my red leather messenger bag and threw it onto my desk. Yesterday, I had really enjoyed teaching this novel to my classes, and now I stared at the book like it would give me leprosy. That damn bastard had taken the joy out of everything!

What really bothered me was that I couldn't actually pinpoint why I was so annoyed. I mean, so the guy had fucked me mercilessly in an airport? Was that truly something that I should let ruin my day? What the hell was my problem? If I were honest with myself, I guess it all came down to faith.

Not my faith in him—I had none of that. But my faith in myself. I could accept that I had succumbed to a one-night stand. I was even almost proud of it, in a secretive, I'd-rather-cut-my-tongue-out-than-tell-anyone kind of way. But I didn't want to be the type of person who did that sort of thing continually.

I just couldn't be that girl. I had told myself before that I was better than his cocky, domineering advances, but my actions hadn't demonstrated that. I could forgive it once, celebrate it even. But never again. This was the kind of behavior that could change a person, and I would never change for anyone, least of all that arrogant asshole Max Samson.

I groaned loudly as the bell rang, dismissing the kids from the cafeteria. *Okay, Lily. Game face.*

I smiled as the kids entered the room and I greeted each by name. I should've been an actress. I had been putting on an Oscar-worthy performance for sure. The goal of today's lesson was to analyze the characters and have the students begin to realize that authors had a purpose for every character they introduced. It was the reader's job, and privilege, to discern that purpose.

As the period progressed, the students became more astute at evaluating the role a particular character played in the progression of the plot and the deepening of the conflict. So far, we had discussed Pony Boy, Johnny, and Dallas. Since we were seriously lacking the female perspective, I decided to move on to Cherry Valance.

Just as I said her name, I heard a knock on the door. I glanced over at the door and my face fell. I quickly looked up at the clock: eight fifty. The bastard was ten minutes early. I had specifically told him that I would meet him out front. Why did he have to be such a pain in the ass?

I wanted to yell at my student Ben, who sat nearest the door, "Stranger danger! Get away from the door! Lockdown, lockdown, lockdown!" But I was too late. As I heard the handle turn, I knew I had lost another battle to Max Samson. Maybe there was still hope for the war.

Max quietly shut the door behind him. He nodded his head to me and then made his way to my desk, sinking into my chair. Did he have to invade every aspect of me? Now, even my chair had been contaminated by his despicable sexiness. I looked back to my room full of students, trying like hell to ignore Max's intrusion. But as I looked at their faces, I knew that was not going to be a possibility. The boys definitely recognized Max, and they stared at him with adoration in their eyes. The girls, clearly noticing his snug-fitting gray T-shirt and faded jeans slung low on his waist, sat mouths agape at this beautiful specimen of masculinity. If they only knew what a dick he was.

I clapped my hands to recapture their focus. They irritatedly turned back toward me as I asked them, "Okay, where were we?"

"We were talking about Cherry Valance," Alicia said.

"That's right, Cherry Valance. What is her role in the story?" As Alicia prattled on about Cherry, I purposefully resisted looking over at Max. Sadly, though, my periphery couldn't look away. He was reclined in my chair, staring at me intently. He made no sounds, no movements. He seemed to be observing me. My demeanor. The way I interacted with my students. Everything.

As the end of the period approached, I wanted my students to leave with a question to ponder tonight so that we could pick up our discussion quickly tomorrow.

"So, here's what we've learned about Cherry: she absolutely detests violence, she agrees to be the mediator between the Socs and Greasers at the rumble to ensure that everything remains fair, she loathes bad behavior, and she will not put up with excessive drinking. Everyone agree?" Eighteen heads nodded assent. "Then, why is she so attracted to Bob and Dallas? On the surface, they are everything she should despise, but she seems almost inexplicably drawn to them. Tomorrow, I want everyone to come in here with a reason for why that may be. You should be ready to explain and substantiate. Got it?" Just then, the bell rang, and I yelled, "See you tomorrow" over the cacophony of screeching chairs and noisy conversations. As I watched them leave, I thought I noticed movement at my desk, but by the time I looked that direction, Max was still.

I started for my desk. The quicker we got this shit show started, the quicker we could end it. As I approached, Max stood and lifted the sole picture I had on my desk up for closer inspection.

"Don't teachers normally have tons of pictures on their desks?" he questioned.

"I don't think it's a prerequisite for employment," I retorted dryly.

His brow furrowed as he stared at me curiously, like he was trying to work something out in his head. Desperate to fill the silence, I explained further.

"She was my dog when I was younger. Charlotte was the best friend I ever had." Why had I said that last part? Why? I was clearly possessed by a complete fucking moron.

After a moment's silence, during which I could almost see the wheels in his brain turning, he asked incredulously, "You named your dog Charlotte?"

*Oh, fuck you, dude.*

"Yeah," I countered defensively. "I was a big *Charlotte's Web* fan. What does it matter?"

He shrugged as he carefully put the picture back where he had found it, touching it gently, as if he had touched on something he was uncomfortable handling.

I wanted him out of my space. Now! I turned and headed for the door. When I reached it, I looked over my shoulder at him. "Ready?" I asked impatiently. I didn't wait for a reply but walked through the doorway and started down the hall without waiting for him to follow.

"Sure am," he said as he sauntered out of my classroom, pushing the door closed behind him and positioning himself directly behind me, leaning in so close I could smell his fresh mint scent. "Lily." He almost growled my name, making me cringe at the images it conjured: his fingers exploring my wet opening, his perfect cock plunging into me, our breaths rapid and needy.

*Lily, get it together.*

I shook my head slightly, as if to clear it. It was a nearly imperceptible movement, but I immediately regretted it.

"Neck spasm?" he inquired with just a hint of amusement tinging his voice.

"No," I replied so harshly, it only served to confirm what he already suspected. He was in my head, burrowing in for the long haul. Why was he always watching me so closely? It unnerved me. My anxiety mounted, and I scrambled to change the subject.

"Guess we may as well start in the gym," I muttered.

"Great idea," he chimed.

*Prick.*

❤

Looking at the outside of the school building, the gym was located to the far right. So it made logical sense that we would start there and work our way to the other end. We walked down the hallway in silence, mine awkward, his scheming, until I finally couldn't take it anymore.

"Principal Murdock mentioned that you wanted to 're-familiarize' yourself with the school. Have you been here before?"

"I went here."

*OOOkay. That's it?* I wasn't going to force conversation if he wasn't going to participate. We walked into the gym, and I gestured with my arm indifferently.

"This is the basketball court," I said flippantly and turned to move on, but he hesitated. He stretched his arms above his head, causing his shirt to ride up and reveal his lower abdominals. It was like a "Flying V" aimed directly at his dick. I couldn't help but wonder if he was going commando again when I didn't see the top of his boxers peeking out from above the waist of his jeans.

"I always like playing a little one-on-one. It helps clear my head."

I glanced back at him abruptly. Had he said that to be purposefully suggestive, or was it just me? Could he have gotten me so worked up that I was now the one with my mind in the gutter?

I started walking again, and he followed closely behind me. I became acutely aware of his imposing presence as we moved. We crossed the court and went to a room that was off to the left.

"This is our wrestling room." *Blah, blah, blah. Who cares about this shit?* The entire floor was covered with blue mats.

"Hmm, those mats look inviting. I'll have to remember this room when I need a nap."

"They're not beds," I replied sardonically.

This comment should have grossed me out. Sweaty boys rolled around on these mats daily. However, the mental image it conjured, him sprawled naked on a king-size bed, was totally alluring. A tingle began to pulse between my legs, reminding me of how physically attractive I found this man.

"Who needs a bed?" he asked slyly.

I cleared my throat and gained my composure to resume the tour. As we made our way around the inner perimeter of the wrestling room, I headed toward the door to the far right that housed our weight room.

I walked in and spun around to look at him. "And this is where our prepubescent athletes act like they're The Rock."

He smiled, but he did not follow me into the room. Instead, he stood in the doorway, placing his large hands on either side of the doorframe, and leaned in. The action made his biceps flex, and I nearly drooled at the sight of him.

Then a curious thought came to me. Why the hell was he wearing a T-shirt? It was friggin' January!

My observations of his clothing made me hyperaware of my own. I was wearing a close-fitting purple sweater and black Editor pants from Express. I tried to purposefully buy clothes that weren't in any way revealing, but that was kind of difficult, considering I was only one hundred and twenty pounds with D-cup breasts. I couldn't hide those puppies if I tried, but I attempted to ensure that they were always tastefully concealed.

Just as my mind began to envision what my breasts would

look like in those giant hands, I decided that it was time to move on. We walked back the way we had come and turned right as we exited the gym, descending a tiny flight of stairs. I pushed open a heavy set of doors that led into the pool and held open the door as he sauntered in and took a deep breath, trying to draw added attention to the next thing out of his mouth:

"I love indoor pools. It always feels so damp and warm inside. Feels great on my muscles."

*Yup, he was saying this shit on purpose.*

I rolled my eyes. "Can we move on?" I asked, exasperated. I meant move on with the tour, but I also wanted to move on from this sexual tension that had been steadily building since my classroom. And the only way I knew to do that was to stay away from Max.

He gave a single nod of his head and followed me out. *God, why did he have to keep walking so close to me?* I felt like he was nearly on top of me, invading my personal space. But he hadn't touched me. Not once the entire tour. My skin prickled with anticipation at the thought that he might graze against me at some point. Damn skin. Who needed it?

Directly behind the pool doors were the boys' locker room doors. I pointed them out to him and kept moving. But he didn't follow this time. He swung the doors open and went inside, returning about a minute later.

"Just wanted to take a look. The lockers are small. It must be a tight fit, trying to get all of your equipment in there."

I couldn't be sure if he had actually just winked or if I had imagined it, but his eyes definitely twinkled at the ingenuity of his comment. I was a jumble of contrasts. I kept telling myself that his comments were inappropriate, that I should be angry. But I didn't feel angry, and it was becoming increasingly difficult to feign emotions that were not there. Almost as hard as it was becoming to repress emotions that *were* there. Part of me, a big part, was flattered by the attention he gave, turned on by the eroticism that laced every word he spoke, and longed for the touch that he was clearly withholding intentionally.

But I wasn't a person of contrasts. I couldn't survive in this paradox. I would suffocate here. So I had to choose, and I chose the easier, less messy route: loathing.

I ignored his last remark, pretended that I hadn't recognized it for what it was: a proposition.

"We have to speed this up. I have a third-period class." I strode briskly away from the locker room, back up the stairs, and out of the gym. He again mirrored my movements, seeming to be magnetically pulled to me.

I showed him the auditorium and got some comment about "putting on a show" and our media room, which got me a mention of how he "would love to do something worth recording." I also showed him the library, nurse's office, guidance office, and assorted other offices he may have to locate throughout the rest of the school year. He must not have been witty enough to come up with any innuendos for these places. Or maybe he had finally given up.

Our last stop was the cafeteria. It wasn't a lunch period, but kids still occupied the tables. The heat had broken in one part of the building, displacing some of the teachers, so some were assigned to bring their classes here. I could feel eyes on us as we moved through—and not just students' eyes. Teachers, cafeteria workers. Everyone stopped to drink up the sight of Max.

"This is it, the last stop on the tour."

Max walked over to a table filled with Mr. Garretty's

biology class. He gripped the edge of the table with his hand and gave it a firm push toward the ground.

"Tables seem mighty sturdy."

*Nope, he hadn't given up.*

I groaned and stormed out of the cafeteria. Halfway back to my classroom, I realized he was still behind me. Instead of continuing to my room, I led him around to a back stairwell that wasn't used often so that I could effectively give him the piece of my mind that he deserved. I was so overcome with fury, frustration, and annoyance that I flew around and directed my hard glare at him as soon as we arrived.

"Listen, asshole, I have to work here. And I can't do that if you're going to be making these ridiculous fucking sexual comments to me all of the time. It has to stop!"

Max looked at me intently, seeming to ponder his reply. Then he smiled, drew a hand to his chest, and said, "Have I been making sexual comments?"

*What. A. Dick.*

I couldn't respond. There was no point. He wouldn't truly hear me anyway.

So I shook my head and left him standing there in the stairwell. This time he didn't follow me. And I was almost grateful for it. Almost. I wasn't capable of any positive feelings toward him or anyone else at that moment. I just wanted to get through the rest of my day and get the hell out of this place.

When I returned to my room, I found Tina sitting in my chair, one elbow resting on the arm as she used her hand to support her chin. She just stared at me for a moment, and I knew from her expression that she had observed Max and me at some point on our route.

"You need a drink. Meet me out front at three fifteen" was

all she said. I nodded my head. Then she rose and walked out without saying another word.

Finally alone, I threw myself into my chair and buried my face in my hands. I only had three minutes before the third-period bell, so I needed to pull it together. I dropped one of my hands to my mouse and gave it a slight jiggle to wake up my monitor. When the screen remained black, I realized that my monitor had been turned off. Dread moved through me as it dawned on me that Max had been sitting here only forty minutes prior. As I hit the button, I inhaled deeply.

There on my screen was a picture of Max, dressed in a hockey uniform from the waist down, shirtless from the waist up. His hair hung in his strikingly blue eyes, his muscled torso sweaty and delectable. I'd never wanted to fuck a picture so badly in my life. When I clicked out of the internet, I realized just how sadistic he was. It wasn't an image up on just Google. The fucker had made this my wallpaper.

❤

The rest of the day passed, and my agitation waned as my students reminded me of what my true focus was supposed to be. The truth was that despite the fact that I jokingly called the kids animals and nerds and complained about my job, I loved being a teacher. And I was damn good at it. I certainly wasn't going to let one man ruin all of that for me.

I decided to check my email one last time before heading out to meet Tina. As I clicked Outlook open, my eyes fell to one email in particular. I eyed the sender's name curiously: *Carter, Adam.* The subject line was blank, so I was forced to click on it to see what it was about.

*Dear Miss Hamilton,*

*I just wanted to follow up on our meeting yesterday and make sure that you had my email address so that you could readily contact me about Eva's progress in English. Also, I was thinking about starting up a book club and wanted to run my first book selection by you. Have you ever read* Water for Elephants? ;) *Though I think it's about a circus, so maybe that doesn't quite pique your interest.*

*Hope to hear from you soon,*

*Adam*

*P.S. Am I too old for the winky face above? I put one in a text to Eva, and she told me I was too old for emoticons. The nerve!*

Once I finished reading Adam's email, I found myself grinning like the Cheshire Cat. So maybe there were men left in the world who could hold appropriate conversations with women. It was refreshing. I quickly tried to think of a witty reply.

*Dear Adam,*

*Thank you for your email, and I will be sure to keep you updated about Eva. In regards to the book club, I didn't know parents of giraffes were all that into reading. Learn something new every day.*

*Sincerely,*

*Lily Hamilton*

*P.S. I thought old men were the only ones who still winked anyway. Therefore, I think you're safe.*

I hit Send, hoping he would find my email humorous. I mean, I basically called him old, but he'd see the humor, right? I was obviously being sarcastic; he couldn't have been more than thirty-five. Now that I was thinking about it, maybe he wouldn't see the humor because it wasn't funny. And what if he didn't remember that Miss Mason had called Eva a giraffe? Was that the sort of thing someone would forget? I was pretty damn sure I'd never forget it, and it hadn't even been said about my kid. Questions plagued my mind as I contemplated all the ways he could react to what I had written.

My cell phone buzzed. I glanced down to see a text from Tina.

*I'm waiting!!!!*

I looked at the time. Three seventeen. *Christ . . . Impatient much?*

I shut down my computer, grabbed my stuff, and walked toward the door. I suddenly thought that I should email Adam again and thank him. For the first time all day, I wasn't obsessing over Max.

# chapter nine

Tina gazed at me hard. "Okay, spill it! You've been a complete wreck since Mr. Sweet-Ass Samson got here yesterday. How do you know him?"

"I don't," I snapped back quickly. The truth was I *didn't* know him. I hadn't wanted to know his name, and he didn't even know mine until yesterday. Now he was going to be in my life for the next few months, whether I liked it or not.

"Bull*shit* you don't know him! I saw you showing him around the school earlier today, and you looked pale as a ghost when he was trying to talk to you. Something's up."

"I need a drink," I replied, resting my elbows on the table and collapsing my head into my hands so I could rub my eyes. "Or two or three."

"I'll get you as many drinks as it'll take for you to let me in on all the juicy details." She looked at me expectantly. "You know him. And when I get back, I wanna know how."

Tina headed toward the bar, giving me a brief respite. I breathed in deeply, taking in my surroundings. The bar was more crowded than I expected for a Wednesday afternoon. It was a casual place, a local haunt that teachers often frequented because of its close proximity to the school. It had a certain *Cheers* quality to it, which made it all the more appealing.

She returned a few minutes later with two shots of tequila and two beers. I drank both shots immediately—before realizing that one of them had probably been for her—and then chased them with a lemon wedge and a few gulps of my Miller Lite. "Thanks." I glanced up, massaging my temples and contemplating what to say next. *Okay, here it goes.* "I met him in the Aspen airport when I was heading home from my parents' over break."

She raised her right eyebrow to let me know that she damn well knew there was more to it than that. "And?"

I briefly gave her the gist of what had transpired: my embarrassment at check-in, running into him at security, his sexual innuendos and forward advances at the bar.

"Aaaand?"

I breathed in deeply and kept my eyes down, preparing myself mentally for what I was about to say. "And...I may have let him finger me during the flight," I said before raising my eyes slightly to gauge her reaction.

"Oh my God, Lily! You go, girl! I didn't know you had it in you." She wore a smile that I couldn't have blowtorched off her face.

I sped up my words, hoping that somehow the last part of what I had said might get lost in the air on its way to her ears. "And I may have begged him to make me come while he fucked me up against a wall in the Philadelphia airport." I shut my eyes tightly for several seconds and then finally opened one when she hadn't responded.

For the first time in my life, I saw Tina Nielson speechless. *This can't be good.*

"He wants you again, doesn't he?" She answered her own question, so caught up in the excitement. "That's why you seemed weird on the tour today! He was hitting on you, and you didn't know how to react." She paused only to catch her breath. "Lily, you *have* to fuck him again. You can't just let that fine piece of ass walk around the building for the next five months without banging the shit out of him on your desk or something." Clearly this dilemma was not as difficult for her as it was for me.

I let out a sigh and allowed myself to sit back, becoming slightly more relaxed in the vinyl booth. "It's not that easy. He's bad news."

"What do you mean 'bad news'?"

"You know he was a professional hockey player, right?" I looked at Tina, and she seemed to be listening closely. "Well, he was pretty good. Really good, actually. He was drafted into the minors out of high school and made it to the pros within two years. He played for the Avalanche for five years until his contract expired and . . ."

"Yeah, he's a hockey player who looks like a fucking god. So what? Get to the point," she interrupted eagerly.

"He couldn't get picked up by another team. He's had a couple short stints, but nothing lasting for the past three years. He was too much of a"—I struggled to find the right word—"a liability, I guess. He wasn't showing up to practices. He stayed out late partying, going to strip clubs, gambling. No team wanted him. And for good reason. He clearly has issues controlling his behavior."

Tina stared at me, taking it all in. "I thought you said you didn't really know him. He told you all this?"

*Shit. Busted.* Out of all of the embarrassing things I had experienced in the past few weeks, somehow this was the only thing that made me feel a hint of shame. "I Googled him." It felt worse to admit it than it had felt when I was actually doing it. *Great. Not only was I becoming sexually reckless, but now I was a stalker too.*

"So what? So he's a playboy who likes to have a good time? You're not marrying him. You're just screwing him." She paused to examine my response. "Please tell me you *are* still planning to screw him."

I said nothing.

"Look, you haven't really been in a serious relationship since you broke up with Chris. I know it was hard for you, but that was like five years ago. I mean, Christ, that's what your twenties are for: fucking hot guys with no strings attached. Have a good time. Enjoy yourself." She raised her voice a bit, clearly enthusiastic about the subject. "For God's sake, if you don't do this for *you*, at least do it for *me*. Now that I'm married, I need some excitement in my life. I need to hear some good stories. It's not every day you get to hear how your friend got finger-banged at thirty thousand feet. And that's the kind of thing I'd like to hear about. Every day!"

"Jesus, keep your voice down."

She stopped to take a few sips of her beer before continuing. "All I'm saying is that you need to get back on that horse…or, in your case, that big dick. Because if you don't, you better stop at the drugstore on your way home and pick up some more batteries for your vibrator. Come to think of it, you better get that sucker a charger, because it's going to get a lot of use for the rest of the school year with all of the sexual frustration you're going to be experiencing."

"I don't own a vibrator."

"Well," she said, as she rose to get us more drinks, "you either take my advice, or you better fucking invest in one."

# chapter ten

My nails scraped against the muscles of his lower back as I worked my way up to his shoulder blades, massaging frantically, until my warm palms found the back of his neck and pushed his mouth even more forcefully against my own.

He was delicious. And soft. And I was urgent as he nipped at my bottom lip, licking his way down my skin from my chin to the front of my neck.

*Yes . . . yes. Oh, God. Keep going.*

My head fuzzed with all of the violent, perfect words I wanted to say as I grabbed a handful of his ruffled hair and pushed him farther down, letting him know of my intent. My back arched slightly as I gripped the muted teal and white comforter with my other hand. I was lost. Passionate. Needy.

With one powerful grasp, he lifted my hips in the air, and my wetness found his mouth at last. His tongue fluttered across my clit as I invited his fingers to invade me and softly stroke my insides. Pulsations of pleasure slid up my spine. My ass again found the bed as he placed me down, sucking wildly at my slick opening.

I was a rush of heavy, demanding breaths. Persuasive moans. And unintelligible ramblings. My heels dug strenuously into the mattress, my legs straining to find the release I needed as I moved his strong hand to my aching chest, inciting him to twist and pull at my nipples gently.

*Oh, shit. I'm close.*

With a quick tug of his hair, I brought his face needily up to my lips again, thoroughly devouring him. Then, pushing on his powerful shoulders, I propelled him to his back, pulled myself ravenously on top of his well-sculpted body, and captured all of him inside me with one rough, abrupt movement. I was impatient as I moved back and forth, creating the friction I craved.

I leaned forward, commanding him to thrust in and out of me furiously while my orgasm built steadily and forcefully. Teetering on the edge, I felt as if I could explode in an instant.

❤

Unfortunately, the sound of my alarm interrupted my erotically blissful slumber. I hit the snooze button before closing my eyes, hoping to pick up where I had just left off.

But it was useless. Why were men the only ones who were granted the pleasure of wet dreams?

My mind was a tornado of thoughts. Sexual. Confusing.

But also surprisingly certain. My dream had added new clarity to my recent desires. *I* had been the aggressor in my fantasy: a sure sign that I could no longer criticize myself for my physical passions. I shivered at the reality that I might even have to learn to embrace them.

However, despite my newfound revelation, there was still one question that remained unanswered.

Why had the man in my dream been Adam?

# chapter eleven

When I arrived at work Thursday morning, I felt invigorated. And free. The bullshit dread was gone. I would accept what the day brought me. And if it brought me Max, so be it.

I was again embroiled in a hearty discussion about the characters in *The Outsiders* during fourth period when I heard my classroom door open.

"Sorry to interrupt, Miss Hamilton, but I wanted to stop by and check on my hockey players."

I scanned the sea of supergeeks, uncoordinates, and shadow-fearers before me.

"None of these students play hockey," I said, confused.

"Oh, then . . . does anyone in here *want* to play hockey?"

Crickets.

"Okay, then. Uh, Miss Hamilton, could I speak to you for a second?"

*Here we go.*

I took a deep breath, plastered a smile on my face, and began walking toward the door.

"Certainly, Mr. Samson."

Once outside, he pushed the door closed. Then he turned to me, wearing a mischievous grin.

"You know all the boys in that room want to fuck you,

right? They probably fantasize about it all day. And night. Some of the girls probably do, too."

*Wait, did I just hear him right? Gross!*

"That's...the most inappropriate thing I've ever heard. And considering some of the vulgarities that have already come out of your mouth, that's really saying something."

"Well, I'm nothing if not truthful." He acted like this was a sufficient explanation and rapidly moved on to a different subject. "There's one place you didn't show me yesterday."

"Where's that?" I asked, still in a slight state of shock from his initial comment.

"I'll take you there. You have lunch next period, right?"

Now who was the stalker? How the hell had he found that out?

"Yes," I replied warily.

"Okay, we'll go then. This period ends in about five minutes. I'll wait in our stairwell for you."

Before I could question him or argue that *we* had no stairwell, he had walked off. I stood still and watched him go for a second before looking back into my classroom. Forty-two expectant eyes were looking back at me. This was going to be a long five minutes.

❤

The bell rang, and my students began to file from the room. I took a moment to get myself together, smoothed out the navy-blue skirt I had worn today, readjusted my white silk blouse, and then headed out the door to find Max. Though I had wanted to pretend that I didn't know what he meant by *our* stairwell, he wouldn't be fooled by it. I knew exactly where I was going. I just wish I could've been as sure about what I was going to do once I arrived there.

I walked into the stairwell, my knee-high boots echoing. He was sitting on the steps, and his eyes found mine immediately. I didn't want to stand in silence, left with my own thoughts screaming at me inside my head, so I spoke quickly.

"So where's this place you're talking about?"

"You'll see."

As he stood and walked out of the stairwell and down the hallway, I concentrated on how much I hated surprises. But I definitely didn't hate being behind him. He wore black cargo pants and a red Nike hoodie. He was very casual chic, and everything fit in all the right ways. As he made his way to the doors that led outside, butterflies began to take flight in my stomach.

Something about this building made me feel safe, like it was a fortress against regrets and bad decisions. But leaving it stripped me of my comfort. I began to fidget as we walked, partly because of the cold and partly because I knew no one would hear me if I screamed. Not that I thought I would need saving from Max. I somehow knew that he wouldn't ever hurt me. However, I couldn't say the same about myself. There was a great chance that I would need someone to save me from myself before this little trip was over.

We walked up a flight of stone steps and turned right into the football stadium we shared with our high school. He led me onto the bleachers and started toward the top. As we climbed the metal stairs, our destination dawned on me. The announcer's booth was directly in front of us. When we reached it, Max took out a key—*where the hell had he gotten that? And more importantly, what reason had he given for needing it?*—

and unlocked the door to the booth. He motioned me inside and shut the door behind him.

One second we were looking at each other questioningly, and the next we were on each other. Hands savagely groping. Mouths tasting salty skin. I had never been up in the booth before, and with my eyes shut as I invaded the inside of his sweet mouth, it was difficult to get my bearings. He spun me around, pressing the backs of my legs against a worn wooden table that looked out over the field. As he lifted me onto it with ease—his able hands clenching my ass—I threw some folders and papers out of our way toward a computer monitor and switchboard while he kicked two chairs to the side and spread my legs so he could fit between them.

"What are you thinking?" he asked, kissing me frantically as he unbuttoned my blouse one handed and raked his fingers against my back with the other.

Um, what was I thinking? *That I hope Mr. Emerson's gym class is planning to play something indoors today.* The thought of twenty-five seventh graders watching me get fucked in an announcer's booth while they were supposed to be playing flag football had not been on the to-do list I had made for myself this morning. But that wasn't what came out of my mouth.

"I'm thinking I want you to get me off," I whispered into his ear. "Twice." *Was that* me *who had just said that? Shit.* If I hadn't actually felt the words leave my lips, I wouldn't have believed it'd been me who had spoken them.

"Well, doll, I do consider myself a competitive person, so I'm always up for a challenge." He retreated from me a moment and began to remove his sweatshirt, pulling his white T-shirt over his head at the same time.

God, he was gorgeous. Tan, despite the winter. Lean but

well built. I could never tire of admiring him. I leaned back to study the muscles of his chest, which were already damp with beads of sweat and glistening in the afternoon sun. I let my eyes trace his tight abs to the little line of hair below his navel. All I could think about was how that hair would tickle the smoothness of my skin when he pounded into me senselessly.

He continued to strip slowly, seductively, as he unbuttoned the top of his cargo pants, granting me a moment to remember what was underneath, before finally pulling them down to free himself.

Leaning over, he hit a few buttons on the control panel. "What do you think? We *are* at a high school football field. How does a quarter sound to you?"

*Huh?* What was he talking about?

He messed with the switchboard for a few seconds and then pointed up to the scoreboard at the end of the field, where "12:00" projected in neon red before beginning to tick down. Holy shit! He was going to time himself. Publicly.

Again, he stepped in front of me, this time looking me in the eyes. "Remove your shirt and your bra," he said without taking his eyes off mine. I did as instructed, but he didn't look down at my breasts, which were already heavy and full at the thought of him touching me. He put his right hand tightly over his thickness and began to pull slowly. Steadily. "Keep your eyes on mine. Don't look away." His breathing increased as he spoke. "Do you know I touched myself like this twice last night and once this morning? And each time I came, all I could think about was you and how hot that tight little ass of yours looked in those black pants yesterday."

*So much for my "conservative" outfit choice.*

I struggled not to look down, especially when I could see his sinewy biceps flexing with each movement out of my peripheral vision. I wanted to watch him touching himself, see what his dick looked like in his hand, while he gave himself the pleasure he had wanted so badly from me.

But the way he stared at me was intimate, so much so that I didn't dare look away during such a private encounter. "Inhale," he directed. "I want all of your senses focused on me."

I breathed in twice, deeply, and smelled a mixture of soap and sweet wintergreen on him. I could see the game clock out of the corner of my eye. "Ten thirty-two," I said, swallowing hard. "You better get started if you wanna make your deadline," I urged playfully. I didn't know how long I could keep my hands off him—or off myself—if he kept this up.

He took his hand away so that he could grab hold of my skirt with both hands and pull it down. My underwear was the next to go.

"Oh, it's not *my* deadline, darling. It's yours. Do you have any idea what the biggest sexual organ in the human body is?"

*Uh, yeah. I'm pretty sure I'm looking at it*, I thought as I glanced down at his throbbing cock, the tip already slick with pre-come. God, I wanted to put my mouth around it. Lick the saltiness from him and suck him off until he exploded with a rush inside my mouth.

"It's actually the brain," he said with a seductive smirk, obviously aware of what I had been thinking. "To achieve maximum pleasure, both your body and your mind need to be stimulated. This is especially true for women," he said softly, allowing his cool breath to run along my shoulder as he spoke without touching me. He leaned in farther to lick and nip along my collarbone, and I felt the tip of him touch my opening. I yearned for him to thrust into me, over and over again, until I was so sore I couldn't walk.

"Don't get me wrong," he continued. "I'd have loved nothing more than to just yank your skirt up and have my way with you like I did in the airport. Quickly. And roughly. And with no concern for anyone's pleasure but my own. And one day I *will* do that again. But what you've asked me for requires a much more . . . deliberate approach." He glanced over my right shoulder at the scoreboard. "Nine minutes left. I've hardly even touched you since I set you down, and I'm willing to bet that you're already fucking wet for me. Let's find out, shall we?"

He pushed his index finger deep inside me, and I instantly tilted my head back against the cool glass window. When he withdrew, he put his finger to his lips, slid it into his mouth, and ran his tongue along it before pulling it out. "You taste sweet. And smooth." Then he put the same finger inside my mouth. "Suck."

Jesus, he could probably make me come with his words alone.

But thankfully he wasn't going to try. He knelt down, pulling me toward his waiting mouth, and positioned my legs over his powerful shoulders. "Watch me," he commanded.

My heart pounded in my chest, my breathing rapid and needy as he swirled his tongue inside me. He was so soft, but his rough stubble against the inside of my thighs created a heavenly combination.

I grabbed on to his tousled hair, pulling, running my fingers down the sides of his head as his speed increased. I felt myself get higher, closer to our mutual goal. I watched as he slid a finger and thumb inside me, spreading me wide as he sucked hungrily at my clit. I moved up and down, rubbing myself against his wet lips, pulling his face toward me farther. "Keep going," I breathed. "I'm so close."

Humming gently against me, he looked up to watch my face. He stared into my eyes as I let myself go, clenching wildly around his tongue and his fingers, never once taking my eyes off him.

Impatient, he pulled away from me and dropped me to the ground. He spun me around and stood behind me, pressing his erection against me and forcing my bare breasts against the cold glass. I felt my nipples harden further. *Four minutes and forty seconds*, I noted. He grabbed at my ponytail and pulled my head roughly to the right with a quick jerk, gaining access to my neck. With urgency, he kissed me along my shoulder blades before letting my hair down and pulling both of my arms up over my head and pinning them against the window with his right hand.

He bent me over slightly, allowing himself better access. With his left hand, he grabbed ahold of himself, slid on a condom, and guided his cock into me, filling me completely. From the field below, there would have been no doubt as to what we were doing. Both naked, my hands above my head, and him driving into me from behind. Unlike my little zoo comment, I didn't have to wonder if I could be fired for *this*.

If anyone caught us, my teaching career would be over. Done. But I didn't care. My physical need for him outweighed anything else. I couldn't resist him. And I was done trying. His hard body, his magical fingers, his soft tongue, his thick cock. And his mouth. God, that dirty fucking mouth. I wanted all of him.

He pumped into me. Harder. Faster. And all I wanted him to do was touch me. Rub his hand across my clit and give me the release I needed. "'We only have a minute left," I reminded him in between heaving breaths.

"*You've* got a minute left. When that buzzer sounds, I'm

going to come so fucking hard in you, whether you're ready or not."

*Forty-five seconds. Fuck.*

"God, I fucking love your hard ass," he said as he swung my hips more forcefully to meet his. "And your tits . . . Christ, I'd like to fucking rub my cock between them."

*Thirty seconds.*

At last, he gave me what I needed. He reached around to the front of me and began to rub his hand in circles with just the perfect amount of pressure. I felt my orgasm building inside me. *Only ten seconds left.*

"Watch the clock," he commanded as he began counting down, continuing to pound into me. "Ten. Nine. Eight." He let go of my hands and grabbed my aching breast, kneading it forcefully. "Seven. Six. You've only got four seconds left. You better hurry." We were both faster. More urgent. "Three. Two . . . Now!" He thrust into me twice more, and my body spasmed uncontrollably as the orgasm ripped through me. I screamed so loudly that I could barely hear the buzzer sound.

He pulled out of me, and I collapsed to the floor to sit against the wood paneling below the window, my legs shaking. "I don't think I can stand," I admitted.

"I'll consider that a compliment." He removed the condom and tossed it into the metal trash can under the table, making no attempt to conceal it.

Once I regained my composure, I stood and began to dress as he did the same. I ran my hands over my skirt one last time to smooth out any wrinkles. As I walked toward the door and began to turn the knob, I just couldn't resist.

"I'm sorry I missed this on the tour yesterday. Have a nice day, Mr. Samson."

I walked away, feeling fully satisfied . . . in every way.

# chapter twelve

I walked in Friday with a refreshed sense of self. Both my body and mind had been completely willing to partake in my romp with Max, and that had been a big step for me. Gone were the feelings of dread and anxiety that flooded into me at the thought that I may see him. I wanted this relationship—or perhaps arrangement was more fitting—as much as he did, and that was okay. I wasn't going to burn in hell for having sex with a hot guy. Or, if I was, fuck it. At least I'd enjoy the journey there.

I was getting into my teaching groove during first period, fully relaxed and focused for the first time all week, when I heard a knock on my door. I turned my head toward the door. It was Max. *So much for focus.*

"Keep working on your plot diagrams," I instructed as I strode toward the door. "What's up?" I asked as I opened it.

"Umm, can I come in? This class ends in about five minutes, right? I wanted to talk to you."

He knew when my prep period was because it was why I had been chosen to be his tour guide in the first place. So this knowledge wasn't what caught my attention. It was the fact that his speech was halted, hesitant, and I didn't know why. I pushed the door all the way open and stepped back, allowing him entrance. He pulled the door closed behind him and sauntered over to my desk, plopping himself down into my chair.

For a reason I couldn't explain, I became acutely aware that Eva, Adam's daughter, was in this class. My mind momentarily drifted back to Adam's email yesterday. I had been worried about his reaction to what I had written Wednesday, a feeling that only built as I didn't hear from him for almost the entire day. But at two fifty-five, after checking my email for the hundredth time, there it was. An email from Carter, Adam.

He didn't reference my comments in the body of his email. He simply asked how my day had been and if Eva had been okay first period. They had evidently gotten into a little spat in the car on the way to school, and since I had Eva first period, he just wanted to check. It wasn't until I came to his closing that I smiled in relief. *Sincerely, The Old Man.* Thank God he had a sense of humor.

But it wasn't the email that made me hyperaware of Eva being here, despite the fact that she had watched Max come in and sit so comfortably at my desk. It was the dream I had had of Adam. It was so realistic that it left me feeling like the need I had experienced was real. And that the need transcended sex. It was like I needed Adam Carter to make me whole.

I turned my attention back to my class, though my periphery was trained on Max. He eyed me curiously, and I knew that he had noticed that I had been somewhere else for a moment. He always watched me so closely, he seemed to notice everything, taking all of me in and examining it with microscopic accuracy. I would never be able to hide anything from him. This was the first time I got a shiver of a feeling that

Max could be dangerous for me.

My class continued to work until the bell, when I told them that we would pick back up with this activity on Monday. I straightened my desks, waiting for the last students to exit my room. When the hallways were clear, I strode over to the door, pulled it closed, grabbed a chair, set it in front of Max, and looked at him expectantly.

He leaned forward, his forearms on his thighs. His hands fidgeted, making it clear that he was uncomfortable. This was the first time I had seen him lacking his bravado, and I wasn't completely sure how I felt about it.

"I'm confused," he said finally. He looked up at me as if he shouldn't have to explain further, like I should instantly know how to respond.

"About?" I prompted.

He sat back and ran his hands through his long hair. I wanted to grab his hair and force him between my legs.

"Do you hate me?" His gaze was intense, almost pained, like asking this question was physically hurting him. "And please don't lie. I'm a big boy and am used to people hating me. I just need to know."

I was lost for words. I don't know what I struggled with more—the thought of having to answer this question, or the fact that he was used to people hating him. I wanted to take the easy road. Tell him I think he's a swell guy so I could get the hell out of there. But I knew I couldn't lie to Max. I had been honest with him from the moment I met him, almost brutally so, never sparing his feelings. Why start now?

"How I feel about you is complicated. I honestly don't even know how to begin to explain it."

"I just . . . I just can't figure you out, and it's driving me fucking insane. You clearly despised me in the airport, yet you let me touch you and have sex with you. Then, I came here, you took one look at me, turned pale as a ghost, and again, hated me. You ripped me a new asshole after our tour, indicated that you basically couldn't stand the sight of me, and left me in a stairwell. But yesterday, you were all too willing to follow me without any idea where I was taking you. You were a ready and willing participant in what transpired in the announcing booth, and then you left with that flirty, suggestive remark. But yet you still won't even say my first name. And I . . . I dunno." He didn't finish his last sentence, and it hung between us like dead space. It needed to be filled, but I'd be damned if I was going to be the one to do it.

I raised my eyebrows at him, encouraging him to continue.

"I don't want you to hate me. I like you, in a weird, self-deprecating kind of way. And if my coming on to you makes you dislike me, then I'll stop. I have zero friends who are girls, but you don't put up with my bullshit, and I could really use someone like that right now. But I also really like sleeping with you, and I could always use someone like that. So, what's the deal?" He expelled this confession in one breath, or so it seemed. His face brightened, and he looked like just saying these words had lifted a weight off him.

Too bad he had positioned that weight squarely on my shoulders. Was I really ready to admit that, on some level, I liked Max? That part of me would probably enjoy having him as a friend and an even bigger part would enjoy having him as a fuck buddy? And how could I tell him that I was intentionally refusing to say his name because I was petty and unwilling to give him that which he had wanted most from me when we first, umm, met? Just when I thought things were getting simpler,

Max turned into a giant pussy and wanted to talk about our feelings. *Hello, Twilight Zone.*

"I don't hate you," I finally said quietly. I shifted uncomfortably before beginning to speak again. "The whole airport thing was totally out of character for me. It's just so pathetic and so far from who I am. I had finally come to terms with the fact that a fling wasn't the worst thing I could do, when you showed up here, at my job. I felt like I had already given you so much evidence to prove what an easy lay I was that I maybe went too far the other way to try to prove that I wasn't. Then, I guess I just said fuck it. I was going to go with my instincts and hope I didn't regret it."

"First of all," he began, "you were far from an easy lay. You definitely made me work for it. Second, I don't find you in any way pathetic. I'm not using you. We enjoy having sex, we're consenting adults, and we're just out to have a good time. Do you agree?"

"I don't want to stop sleeping with you," I admitted. I said it so matter-of-factly, I almost thought another mouth had spoken it. Was I really becoming this comfortable with casual sex? "As long as we both are on the same page about it," I continued. "We both have an urge and enjoy when the other satisfies it. No tangled strings, messy feelings, or complicated plans. Okay?"

"Okay." He nodded his agreement, smiling for the first time since he had asked to come in. "And the friendship?" He was so full of annoying questions. Though hopefully he wouldn't ask the one I wanted to avoid most: why I wouldn't call him Max.

"I think we can be friends. I feel like it would be weird to be banging some random guy I see in the halls occasionally."

He laughed briefly at my remark. "Great, I'm glad we got this ironed out," Max said as he stood. "I need to go check on supplies that just came in. I wasn't able to concentrate on it before, with all that shit running through my head." *Wait, he was leaving? So we weren't going to christen our new friendship by, say, having a quickie on my desk?*

I was just about to renounce all I had just said, declaring that I did hate him and never wanted to see him again, when he added, "If I don't see you, have a great weekend, Lily."

It was spoken so sincerely, my irritation immediately dissipated.

"You too."

# chapter thirteen

Whew, Friday! This had been one long, crazy week. And while I was glad just to have survived it, part of me was sad to see this week end. What had appealed to me most about the events I had endured—and enjoyed—was the *living* that had taken place throughout. It was like I was breathing fully for the first time since, well, ever.

All that was left to do was make it until three fifteen, and then I was free as a bird. I had intentionally not made plans for this evening because I knew that I would be exhausted, and I also didn't feel like dodging a ton of questions from my girlfriends. "So, have you met anyone interesting?" "Do you like being all alone?" "Doesn't your pathetic life make you so sad that you think about taking a bath with a toaster?" *Fuck that.*

I hadn't told anyone except Tina about Max, and I planned to keep it that way. Even though they may be intrigued and impressed by my recent conquest, they may also be judgmental, and I didn't need that right now. I had finally stopped judging myself, and I definitely didn't need a pack of hyenas taking over the job.

I decided to check my email to keep myself occupied for the next fifteen minutes. I immediately was drawn to one that was from *Samson, Max.* Guess he had gotten a school email account. Before I opened it, I braced myself for the obscene material it would surely include. He didn't disappoint.

*Lily,*

*Thought you might want a visual for when you're pleasuring yourself to the thought of me this weekend.*

*See you Monday, doll.*

*Max*

My mouse hovered over the attachment. Surely he wouldn't send a graphic picture through work email. We would already need to have a serious conversation about what he had written in it. I admit that there was a bit of hypocrisy in my having fucked Max on school grounds but now getting all worked up over an email. However, if being the daughter of lawyers had taught me nothing else, it was that you never put *anything* in writing.

I finally grew a set and clicked open the attachment. The picture showcased Max's dazzling smile. And upon closer inspection, I knew he must have taken it earlier today. The vision of his tight black T-shirt clinging to his firm biceps and chest was a sight that wasn't easily forgotten. And now I had an actual picture of it that wasn't just an image in my mind. I grew warm at the sight of it, smiling slightly, before clicking it closed, forwarding the email to my personal account, and deleting it from Outlook. I couldn't explain why I had decided to forward the email; I just knew that I wanted to, and that was enough for me.

I scanned the other junk that littered my inbox: something

about our school's choir taking *another* field trip—probably to some street corner to sing for change—our seventh-grade boys' basketball team making playoffs—didn't everyone make playoffs at this age?—and something about someone losing their keys.

Then, I saw it. I brightened as I recognized the sender, which made me realize that I had actually been hoping to get an email from him.

*Miss Hamilton,*

*Thank you for getting back to me about Eva yesterday. I swear, she will be the death of me. I can't wait until she's a teenager and begins telling me off daily. Good times! Thanks again. Enjoy your weekend,*

*Adam*

*P.S. I was planning on visiting our favorite coffeehouse tomorrow morning around 8. Just thought I'd let you know in case you were in the area.*

Wait, what? Had I just been asked on a date by the father of one of my students? No, it wasn't a date invitation. Just a friendly FYI. But why would he want me to know he was going to be there? Did he want me to join him? Or was he telling me so I knew *not* to show up? No, that didn't make sense. Why would he mention if he didn't want me to show up? Should I go? And more importantly, why the hell was I smiling so widely?

# chapter fourteen

My decision had fluctuated all morning. To go or not to go, that was the question. And as I pulled on my coat and locked my apartment door behind me, I still wasn't sure of my answer. I had been up since five, unable to force myself to pretend to sleep any longer. And since I couldn't stand staring at the walls in my apartment for another second, I decided to leave around seven fifteen and walk the three blocks to the coffeehouse.

But the three blocks did nothing to firm my resolve. As I approached the shop, I still wasn't sure I wanted to be there. Well, that's not true. I definitely wanted to be there, but *should* I have been there? I passed the giant window at the front of the store, and my eyes immediately homed in on him. I looked at my watch. It was only seven thirty-five. I stood there, locked in place, as I gave serious thought to dropping to the ground and crawling out of eyesight before he saw me. But as usual, I was too late.

His radiant green eyes glanced up, recognized me, and instantly warmed. Adam waved to me, and I smiled in return, resuming my pace to the door. As I stepped inside, I was met with the heavenly smell of coffee beans and the intense warmth of the blazing drinks. I walked over to where Adam sat at a high table in the middle of the seating area. He watched my entire approach, his eyes glued to me. When I reached him, I wasn't quite sure what to do next. Thankfully, he rescued me from my indecisiveness.

"Miss Hamilton, I'm glad you made it. Please," he said as he motioned to the vacant chair across from him.

I shrugged off my coat, revealing the pink Under Armor sweatshirt beneath. I hadn't wanted to overdress, nor look like a hobo. The sweatshirt was casual, but pink always added a hint of femininity to any ensemble—or so I hoped. But I didn't sit.

"I'm going to get myself..." I started.

"Oh, I hope you don't mind. I already ordered for you." He turned and pointed to a young barista behind the counter, who nodded and began preparing a drink. "Caramel macchiato, right?"

Just then, the barista brought over my drink and a blueberry muffin and placed them in front of me.

"Thank you, Rachel." He smiled kindly at her. He then turned his attention back to me. "I didn't want to order it before you got here. I thought it would get cold. I come here pretty frequently, so when I was in line obsessing over the decision of whether to order it now or wait and see if you came, Rachel offered to bring it over when you arrived."

His action was so incredibly thoughtful, but my brain had such inexperience with "thoughtful" as of late that the only thing he said that really struck me was the "see if you came" part. *Jesus Christ. I was becoming a real horn toad.*

"Thank you so much," I finally said as I took the empty seat. I glanced down at the table and then eyed him incredulously.

"You're really reading that?" I asked with a smirk.

"Of course. I said I was starting a book club," he replied with feigned seriousness as he touched the cover of the book he brought. Fucking *Water for Elephants*.

I shook my head. "So who's in this book club?"

"As of now, just me."

"It can't be a club if you're the only member," I pointed out, picking at my muffin.

"I'm very particular about who I include in my clubs."

"You have more than one club?"

"Well, no, but since this is my first, I plan to be selective."

"Always good to have a plan." I could barely hold back my smile. This banter came so easily with him, like we had known each other for years.

"Would you like to join my book club?" he offered.

"Nah, reading sucks."

He nearly spit out his coffee at this comment, and I sat back, pleased with myself.

"Aren't you the one teaching my little giraffe the finer points of *The Outsiders*?"

I laughed at his words. But for some reason, it struck me that he knew about the book we were reading. I felt that most parents really had no clue what their child was learning in school, and I found this to be a great tragedy in the parent-child relationship. I was impressed that he knew, appreciated him for it.

"Yeah, but I haven't actually read it. That's what SparkNotes is for."

"Valid point, Miss Hamilton. Valid point."

I almost told him to call me Lily, but I didn't. I liked hearing his deep, raspy voice call me Miss Hamilton. I also liked that he didn't assume he could call me by my first name, like some other arrogant man, who shall remain nameless, had. Maybe I felt a little power in it, with my calling him Adam but his referring to me more formally.

"So, you come here often, huh?" *Very original, Lily.*

"Pretty frequently, actually. It's on my way to work," he said as he sipped his coffee.

"Me, too. Though, I don't normally come here on weekends," I admitted.

"I don't usually either, but I made an exception today."

"Why? What's special about today?" I questioned.

"That you might be here," he replied casually.

I was dumbfounded by how calmly he had revealed this. He was clearly extremely confident in his own skin, which sharply contrasted with how awkward I usually felt in mine. It was such a fucking turn-on, I wanted to flip the table over and jump on his lap.

"That may be the nicest thing anyone has ever said to me," I shyly declared.

"Well, now, that's a real shame, because I can think of many nice things I could say to you."

We sat there silent for a long moment, allowing the electricity between us to build until I was sure I could hear a distinct hum. His eyes stared into mine in a totally different way than any other man's ever had. His pull was so strong and necessary that I felt myself inching my chair farther under the table, trying to close any excess distance between us. It was then that the craziest, truest thought popped into my head.

*I could love this man someday.*

"So," he said, breaking our trance, "do you like Italian?"

*Did I ever.*

# chapter fifteen

Monday had begun like any other, and I found myself settling back into my normal routine. Fifth period arrived before I knew it, and I headed to the faculty lounge for lunch.

I took my seat at the middle of the table near Tina and a few of the other teachers. I had ordered the only thing that looked somewhat edible: tuna on a whole wheat roll, courtesy of Mrs. Obama's new healthy lunch initiative. It was between that and a taco salad made with ground chicken instead of beef and infused with some kind of a neon sauce that was meant to make it look more authentic. It instead ended up giving it a radioactive quality that I couldn't ignore.

With everything that had been going on lately, I looked forward to shooting the shit with the other teachers. We usually enjoyed our own version of the game Jeopardy, in which we broke into teams and bet quarters while someone read trivia questions. And I was thankful for it. As a new teacher five years ago, I was advised by a veteran teacher never to miss lunch. And he was right. It was a chance to escape the daily grind of my classroom—although lately that daily grind had involved Max.

"You're not really gonna put that in your mouth, are you?" Immediately, I knew who had said it. I would recognize that deep, sultry voice anywhere. "You wanna get something real to eat? Something not manufactured in a lab, perhaps?"

I knew he was referring to my substandard choice in cuisine, but as I turned around to look at Max, with his dick at my eye level, I couldn't help but picture something else in my mouth.

"Um, maybe I *am* in the mood for something else," I said, standing up to toss my sandwich in the trash. "What'd you have in mind?" I noticed Tina's eyebrows rise slightly, and she gave a subtle nod of approval as Max and I exited the room.

We slipped out the back doors and cut across the field on the side of the building, heading to the parking lot. I felt like I was back in high school again, skipping class and hoping no one saw us get into his car and began to think that our relationship was not purely platonic. As we got to the parking lot, I realized I had no idea what Max even drove. But as I walked among the rows of Camrys, Odysseys, and Priuses, I spotted Max's car almost immediately. The lights on the new black Range Rover blinked as he unlocked the door and held it open for me to get in. It was luxurious in a rugged sort of way. This thing had Max written all over it.

He climbed into the tan leather seat beside me and revved the engine before quickly pulling out of the parking lot. "So what are you in the mood for?" He looked over, eyeing me curiously with a seductive smirk.

*Oh, I don't know. A slice of pepperoni and an orgasm.* I reached over to his lap, cupping him. *Might as well get to the point.* He was already semi-erect and grew even harder at my touch.

His only response was a groan as he leaned his head back against his scat and ran a hand through his hair, which always looked as if he had just woken up but had fixed it just enough to make himself look incredibly sexy. He wore khaki cargo pants, a dark-gray T-shirt, and a black leather bomber jacket. The look suited him well.

I was overwhelmed by my need to touch him. To put my mouth on him and feel him grow even larger as I swept my tongue across his tip. He placed his hand over mine and began to move me faster, more vigorously against his shaft.

"Just drive," I instructed quietly as I reached over with my other hand to unzip his pants. Pulling his thick cock out with one hand, I took a moment to close my eyes and imagine how it felt inside me. I grew wetter at the thought of straddling him while he accelerated faster down the road. It crossed my mind that I might need this image for later, but right now I wanted it to be about him, just as he had made it about me last time. I wanted to return the favor.

I wasted no time leaning over to envelop him in my moist mouth. He moaned deeply as I swirled my tongue around him greedily, taking all of him at once. The muscles of his ass and thighs tightened with every subtle and insistent thrust into my mouth. With more pressure, I tugged his length with my hand and sucked urgently. I could sense him fill, feel how close he was to climaxing.

"Fuck, this feels good. I'm gonna come," he warned, pushing gently on the back of my head while he flexed his hips toward me.

I was glad. I wanted this to be quick. I wanted him to lose control so I could know for sure that I had the same effect on him that he had on me. With his warning, I was more impatient than ever. I flicked my tongue across his head and pulled powerfully with my clenched hand.

In a rush, he let go, pulsing in rapid spurts into the back of my throat. I slowed my pace, becoming increasingly gentle as his orgasm tapered off. I didn't pull away until I knew he had finished completely, licking every drop off him and swallowing hard.

"So, do you like hamburgers?" he asked casually.

I just shook my head and laughed at his comment. "Sure."

# chapter sixteen

For some reason I couldn't really explain, I had been nervous since Saturday. It took three days for it to sink in that I was going on a date, a real date, with Adam, and I'd begun to obsess over every minute detail.

What would I order to drink? Would he think I was no fun if I just got water? Maybe he'd think I should be a member of AA if I ordered some kind of martini. What would we talk about? Him? Me? Eva? Our jobs? Hobbies? It had been so long since I'd been on a *real* date with someone I didn't already know. I couldn't be certain, but I was pretty sure giving road head during my lunch break didn't exactly qualify as a date.

And what would I wear? I didn't want something too revealing, but I wanted him to look at me, to really notice me and find me attractive. Should I wear something bright? I wanted to appear cheery, but it *was* the middle of winter. Pastels were definitely out. Black was too dark. And what about my heels? Though he wasn't quite as tall as Max, maybe five-foot-eleven, I could still get away with a pretty high heel. But how high? I didn't want him to think I looked like a streetwalker. After all, I was his daughter's teacher. "Christ, his daughter's teacher," I said aloud to no one as I dressed for our date, finally deciding on a navy-blue wrap dress and two-inch heels that I hoped screamed sexy but sophisticated.

*What am I doing?* Was it even ethical for me to be dating a student's dad? After a few minutes of silent rationalization, I decided that it had to be okay. I mean, it was too late to cancel the date anyway. He would be here any minute, and that would just be plain rude. I wasn't rude, was I? And if I were being completely honest with myself, I did not want to cancel it. Plus, it's not like I was going to sleep with him. At least not tonight. But since I clearly had become sex obsessed as of late, I couldn't rule it out forever.

And that thought was confirmed when I opened the door to greet him. He was more beautiful than I'd remembered. And if one of us was pulling off sexy-sophisticated, it was definitely him. He wore crisp black slacks that fit snuggly in all the right places, a dark-gray button-up shirt, and a vest. His hair was freshly cut, trimmed neatly on the sides and short but slightly messy on top.

He flashed a confident smile and handed me a single pink rose. "You look absolutely beautiful."

My first reaction was to say *You too*, but I decided on a more humble and less aggressive "Thank you" instead.

I followed Adam down the stone path, careful not to trip in my heels. He opened the door to his red GMC Yukon and helped me in. "So where are we headed?" I asked as we pulled away.

"A new place in the city. Everything's supposed to be great there. A friend of mine and his wife went a few weeks ago, and they loved it. I figured we'd try it out."

❤

The restaurant was two stories, with a bar on the main level and dinner seating on the lower level. Dimly lit with small cozy tables sprinkled throughout, it had a kind of comfortably intimate quality to it.

Adam checked in with the hostess, a girl who looked to be in her early twenties and was dressed in a black skirt and black top. She was pretty, and I suddenly felt self-conscious of the way I looked next to her. She led us downstairs, seated us at a small table against a brick wall, and handed us our menus. "Your server will be right with you," she said.

Our waitress arrived shortly after, and as I studied my menu, Adam ordered a hot seafood antipasto as an appetizer and a bottle of something I couldn't pronounce. He looked up from the wine list and over to me. "Did *you* want something to drink?"

Was he serious? Did he plan to drink the entire bottle of wine himself? I thought it had been for the two of us. "Uh . . ." I just stared at him.

Thankfully he interrupted my puzzlement. "Just kidding," he said with a boyish grin. "I figured you'd know I was joking. Do I strike you as a raging alcoholic or something?" He chuckled as he turned toward the waitress. "I think that'll be all for now. Thank you."

We sat in silence for a few moments before he finally broke it. "So what are you in the mood for?"

My mind flashed back to yesterday afternoon. It was the same question Max had asked me in his Range Rover before our little tryst but said in such a different way. More innocent, more genuine. But in my mind, no less seductive.

I busied myself reading over the menu, still slightly embarrassed that I actually thought he was only ordering the wine for himself. "Everything looks great here. I have no idea what to get."

"I guess that explains the name."

I looked up at him, confused.

"La Scelta," he said. "It means 'The Choice.'"

❤

"So you obviously know more about me than I do about you," I prompted. "Tell me a little about yourself."

"Well, you know more about me than you think. You know I have a twelve-year-old daughter, I enjoy coffee, and I like to start clubs. What more is there?" he said with a little laugh.

I loved the way I felt when he smiled. Like he righted the world with it. It was the kind of smile that begged to be returned. So I did.

He continued. "I'm really an open book. But I guess I'll start with the small stuff. I grew up in Montgomery County and went to Drexel for architecture. I've worked for a local firm now for about eight years."

"What do you design?" I was genuinely interested.

"I've designed commercial buildings in the past, but now I work mostly on custom homes. People pay us to design the house of their dreams, basically. It's fun. I design the blueprints and then oversee the construction here and there as well. It gets me out of the office. I like to get my hands dirty every now and then."

The thought of this man, who was so well-dressed, so put together, getting dirty was such a turn-on.

"Drexel is actually where I met Eva's mother. Not first-date material, I know, but you heard me mention her at the conference, so I figure I'll just tell you sooner rather than later.

Eva was born when I was twenty and we were sophomores in college. Jessica and I . . . we just weren't good together. We tried to make it work for Eva's sake for a few months after she was born, but things ultimately started to fall apart. Jessica couldn't take it. The stress, I guess. She left." He was struggling to maintain eye contact throughout his explanation, as this was clearly something he seldom discussed. "The rest is history, really. I started working full-time and was able to finish school and still raise Eva with the help of my parents."

The thought of him with a tool belt had nothing on what he just shared, and it turned me on thoroughly. My body and soul felt for him, were attracted to him. This man was a single father and had finished school to make certain that his daughter could get everything she deserved.

"How about you?" he asked casually. "What's *your* story?"

"Not as impressive as that, I'm afraid." I was still blown away. I described my upbringing and my history with my parents, how I'd gone to Penn to become a lawyer but just couldn't go through with it.

"Well, I'm glad you decided to become a teacher. Eva really likes you." He reached across the table and took my hand, stroking the top gently with his thumb. "And I think I'm beginning to see why."

❤

As Adam walked me to my door, I realized my fears about what we'd talk about had disappeared as quickly as they'd arrived. Conversation with Adam was easy. He'd told me he had a chocolate lab growing up, was a fan of The Killers, Zac Brown Band, and Pearl Jam, and loved to cook even though he wasn't great at it. I had divulged my secret obsession with *The Real Housewives* and MTV's *Teen Mom* and told him that the only sport I'd ever really loved was track and field. I had run throughout high school and was training for the next Broad Street Run.

"I hope I can call you sometime," he said, his green eyes staring right at me.

"I hope so too." I smiled sweetly at him. I wanted to grab him. Pull him close to me and feel his perfect lips pressed up against mine. Taste his tongue as he moaned inside my mouth. But my attraction to him was deeper than the sexual one I had become so comfortable with as of late.

"Would it be weird for me to kiss you right now, Miss Hamilton?" The way he said it was seductive, cautious, kind.

I laughed softly. So low, I couldn't be sure he had even heard it. "Under one condition," I urged.

He squinted his eyes slightly, curious. "What's that?"

"Call me Lily."

The corners of his mouth lifted slowly as he leaned into me. His lips found mine, and he parted them slowly with his tongue, exploring me. His hands held me tightly to him before he pulled away and kissed me on the forehead. "Good night, Lily."

I watched him stroll to his car. Partly because I couldn't believe I was letting him go without inviting him inside for a drink, and partly because I just wanted to get a good view of his ass one last time.

As I entered my room, I leaned against the door for a moment. I felt invigorated. I felt like I might actually be able to commit to a real adult relationship with someone. I felt... aroused. By the kiss? Certainly. By his confident, self-assured attitude? Absolutely.

I changed out of my dress and got into bed, willing myself to remember his voice, his strong features, and the smell of his aftershave on his smooth skin when he kissed me. I ran my hand down my stomach to the throbbing between my legs. But for some reason I couldn't explain, I reached over to my phone, logged into my email, and opened the picture of Max.

# chapter seventeen

The next two weeks passed quickly. My days were filled by Max, but they all ran together and became a hazy blur in my memory. We were spontaneous, and slightly sex-crazed. And even though I still hadn't called him Max to his face, we knew each other intimately. I couldn't deny my attraction to him. I was definitely addicted to sex with Max.

But despite the heated desire that bloomed between us, there were other moments, still moments. Moments where time slowed and I found myself looking at him differently: not as an object of my wildest desires but as something more. Something resembling a good friend. I caught myself lost in staring matches with him, like we were having an entire conversation without uttering a word, especially during our lunches together, as he often joined us in the teachers' lounge now.

There were also instances where our need to touch one another seemed to represent something beyond the physical. It was almost emotional, a support the other could count on. I found myself often brushing my shoulder against his arm, wanting to feel him there. I began to realize that the sex wasn't going to last forever, but maybe the friendship we had forged could.

While I had found a friend in Max, I hoped I had found a boyfriend in Adam. My time with him was a stark contrast from Max. Everything about Adam was deliberate, focused. He wanted to make the most of every moment we spent together, and I adored him for it. Our conversations covered a wide expanse of things: fond memories, our past relationships, our hopes and dreams for the future. All of the things you talk about in order to ensure compatibility. And Adam and I were compatible.

It was more so the small, unsaid things that assured me of this, though. Last week, he had taken me to a Philadelphia 76ers game. We'd sat damn near on the court, watching the Sixers get trounced by the Miami Heat.

"Do you come to basketball games often?" I had asked about midway through the first quarter.

"All the time. I'm a season ticket holder."

"Wow, really?" I asked. What came out of my mouth next was something I instantly wished I hadn't said. "Why?"

Adam smiled at me, showing that he understood why I was asking. The team was terrible. How much fun could it be watching losing season after losing season?

"I grew up watching basketball with my dad," he explained. "He brought me to games often, and we had the best times watching Julius Erving, Maurice Cheeks, and Charles Barkley. I guess I want to recreate those great memories with Eva. The family that plays together stays together, right? Besides, I'm not a bandwagon jumper. I'm a Philly sports supporter through the good, the bad, and the downright ugly."

I warmed at his explanation. I thought back to my own childhood, and while I could recall good times, nothing I would describe as the "best" came to mind. I hooked my arm through his as I thought about what a tremendous father he was. I wondered if Eva knew what she had.

I'd heard that a woman subconsciously examined potential mates for the things she most wants present in her offspring. But even though this was supposedly done without the woman ever realizing that she was doing it, I always noted the things that I would want passed down to my children. Adam's capacity to love was definitely one of them. But he demonstrated another at a Killers concert in the city.

Of course, Adam being Adam, the evening was first class all the way. We took a black stretch limo into the city and had front-row seats and backstage passes. I loved The Killers and was so excited to go, I could barely sit still for the entire ride there. And since traffic on 76 was awful, the ride seemed interminable. We arrived, got drinks, and took our seats just as the show was beginning.

I had to hand it to Adam. For such a gentleman, he could definitely let loose and enjoy himself freely. It was a duality I found extremely attractive. About midway through the show, people started working their way forward, trying to crowd the barricade that denied them access to the stage. It was such a gradual filling, I barely noticed until we were pushed together, asshole to belly button. The crowd grew rowdier, and Adam put his arm protectively around my waist.

Then, out of nowhere, I felt a pair of large, slimy hands on me, trying to pull me backward. I jerked away and turned to where the hands had come from. They belonged to a sweaty, slovenly, drunk prick who looked to be about my age.

"Come over here and finish what we started," he slurred, reaching for me again.

I tried to move back, but there was nowhere to go. Just

as the man was about to make contact with me again, Adam stepped in front of me, shielding me from the groping hands.

"Walk away" was all Adam said. His tone was calm but menacing, and I could hear the rage behind it as his back muscles tensed against my breasts.

"Fuck you. That little tease was rubbing up on me and . . ."

The man's sentence was cut off by a punishing blow to the jaw, inflicted by Adam. The disgusting man fell to the ground, knocked out cold. As the audience began to realize what had just occurred, Adam grabbed my hand and led me through the chaos.

He led me through the concert arena, out the exit, and back to the safety of our limo before he spoke.

"Jesus Christ, are you okay?" His eyes were filled with worry, his brow furrowed.

I nodded. "Are you?" I asked, gesturing toward his hand. I could already see a bruise forming at his knuckles. He had hit the man with such force, I actually expected to see blood running down Adam's hand.

"Yeah, yeah, I'm fine." He sat back and drew me to him, draping his arm around my shoulders. He told the driver to start home, and then we sat in silence.

"Not quite the evening I had envisioned," he said with a slight smile, the twinkle returning to his eyes.

"No, but I have to say, you were a real badass." I returned his smile.

"I was, wasn't I?" he said with a laugh. "Guess all those kickboxing classes really came in handy. I should write the instructor a thank-you note."

I was happy to have the humor between us again, but it didn't capture how I was truly feeling. Laughter wasn't where I wanted this moment to go.

I put my fingertips on Adam's cheek and slowly turned his face toward mine. "Thank you," I whispered against his lips.

"My pleasure."

# chapter eighteen

Since the concert, all I could think about was Adam and how hot it was that he had protected me. He had even called me Sunday morning to see if I was okay because he knew that I'd been a bit shaken up from everything that had happened the night before. No one had ever gotten into a fight for me. Ever. And I was completely turned on by it. By him, really. It was becoming difficult to hold myself back. Our makeout sessions were great, but we needed to turn up the heat. Now!

I wanted, or rather needed, some sort of sexual contact with him. I had to know what it was like for Adam Carter to get me off. But more than that, I wanted to feel close to him, closer than I did now. He seemed so timid at times, somewhat uncertain of how fast we should be moving. So I made a vow to myself that the next time I saw him, I would make the first move. Until then, I would be fucking the daylights out of Max. A girl still had needs.

On Tuesday, I beamed when I saw I had a text from Adam:

*I was hoping you might want to see a*
*movie Thursday night with me. Your pick.*
*I was thinking of dropping Eva with my*
*parents for the night and going late. But*

*I know you have to be up bright and early*
*to teach, and I wouldn't want to wear you*
*out. Let me know.*

My eyes were drawn to his use of the phrase "wear you out." Did he mean what I thought—or hoped—he meant, or was he just being considerate of my need to sleep? Damn text messages! I responded with something I thought would work, no matter what his intentions were.

*How about* Warm Bodies *at 10:50? I'm*
*fine with you wearing me out : )*

❤

Thursday night finally arrived, and with it, Adam. He was dressed in dark jeans that were intentionally worn at the knee, a four-pocket khaki jacket, and a crisp, button-down white shirt that he left untucked. Revealing a peek at his smooth chest because his top two shirt buttons were undone, he looked like he should be on the cover of *GQ* instead of my front steps.

I wanted to skip the movie and make our own version of *Warm Bodies* in my bedroom. It was all I could do to keep from pulling him inside my apartment and then inside *me.*

As we walked to his car, he told me I looked beautiful. I blushed at his compliment, appreciative of it his thoughtfulness. I had tried on about fifteen different outfits before settling on a loose black shirt, skinny jeans, and knee-high boots. At least the wardrobe changes had been worth it!

Adam ordered us a large popcorn to split and two iced teas.

With the exception of two other couples and three teenagers toward the front of the theater, it was empty. I picked at the popcorn slowly for the first half hour or so, my hand grazing against his every now and then.

Each time I felt his skin against mine, my chest clenched at the anticipation of what I hoped would happen later. I found it increasingly difficult to concentrate on the movie as, out of my peripheral vision, I was busy focusing on Adam slowly licking the butter off his fingers. One. By. One. I squirmed in my seat at the thought of those same fingers moving inside me, that tongue licking up and down the insides of my thighs. My stomach tightened in response to my daydream. *Christ, Lily, focus on the movie, you hornball.*

Adam reached over to put his arm around me and began to rub my bicep softly. I leaned into him and rested my head against his shoulder. I could smell that same aftershave that I remembered so well from our first date. I needed to find out what it was so I could get a bottle and smell it when I needed an Adam fix.

From this angle, it was easier—and much more fun—to stare at his lap than it was to watch any of the zombies on screen. I placed a hand just above his knee, and he began to trace his fingers across my forearm with his other hand. As he moved his hand back and forth, I couldn't help but close my eyes and picture him touching himself while he thought of me. Like Max had. But Adam was nothing like Max, so his doing it would mean so much more.

As I subtly stroked his leg, I thought I could see him get slightly hard at my touch. He shifted in his seat involuntarily and cleared his throat. After all that I had done with Max— and the places we had done it—it was strange to find myself wondering if I could work up the nerve to do this. After all, I was just going to touch him above his jeans. Feel how stiff he was and make him even harder so I knew I could have him later. Eva was sleeping at Adam's parents' house. Tonight would be perfect.

*Just do it, Lily.*

I couldn't wait for courage that would never arrive, so I just acted. If I could attribute one piece of solid advice to my mother, it would be that "action comes before motivation." If only she would have known that her words of wisdom would lead me to this. I laughed internally at the thought and placed my hand firmly on his dick, beginning to massage him over his jeans. I only got far enough to confirm that I had been right about his erection when he put my hand in his to stop me.

Until this moment, I had never realized that one silent gesture had the power to make me feel so physically and emotionally broken. I had been rejected. And this time it hadn't been by some stranger who had moved my hand away just so he could fuck me later in an airport hallway.

❤

Silence filled the car like smoke on the ride home. With every breath, I could feel my chest tighten as the air seemed to thicken. Even on this cold February night, the warmth of the heater burned my cheeks. And the early morning darkness made me wish I could just close my eyes and forget this had ever happened.

*What have I done? What kind of person tries to give someone a hand job in a fucking movie theater?*

I didn't have to look far for the answer:

*Probably the same type of person who uses her lunch break to get a piece of ass instead of a piece of pizza.*

But if I were being honest with myself, I knew why I had wanted to do that in the movie theater. I wanted Adam to be a little adventurous. I wanted him to know how much I couldn't resist him. And I wanted him to feel as aroused as I felt constantly when I was with him. But most of all, I had just wanted him to *want* me.

# chapter nineteen

My date with Adam kept replaying in my mind. I didn't know how to feel about it, so by eight o'clock Friday evening, I decided that I should attempt to feel nothing. And there was only one way to thoroughly accomplish that. It was time to call the hyenas.

Four phone calls, a blue skintight dress, three-inch heels, and about two hours later, I was waiting in line outside of Fire and Ice Nightclub in Old City, Philadelphia. My friend Kaylin decided that, after five minutes, we had clearly waited long enough. Even though I hated pretentious bitches who did what she planned to do, I still allowed her to drag me to the bouncer, flashing a smile as he unhooked the red ropes and allowed us entry, simply because we were good-looking and scantily clad.

Inside the club was dark and hazy, the only light supplied by the strobes flashing from the stage. The DJ was playing music that instantly made me think of the cast of *Jersey Shore*. It was a pretty small place, maybe fifteen hundred square feet, with bodies packed in like sardines.

"Shots!" my friend Leah yelled, though we could barely hear her over the bass.

We eagerly followed her to the bar, ordered five redheaded sluts, and downed them with the ease of seasoned professionals.

These had been a staple for many of us in college, and tonight was a night for good memories. As the warmth from the alcohol filled me, I began to loosen up. I was incredibly thankful for my friends, who had asked no questions once I had declared that I was in desperate need of a night out. I was also thankful for the loud music, which prevented me from explaining why I needed this escape.

We stayed at the bar for another round before venturing onto the dance floor. I nearly danced myself into oblivion with my wall of girlfriends. Every time a man approached one of us, the wall would close, effectively shutting him out. Tonight wasn't about men and their mixed signals. It was about fun.

A while later, after we were sufficiently sweaty and thirsty, Chelsea made a motion of throwing back a shot, a universal signal for "let's hit the bar." We ordered another round of redheaded sluts, and I felt the liquid cascade down the back of my throat, effectively beginning to erase my self-consciousness. I needed another.

"Bartender," I yelled, "gonna need another round."

He obliged with a clear look of agitation. It was common knowledge that bartenders hated making copious amounts of mixed drinks on a packed night. *Oh, well.*

The drinks he put in front of us were immediately scooped up and downed. I opened my clutch to check my phone. The time flashed twelve thirty. *Christ, where had the past two and a half hours gone?*

"I gotta pee," I said in Amber's ear. "Be right back."

Amber nodded her head and turned toward the rest of the group. I sauntered to the back of the club, where there was a bathroom with only two stalls. Eleven women were in front of me, all swaying with inebriation and full bladders. Or maybe I was swaying and they were still? It was becoming hard to tell. The alcohol was beginning to dull my senses, causing the room to shift slightly under my feet. I was drunk. *Mission accomplished.*

When I finally returned to the bar twenty minutes later, my friends were not where I had left them. I ordered another drink and made my way onto the dance floor, hoping to find them there. I searched through the thick crowd but with no luck. *Where did those bitches go?* I pulled out my cell phone, huddled against a wall, and began calling them. I had already called Kaylin and Amber, but to no avail. Finally, Chelsea picked up.

"Where the fuck are you guys?" I yelled angrily into the phone.

"What do you mean? Amber said you left, so we had one more drink and did the same."

"*What?*" I wailed, incredulous. "I told her I was going to pee. I didn't say anything about leaving. I'm still fucking here." I would've felt completely helpless had I not been so wasted. Instead, I was pissed.

"Oh," said Chelsea simply. I could hear her telling the others what had happened.

"Can't she take a cab?" I heard one of those dirty whores ask.

"Is she fucking kidding? A cab? You bitches totally left me, and now I'm supposed to spend a hundred dollars getting home? Fuck you. I hope you run out of gas and get stranded too."

The last bit had not been the most mature statement I had ever made, but maturity wasn't my prime concern right now. I ended the call and dropped my arms to my side, trying to decide what to do next. There was only one person I felt I could count on enough to drive into the city at one a.m. to pick me up. I lifted my phone, found his name, and called him.

"I need your help. My asshole friends left me at Fire and Ice in the city, and I have no way home. I'm really sorry to call, but could—"

"Jesus Christ, some fucking friends!" he interrupted. *My thoughts exactly.* "I'll be right there, Lily. Go to the bar and wait there for me. Stay at the bar." His repetition of the last statement let me know that he was fully aware that I was drunk. *Was I slurring?*

"Thanks, Samson."

"No problem, doll."

I hung up and did as I was told, though I held on to my phone, just in case Max tried to call me. Then I returned to the bar and ordered another drink. *When in Rome.* I swallowed the shot in one gulp and ordered another. The bartender eyed me warily before sliding another shot in front of me. I raised my eyebrows at him. *What the fuck was he looking at? Douchebag.*

I left the drink on the bar, cupping my hand around it, but I didn't lift it to my lips. I was starting to feel a little woozy. So I placed both arms on the bar to steady myself, my drink in one hand, my phone in the other. I felt my phone buzz. It was a text from Chelsea.

*Did you find a way home?????*

I giggled to myself as I wrote my response:

*Nope. I was dragged into an alley,
mugged, and I'm currently bleeding out*

*all over the street from the multiple stab
wounds my attacker inflicted. Make sure
you watch the news tomorrow!*

I was super morbid when I was drunk. Chelsea never replied. *What a bitch.*

When my phone vibrated again, I thought it was one of my other whore ex-friends, but it was Max.

*How ya holding up, doll? Should be
there in ten minutes.*

His concern made me smile. Now *he* was a true friend. Not like those other trollops. Feeling better about my situation, I finally tilted the shot to my mouth and drained the glass. I noticed that I was beginning to rock back and forth a bit, but I didn't care. Max was coming, and he would make the world steady again.

I wasn't sure how much time passed. I wasn't actually sure I was even still awake. But I was brought out of my daze by a growing murmur building amidst the crowd.

"Move!" was all I had to hear to know that he had arrived.

He made his way toward the bar, his eyes registering first relief and then annoyance at the sight of me. Just as he was about to reach me, a scantily clad waif stepped in his path.

"Hi," she crooned.

"Hi." Max smiled weakly, trying to get around her.

"I just wanted to let you know that I am a huge fan. Can I buy you a drink?" she propositioned.

"Thanks, but I'm just here to get someone," he said, motioning to me.

The dirty pirate hooker turned to look at me, scowled, and turned back to Max. "Trust me," she said in a low, husky voice, "I'm definitely your better option."

"No, you're definitely not. Now move the fuck out of my way." Max was enraged by her comment. *Oooh, Max angry. This was going to be hot.*

Max side-stepped around her and grabbed my elbow firmly so as not to lose his grip on me. "Ready, doll?" he asked, already beginning to move without waiting for my response. "And why the fuck didn't you respond to my text? I was worried you'd been roofied and murdered out behind the club." *Guess I wasn't the only morbid one.*

As we passed the stunned woman, her shock at Max's words wore off and she found her voice again. "Fuck you, you washed up has-been. You're not going to talk to me that way, you fucking asshole."

Even though Max had me by the arm, that didn't prevent me from jerking around violently so that I was face-to-face with that bitch. It was so unfortunate that I was slurring, because it really hurt my delivery.

"You're calling him a has-been? You just threw yourself at him not sixty seconds ago, and now you're going to act like *you're* too good for *him*? How is the weather in Delusionalville this time of year?" *Ha, take that, Crypt Keeper.*

"Whatever, skank. Clearly he's into slumming, because that's the only reason he'd choose a dumpster slut like you over me."

*Hmmm, that was a good one.* I was going to have to hit below the belt to win this one. "You're just jealous, you sloppy cunt!"

With that, Max wheeled me around and stared at me,

shocked. His eyes were wide, and his mouth hung open. "Did you really just say that?" he asked incredulously.

"I'm really drunk."

"Let's go, you fucking sailor, you."

Max half supported, half carried me out of the club and into his Range Rover that was parked directly outside. He reached into his pocket and pulled out his wallet, slipping the valet some cash, even though Max had clearly never given the guy his keys. He must have pulled up out front and just left his car there. I smiled slightly, realizing that he must have been in a tremendous hurry to get to me tonight.

He helped me into the passenger seat and buckled my seat belt for me like I was a four-year old before walking around the front of the car and climbing into the driver's seat. He looked at me, grinning sweetly.

"Doll, do me one favor?"

I was feeling generous in my compromised state.

"Anything."

"Don't puke in my car," he said dryly as he threw the car in drive and pulled out onto the road.

*What a charmer.*

❤

I must have fallen asleep pretty quickly because I remember nothing of our trip home. At some point, I think Max asked me my address, but I don't remember answering. I awoke slightly when Max lifted me from the car and carried me up the flight of stairs to my second-floor apartment. *Praise the Lord for strong men.*

He told me to get my keys out of my purse.

"Clutch," I groaned sleepily.

"What?" he questioned.

"It's not a purse; it's a clutch."

"Lily, Jesus Christ, just open the damn thing and get your keys," he exclaimed, clearly exasperated.

"All right, all right, don't get your panties in a twist," I mumbled as I sloppily sifted through my clutch. "Got 'em." I held them up and jingled them triumphantly.

"Okay, now how about using them?" His amusement at drunk Lily had worn off right after I had said the C-word. *God, had I really said that?*

After missing the lock a few times, I finally managed to get my door open. Max carried me in and asked me which room was mine. I threw my arm up in the general direction I thought my room was and plopped my head down on my shoulder. He nudged open my bedroom door with his foot and gently lowered me onto my bed, pulled back the covers, and tucked me in.

"You need anything before I go?"

I grunted into my pillow.

"I'll take that as a no. Text me if you need anything."

I think I was already asleep again, because I don't remember responding.

*Christ, that harlot at the club really had been the better option.*

# chapter twenty

I didn't hear from Adam the rest of the weekend, and I tried not to care. I was busy nursing a hangover all day Saturday, and I wasn't about to make my headache worse by attempting to talk to him. I thought back to what I could remember from Friday night. Dancing, drinking, those bitches leaving me. Calling Max. More drinking. Telling some girl she was a "cunt." *Real classy, Lily. Way to go!*

But what I couldn't remember was why I had chosen to call Max instead of Adam. I tried to dissect my decision in my mind. I mean, I didn't really have any reason to be mad about what Adam had done. Or, in this case, *not* done. Plus, I must have known that Adam would have Eva at home and wouldn't have been able to get me even if he'd wanted to. What would he have said? *Eva, honey. You have to wake up, sweetheart. We have to drive into the city at one in the morning to pick up your shitfaced English teacher from a nightclub. No need to worry; she's clearly just upset because I wouldn't let her jerk me off in public last night.*

I mean, obviously I couldn't let Eva see me like that. And if I were completely truthful with myself, I couldn't let her father see me like that either.

Max, on the other hand, wouldn't judge me. He didn't

have room to. Though we had never actually discussed it, it was common knowledge that he was only starting up the hockey club to advance his career. Apparently he had been offered a broadcasting job with a local sports network but needed to clean up his image first. If anyone knew what it was like to make mistakes and be vilified for them, it was Max.

Monday morning rolled around, and I brewed my own coffee at home—a task I hadn't completed in months. I couldn't risk seeing Adam at the coffeehouse before I had a chance to gauge his opinion of me. Did he think I was a slut? Was he second-guessing if he even wanted to be with me? I had no idea.

By the end of first period, I was a hybrid of emotions. The kids were taking a test today, so I was hoping to get some grading done during class, but I just couldn't focus. I sat at my desk, red pen in hand, staring at my phone hidden inconspicuously on my lap, checking it over and over for a text that never came. I was no better than my students.

The bell rang, and I realized I had lost track of time, despite the fact that I had been doing absolutely nothing all period. Chairs screeched, and my desk was suddenly bombarded with tests. When I finished organizing them, I looked up to see Max standing over me. He wore ripped jeans and a gray vintage Philadelphia Flyers T-shirt that clung to his chest and hung just below the waist of his jeans. "Just checking to see how you survived the rest of your weekend. You were pretty banged up Friday night."

"I don't even wanna think of what a hot mess I must have been," I said, putting my head in my hands.

"You *were* a hot mess. But *my* emphasis is on the 'hot' part."

I looked up to see him wearing a teasing grin. "It's just an expression," I snapped. "I'm not really in the mood right now, Samson."

"Doll, don't kid yourself. You're always in the mood."

"You know what I mean." I rolled my eyes. "I'm not having a good day."

"You wanna talk about it?" he asked, tilting his head to the side, obviously concerned.

"That's actually the last thing I wanna do."

"Well," he said seductively as he took my hand and pulled me to my feet, "come with me. I have something that'll make you feel better. And lucky for you, I'll be the one doing all the talking."

*Yup, he was right. I was always in the mood.*

❤

We strolled quickly down the hallway, and Max led me down a flight of steps and then took a left toward a part of the school I rarely used. It dead-ended at the entrance to the backstage area of the auditorium. How did he even know where this was? I had never gone back there myself, and I had worked at this school for five years.

He opened one of the double wooden doors and hurried me inside. Backstage was a mess of cardboard props, costumes, and painted plywood structures that would be used in the spring play. But once the door shut behind us, it was so dark, I could barely see my hand in front of my face.

"You have to stay quiet," he said.

I could hear a man speaking on a microphone just beyond the black velvet curtain toward the front of the stage.

"The eighth grade is having an assembly," Max whispered. "Some shit about making bad decisions or something."

The speaker droned on monotonously for a few moments about the dangers of drugs and alcohol before directing the students to watch the video on the large screen. I wondered if the presentation would mention any of the dangers that came with getting fucked in a middle school auditorium. Certainly *I* hadn't bothered to consider *any* of them.

My eyes were still trying to adjust to the darkness when, without warning, Max's tongue penetrated my mouth, its softness exploring me deeply, almost violently. I gasped, suddenly feeling the need for air. My heart was already racing. The blackness. Van Halen's "Right Now" coming from the video on the other side of the curtain. The uncertainty of who was around. It was thrilling, unlike anything I had experienced before.

His strong hands traveled down my back to my ass, squeezing it roughly. "God, I could fuck you anywhere," he groaned into me as he bit my earlobe. "I can't get enough of you, Lily. You're like a fucking addiction."

"I know the feeling," I managed to expel between labored breaths.

"Shh, no talking. Remember?" he reminded me, putting a finger to my lips. He let go of me with one hand, and I could hear him frantically fumbling with his belt buckle.

I reached in front of me, feeling my way down his firm stomach to undo his jeans, and I smiled internally at the appropriateness of the music. I needed this. *Right now.* But before I could pull his pants down, he scooped me up, and I wrapped my legs tightly around his waist as he carried me a few feet to my right, closer to the curtain. When he placed me down, I expected to land on a table or desk of some sort, but I was surprised to feel hard wooden steps digging into my back.

He had put me on a makeshift staircase of some kind. Leaning over me, he pulled his pants down just enough. We were hurried. And frantic. I heard him tearing the foil package, and then his hands removed my shoes and pants in one swift motion. *Swift.* The word brought me back to where I actually was: our middle school auditorium with students no more than twenty feet from us. Maybe our school had been intended for actions such as this. The thought made me smile. *Well, maybe not actions exactly like this.*

I leaned back as he slid my thong to the side forcefully, not even bothering to remove it. As he thrust himself deep inside me, I wondered how wooden steps could possibly feel this good against my spine. He stood in front of me and dug his powerful fingers into my hips, pulling me back and forth.

"Is this what you fucking want? You want me to make you come like this? Huh? Thrust my fucking dick in you so far that it practically hurts?"

I knew he didn't want me to answer. All I could do was feel him as he tugged at my nipples under my shirt and pushed into me more rapidly, more urgently, his lower abdomen rubbing up and down against my clit. I smelled his fresh body wash mixed with sweat. Already, he smelled like sex. I felt the pressure build like a rush inside me.

I dug my nails into his shoulder blades, gripping his T-shirt tightly until I couldn't scrunch it any more firmly inside my sweaty palm. With my other hand, I pulled on the curtain, letting the soft velvet brush against my forearm as I held on tightly. As I felt him swell even bigger, the gentle pain on my back mixed with the pleasure deep inside me made me lose control.

I couldn't wait any longer. And I didn't want to. My orgasm pulsed through my entire body, and I urged him even farther inside me as my legs clamped around him harder, pinning him in place. I wanted to cry out. To moan. And to yell every vulgar word I could think of. Instead, I bit delicately into his bicep. Not hard enough to break the skin but hard enough to leave a mark that would hopefully remind him of me when he got undressed for bed later.

He sped up, pounding into me more vigorously. I felt him tremble as he cursed under his breath and moaned a deep, raspy sound. Our muscles weakened and our bodies went limp as we collapsed, a heap of tangled limbs, to the bottom of the stairs.

When we were finally ready to get up, he stood first and put out his hand to help me rise. A strange feeling of déjà vu coursed through me. Though it was the same hand that had reached out to me a month and a half ago when I was on an airport floor, it felt like a different man extending it. This man knew exactly what I always needed: whether it was a friend, a phenomenal lay, or something that now seemed strangely in between.

I placed my hand firmly inside his, and I spoke the only words that came to mind. The only words that I knew for sure he'd let leave my lips, despite my backstage vow of silence. "Thanks, Max," I whispered just loudly enough that I was sure he had heard me.

❤

Max had done a sufficient job of helping me forget about Adam—at least for a little while. I made a pact with myself that

I wouldn't check my phone again until after school, and to my surprise, I was able to keep it.

But barely. When the last bell rang, I looked at my phone immediately and saw a text from Adam.

*Lily, sorry I haven't called. Things have been crazy at work. I've been on a job site off and on since Saturday morning. Having some issues with some of the contractors. Boring stuff, really. Thought we should talk. I'll be done here by 3:00 or so and thought you might be able to meet me outside for a few minutes before I pick up Eva from mural club. 3:30? Let me know.*

I looked at my watch. Two forty-seven. I had to make a decision. My mind spun. Were we really going to talk about what happened on Thursday? Outside of his daughter's school? By now, I just wanted to move on with him. What was there to discuss? Maybe he was going to tell me he didn't want to see me anymore. But he wouldn't tell me that in the parking lot, would he? The whole thing was just plain awkward. I was hurt, embarrassed, and really had nothing to say.

But I decided I had to see him and give him the chance to talk, even if I felt uncomfortable doing it.

*Sure. I'll meet you out front around 3:30.*

I didn't want to seem too eager, so I waited until three thirty-four before heading down to the lobby. *Real smooth,*

*Lily. Show him who's boss.* I spotted Adam's Yukon waiting for me out front. He reached across to open the door for me, and I climbed inside.

Though I made every effort to look straight ahead once seated, I couldn't help but notice him as I pulled myself into the seat. In ripped, faded jeans and a green and tan plaid shirt rolled at the sleeves, I was suddenly conscious of how sexy he looked without even trying. He'd been working outside all day, and though it was still pretty cold outside, his face looked flushed, and I could tell he'd been sweating. I wanted to jump him right here in the parking lot. But I wouldn't make that mistake twice, so I kept my eyes directed on the windshield.

"I think I owe you an explanation," he began.

*Yup, we're really gonna talk about this.*

"You really don't owe me anything," I said, and I meant it.

"Lily, I know you're upset. I can see it on your face. Would you look at me? Please." His voice was kind, almost pleading.

I turned my body toward him but struggled to maintain eye contact. "I'm not upset. Just embarrassed, I guess." I let out a low, nervous laugh.

"There's nothing to be embarrassed about. Really. I think I understand, and we don't need to make a big deal about it. I just want you to know that it doesn't change how I feel about you, if that's what you think."

I was relieved at his confession. It took everything I had to ask him this next question, but I had to know the answer. "How *do* you feel about me exactly?"

He breathed in deeply, clearly considering his answer. "A middle school parking lot probably isn't the most appropriate place to be discussing all this. I really just wanted to make sure you were okay. I didn't mean to hurt your feelings. Let me take you out Saturday night, and we'll talk about it then." There was a hint of a smile in his eyes. He put his hand softly on my chin and lifted it gently as he leaned in to give me a small kiss. It was innocent enough. His lips barely grazed mine, but they lingered just long enough to leave me wanting more. "What do you say?" he whispered with his mouth still almost touching mine.

"I say I'll see you Saturday."

# chapter twenty-one

The rest of the week passed without much excitement. I tried to stay focused on work and even managed to take advantage of the unseasonably warm weather to run a couple of miles on Tuesday and Thursday. Adam and I spoke on the phone once and exchanged a few text messages about nothing in particular.

On Thursday, he called to tell me that he'd pick me up at seven o'clock on Saturday. He told me to dress formally and that he'd take care of the rest. I couldn't help but tingle with excitement, though anxiety wasn't far behind. He had promised me a conversation, and no matter the awkwardness it may cause, I intended to have it.

I didn't see much of Max. He came down to lunch once or twice but no visits to my classroom or run-ins in the halls. By Friday, I was starting to wonder if I had done something to cause his sudden absence from my day-to-day routine. Friday afternoon rolled around, and I was contemplating sending him a text to see if he'd respond and to get a gauge of whether he was mad at me or not, when I heard him.

"Hey, doll." His voice sent shivers down my spine as I realized that I had missed that voice this week, as well as the man behind it.

"Hey, yourself. Where have you been, stranger?" My tone

was more accusatory than I had intended. *Christ, Lily, he's not one of your students.*

"Sorry I've been MIA. A lot of stuff needed to be done this week. I had to finish putting the schedule together, going through the purchase orders and making sure all of the new equipment was accounted for, and a ton of other shit that really sucked. How was your week?"

"Fine. Nothing interesting to report." My voice was disinterested, dismissive almost. I was feeling a well of emotions, but I couldn't explain any of them. Was I actually *angry* that he hadn't made time for me since Monday? That couldn't be it. *Could it?* I needed to get over whatever it was that was causing this emotional upheaval. I had no right to be angry. We were just friends. I sometimes went weeks without talking to a lot of my other friends. Of course, I wasn't fucking any of *them.*

"Any plans for the weekend?" I asked in an intentionally sweet voice, hoping to overshadow my initial bitchiness.

"No, not really. That's actually why I stopped by. A bunch of the teachers are going to Flanagan's for happy hour. I was thinking about stopping by. Do you wanna go?"

"Sure," I said, entirely too eagerly. *Did I have Multiple Personality Disorder?* One minute I was pissed at him for no reason, and the next I was nearly jumping up and down to spend time with him. "I'll meet you there in about twenty minutes."

"Great," he said, smiling.

I found my own smile lasting long after he had left my room. I had never spent time with Max beyond the confines of normal school hours. I was excited to hang out with him outside of this building, though I couldn't have told you why.

I shut down my computer, grabbed my coat and purse, turned off my lights, and headed to Flanagan's.

♥

I parked my car next to Max's and headed into the bar I had sat in with Tina only a month prior. So much had changed since then; it almost felt like an entire lifetime had been lived between then and now. I walked in and smiled at a few other teachers before my eyes settled on Max. He was sitting at a high-top on the far side of the bar. He was holding a pint of beer, talking to a few of our male teachers about who knew what, though one could guess. Sports.

The females on the faculty were mostly huddled together, and an amateur observer may think they were partaking in gossip and exchanging beauty secrets. However, I knew better. They had gathered about ten feet from Max, directly between him and the bar. A few stood there with their backs against the bar, their elbows resting on the counter, effectively pushing their breasts out as far as they could.

If Max wanted another drink, he'd have to push through them, and if one of them were lucky, his chest would meet theirs in a pseudosexual encounter they could thrive on for weeks. *Poor, bitches,* I thought as I walked toward Max's table.

With every step I took, I felt more powerful, more important, more confident. Because I knew damn well that if anyone was going home with Max Samson tonight, it was going to be me. *Watch and learn, ladies. The master is here.*

"Hi, guys," I said cheerily. The men mumbled hellos, anxious to get back to their conversation.

"Here, Lily, I saved you a seat," Max said as he pulled a

barstool from under the table and pushed it toward me.

I laid my coat down on it and then turned toward the bar. "I'm going to get a drink. You want one?" I asked Max. I almost asked if anyone else would like a drink but thought better of it. I was not about to buy all these guys a beer, and since they were teachers, I knew they'd take me up on it if I offered.

"I'll go. What do you want?" he asked, rising from his stool.

I sat down on mine as I said, "Surprise me."

He smiled mischievously as he began walking toward the bar. "You guys all good?" he asked as he walked away, not allowing them time to actually respond. Clearly Max didn't want to buy these guys a round either.

I watched with interest as Max approached the estrogen snake pit. The women saw him coming and instantly improved their postures: shoulders back, chests out.

"Excuse me, ladies," Max said amicably. The women had clearly hoped that Max would push through them, giving them opportunity to brush up against his rugged form, which was only slightly covered by a white thermal shirt that showcased his muscular arms and khaki cargo pants that snuggly hugged his hips.

But he didn't even attempt to climb through their web of palpable desire. He actually waited for them to move out of his way. I damn near laughed out loud. I could only imagine the disappointment flooding through each one of them, and I almost felt bad. After all, I liked most of them well enough. I wouldn't call them friends, but I had carried on conversations with all of them at one time or another. I even ate lunch every day with a few of them. But I didn't appreciate anyone trying to get cheap thrills from Max. He was worth more than that.

As he walked away from the bar and back to our table, I could feel the hate emanating from the den of lions. Not true hate, but a jealous hate that would ebb away as the weekend progressed. *Don't hate the player, hate the game, skanks.*

"Tequila sunrise," said Max as he placed the drink in front of me.

I glanced up at him questioningly.

"It looks pretty," he explained as he sat down, shrugging his shoulders.

The other men drew away from our table, realizing they no longer held Max's attention.

"So," he said.

"So," I replied.

We both laughed. Max and I typically fell into conversation so easily, this hesitation was foreign to us. It was like neither of us knew the other outside of Swift Middle School. We were starting from scratch.

"So," I began again, "why did you come back to Pennsylvania?" I already knew the answer to this, but I wanted to hear his version of it. I also wanted to know if he'd tell me the truth.

"Long story," Max exhaled, staring at his beer. When he finally lifted his eyes to me, I raised my brows, prompting him to proceed. "I'm sure you already know most of it. It's been all over the press."

"Are you insinuating that I use my free time to scour the internet for information about you?" I asked jokingly, though the joke was on me. I had, in fact, done just this on numerous occasions.

He chuckled silently and then stared at his hands as they cupped his glass while he continued. "It seems that the dashing man before you has a bit of an image problem. Since I decided to retire last season, my agent said that there has been some interest from a few sports stations in having me join their broadcasting teams. But they were all reluctant to hire me because I'm notoriously difficult to work with."

"You? Difficult? I would never have guessed," I teased, trying to keep the atmosphere light.

"I know, can you imagine?" Max laughed, but it didn't reach his eyes. My heart felt for him. It was clear that the judgment that followed him around weighed on him. "It's my own fault," he continued. "I know that. I'm really such a prick." As he said this, he ran his hand through his hair, clearly disconcerted by his own openness.

I sat silently, giving him the time he needed to decide whether to continue or change the subject. Ultimately, he continued.

"Confidence is one thing I have never lacked. I have been an arrogant son of a bitch since I could walk. And when I made it into the NHL, I got so caught up in my own importance that I thought I could walk on water. I felt impervious and got involved in self-destructive behaviors just to prove that nothing could touch me. Gambling, drinking, womanizing, not going to practice, not running plays the right way, grandstanding in front of my teammates. It was really fucking disgraceful.

"Then, three years ago, I found myself without a team. No one wanted me. I went from being one of the best players in the game to being a liability that no one wanted to employ. And even then, I couldn't get it together. A few teams gave me a shot, and I fucked all of them up. It wasn't until this past season, when there wasn't even a slight whisper of an interest, that I knew I had no choice. I either willingly retire with a tiny shred of dignity, or I go unsigned and deal with all of the embarrassment that comes with that. My agent told me he could get me into ESPN or one of the other major networks if I showed that I wasn't a total asshole. So, here I am, trying to do just that."

When he was finished, he looked up at me, trying to gauge my reaction. I didn't know what to say, so I went with the first thing that popped into my head. "That really sucks." *I could be really eloquent sometimes.*

"Yeah, yeah, it sucks." He laughed again, and this time, it showed in his eyes. I breathed easier, happy that I wasn't going to have to keep him from swallowing a bottle of painkillers or anything.

"Uh, so, the womanizing. Give me a ballpark figure. Exactly how many women have you picked up in airports?" I spoke in an easy, casual tone, but that's not what I felt. I wanted to know the answer to this question. I had to know it.

"I have no idea. Couldn't even give you a ballpark. I can tell you that I was tested by our team doctor monthly, at my own insistence. And I always wore a condom. I was definitely not trying to knock up some gold digger, that's for sure."

I felt mildly better but not completely. Of course, I was concerned about any sexually transmitted diseases that could be coursing through those veins across from me. But I think what really affected me was that I hadn't been special. Not in the least. Max had picked up girls all over this country, and probably some in a few others, and had had his way with each of them. That was what was truly bothering me when I asked my next question.

"Did any of the relationships last for any significant amount of time?"

Max stared at me a moment, as if trying to read on my face how he should answer this question.

"Tell the truth," I urged.

"If they did, it was out of convenience, not attachment," he replied simply.

"You never met a single girl who you thought you could have a meaningful relationship with?" I couldn't believe that Max had never loved a woman, never let himself emotionally invest in someone. I suddenly found him very hard to relate to.

"Lily, you saw firsthand the kind of girl I attract at the bar last week. Those vapid bloodhounds are not *settling down* material. Besides, I never thought myself capable of committing to one woman before."

My ears pricked up at his words. "Before?" What did that mean? Did he mean before I had forced him to discuss it? Or, did "before" include the present? So, could he see himself committing now? I desperately wanted to ask these questions. My mouth opened to unleash them, but . . . I couldn't.

If I were honest with myself, which I had forced myself to be almost too often lately. I didn't ask out of fear. Fear that he would say that he never thought about commitment before *me*, that I had been the one to change Max Samson. That I was the one he could commit to. I didn't want to shoulder that responsibility, especially when I didn't feel the same.

But an even bigger part of me feared that wasn't what he would say. That I was no more than the laundry list of others whose names had faded from his memory before they had any real chance to stake claim there. It was better not to press it any further than to risk completely blowing my ego to shit.

"I'm going to get us another round," he said, effectively pulling me out of my head and back into the moment.

"No, you got the last one. I'll go," I replied, starting to move before he had a chance to stop me. As I walked, I noticed that the herd of teachers had thinned considerably. Now only a few were sprinkled here and there, deep in conversation with one another. The flock of females had left, probably off to find a virgin's blood to drink or something.

"Can I have a tequila sunrise and whatever beer Mr. Samson is having?" I asked the bartender. As he handed me my drinks, I laid a ten-dollar bill on the counter, telling him to keep the change. I put Max's beer in front of him and sat back down with my own.

"So, why did you choose your former middle school as your image booster?" I hoped that this question would steer us back to comfortable ground.

"I liked Swift when I went there. And my agent said working with kids was always a winning option. Teenagers suck, so that left me with middle schoolers." *Yup, this was the Max I could relate to.*

As we drained our drinks, Max eyed me curiously. "You wanna get out of here?" He smirked as he awaited my response.

"I thought you'd never ask," I replied, already grabbing my coat and heading for the door.

❤

As I followed Max to his house, I pondered why, after all he had told me tonight, I was still overwhelmed with the need to fuck him. I practically ran out of the bar as soon as he hinted at continuing our private party elsewhere. Truth be told, he probably could have convinced me to fuck him at the bar, maybe even on it. Thankfully, I wasn't alone with my thoughts for long. Max lived only about ten minutes away.

As I pulled into his driveway behind him, I was surprised by his house. I had expected some kind of extravagant, almost tacky thing in a gated community somewhere. But this was a simple two-story house, made of brick with dark shutters. It had a two-car garage and a well-manicured lawn. We walked up the stone path and climbed two stairs to his front door. "You're not afraid of big dogs are you?" was the only thing he had asked since we arrived, and it wasn't until he opened the door and I saw two gigantic Great Danes galloping at me that the question registered.

I ducked behind Max, trying to figure out if these dogs were friendly or not. Once it became clear that they were not going to eat me, I began petting them excitedly. I *loved* dogs, but they were prohibited at my apartment complex.

"Well, I see I'm not the only male in this family who likes you."

I ignored Max's comment, unsure of how to take it. "What are their names?" I asked instead.

"The brindle one is Hercules, and the tawny one is Achilles."

"And you thought it was weird that I named my dog Charlotte? Why would you name this poor dog Achilles?"

"Because Brad Pitt was badass in that movie."

*Boys.*

"Do you want a drink?" Max asked as he walked farther into his house.

I followed him, looking around, taking everything in. The light-colored hardwood floors contrasted with rich brown furniture. His house was tidy, with not a thing out of place except for a few dog toys sprinkled on the floor. He led me into the kitchen and motioned for me to sit at his glass table. The appliances were all stainless steel, and his cupboard doors were made of glass so that one could look into them. It was simple and modern. Very much like Max.

"I have beer and wine in the fridge. Or we can go downstairs. I have a full bar down there."

"Wine works." I usually had a rule not to mix my alcohols, but I always broke all the rules with Max anyway. Why stop now? He poured me a glass and grabbed himself a beer. I stood as he handed it to me.

"I'm giving myself a tour," I said, smiling and hurrying out of the kitchen before he could stop me. I left the kitchen and found myself in the formal dining room that housed only two large dog beds. I made my way back down the hall toward the living room, where I had entered the house. As I passed the kitchen, I saw that Max was still there, sipping his beer as he leaned against his granite countertop.

I entered the living room, and my eyes scanned the rest of the room that I hadn't noticed when I first arrived. There was a huge flat screen TV mounted on the wall, as well as a pretty impressive surround sound setup. *Boys and their toys.*

Then, I walked over to a glass display case. It housed all of Max's hockey awards, including an all-star medal and an MVP plaque. I wondered what it must be like to be so good at something. His walls were bare, except for a few framed pictures of people I didn't recognize next to the display case—*family maybe?*—and a menagerie of framed pictures on the wall behind one of his couches. I moved closer, trying to get a better look at what they were of, when I stopped in my tracks, completely surprised.

I reached out with my hand to touch the frames. *Had*

*Max taken these?* That was a stupid question; clearly he had. I processed the photos slowly: a picture of the Swift Middle School sign in front of the building, pictures of the boys on his hockey team practicing and goofing around in the weight room, a few shots with Max and some of the teachers—*I hadn't even known he'd been friendly with any of the others*—and there were some of me.

One captured me teaching. He must have taken it from the hallway. And another of me from the side. *When had he taken that?* The last was one we had taken together at lunch about two weeks ago. We were making silly faces, trying to mimic the self-portraits the kids were always taking.

As I stared at them, I felt my skin prick to life, sensing him before he actually touched me. When he did make contact, his touch was soft, affectionate, caressing. My nipples immediately hardened as my mind reeled. Should I feel awkward that he had these pictures of me hanging in his house? Perhaps I should have, but I didn't. My feelings were actually leaning in the opposite direction. I had never felt more aroused by Max. And that was really saying something.

He took my drink from my hand and put it down on a table somewhere beyond my senses. He was then behind me again, splaying his right hand over my taut stomach, gently pulling me against him, his erection hard against my ass. He nuzzled my head to the side as he began showering my neck with short, sweet kisses. I began to grind against him slowly, eliciting a deep exhale from this god among men.

Our pace quickened, his kisses became harder, more passionate as I pushed myself into him. I could already feel my orgasm building despite his barely having touched me yet. He lifted my shirt, pushing my bra up with it as he cupped my breast and massaged it with a force that only he could make sensual. I reached behind him, found his hair, and ravaged it, pulling and stroking it with the same rhythm that the throb deep in my pelvis had.

Suddenly, he put both of his hands to my waist and turned me toward him, hoisting me up, his hands firm on the backs of my thighs. I kept grinding into him, needing to feel his full length. He thrust his tongue into my mouth as the slow, soft Max disappeared and was replaced by this wild, commanding one. I knew then that this was why I craved Max so intensely. I didn't have to offer myself to him. He just took. And God, did I love being taken.

It took me a moment to realize that we were moving. And as my back felt the wall, I arched against it, bringing it into our erotic exchange. Max pulled back from me for a single moment. He looked at me, seemingly into me, and told me all that I needed to know. I was the one he could change for, would change for, if only I gave him that chance.

But I was too high on my need for him to do anything other than pull him back to me. His mouth went to my neck, frenzied and full of fire as he kept one hand under my ass for support and raised the other to begin loosening the buttons on my pants. My hands groped for his zipper, unable to stand the distance these clothes caused. He lowered me just long enough to pull my pants off and step out of his own.

His length sprung free and pushed at my panties, trying to breach the soft barricade that separated us. I threw my arms up and pulled my shirt over my head, tossing it to the floor as Max began to carry me up the stairs. We made it about halfway before he lowered me again, laying me on the stairs. He knelt between my legs, quickly removing his shirt before putting his hands to my panties. He lowered them with such slowness, I wasn't sure where he had found the restraint. I moaned at his erotic action as my own hands rushed to my breasts, pulling my nipples, unable to quell the beckoning of my skin for contact.

Max then crashed down upon me, leaving no shred of skin without the moisture of his tongue. His cock was at my opening, the tip gaining entrance and then being hurriedly removed. I wanted, needed, to feel the fullness of him. I groaned in anticipation of his thick, hard cock plunging into me, forcing me to stretch to accommodate him. I rocked my hips into him, trying to force him inside, but he pulled back. I groaned again, my heightened senses becoming too much to withstand.

He lifted me skillfully, with a grace possessed only by one who has done this before. I pushed that thought to that back of my mind, not wanting to dwell on the inevitable truth: Max had fucked on every known surface of the planet. But I didn't care about that in this heated moment. All that mattered was that he was currently exploring *my* surface, navigating me with efficiency and patience.

My mouth devoured him as we moved, our destination unknown to me. One of his hands continued to support me while the other reached up and applied pressure to the nape of my neck, causing my head to loll back, giving him greater access to the soft flesh there. Suddenly, I felt my world shift as my eyes found the ceiling and my back felt the smooth coolness of his comforter. He lowered us both onto his bed, managing to maintain our closeness as his kisses moved to my breasts. His teeth toyed with my nipples, elongating them, inflicting that brutal balance between ecstasy and anguish.

I was his in this moment. He possessed me fully and

without apology. My attention focused on his every movement, every moan, every brush against my skin. I doubted whether I would ever be able to walk away from this. I lay there, hypnotized by the sexual power he exuded. I wanted to taste it, feel it, suck it from his cock and let it flood me. I finally gave him what I knew he wanted.

"Please, oh God, please,"

My voice was hushed and raspy, raw with the need that quaked between my thighs. But he didn't respond, nor did he enter me as I so desired. Instead, he raised his eyes to me, telling me that it wasn't enough.

"Oh God, I want you so badly. Please. Oh, please. Max." The uttering of his name was enough, and he thrust into me, forcing me to take all of him. His hands fell to either side of my head, and my own roamed his body, scratching his back, pushing down on his hips to increase his speed. He then lifted one arm at a time and captured my hands in his, pinning them by my head. He continued to pound into me as my own wetness coated him, allowing him to slide without friction or resistance. I arched my hips as my clit begged for more stimulation. He lowered himself slightly, as if sensing my need, so that his pelvis gave me the contact I craved.

He plunged deeply once more, and my climax peaked. The euphoric climbing ended as I reached my destination. An uncontrollable spasm ripped through my body, causing all parts of me to clench and prohibit any further movement. He had spent me thoroughly. I yelled my satisfaction, unable to keep it inside my body. Max grunted, a sound full of heady desire, as he expelled his passion into me. He then crumpled atop me, both of us panting from this incredibly demanding and satisfying sexual experience.

I didn't know how long we lay there, our limbs tangled together, soft kisses floating from our already sore lips. But I was suddenly overcome with the need to get up. I told myself that it was because, if we kept kissing, he was going to have to take me again. And physically, I didn't have it in me.

But it was more than that, deeper. Our encounter had been intimate, too full of meaning and blurred lines. I had to escape from it, get away from the tantalizing scent and feel of Max Samson.

"I'm going to use your bathroom," I said as I climbed off him, disengaging myself from this moment. He followed me up, and my eyes couldn't help but steal a fleeting glance at his cock. *A condom! Oh, thank the Lord! When had he put that on?* Despite my having been on birth control since I was eighteen, I still wanted to use condoms with Max, for obvious reasons. But, in the heat of our passion, I had never even thought about it. At least one of us was thinking with the right head.

His bedroom was large, with vaulted ceilings and exposed wood beams. But the room itself was simple. The hardwood floors continued up here, the walls were white, and his comforter was a light gray. He had a master bathroom that was big enough for two, with a shower stall and Jacuzzi tub. *Man, would I like to climb in that thing right about now.*

Max lagged behind me long enough to let me pee in privacy. I opened the bathroom door when I was finished, letting him know that he could join me. I felt suddenly uncomfortable being so naked. I quickly grabbed one of his towels and wrapped myself in it, inspecting my freshly fucked hair in the mirror. *What a mess.*

I noticed Max's reflection in the mirror as he approached. My chest felt heavier with each step he took toward me. It was like the air was being choked out of me. Max's reflection looked different now. More vulnerable? Open? I couldn't stand the air of change that surrounded us. I had to force us back into the familiar, weigh us down so that we never scratched this surface again.

"You know, about this whole image thing."

His head jerked up as something clouded his eyes. Disappointment. This wasn't what he hoped I would want to talk about after . . . I guess it could only be called lovemaking. His gait slowed and his demeanor changed. The peace our encounter had brought to him was fading. My next words would erase it completely.

"This *Mighty Ducks* routine you've got going isn't going to convince anybody that you're a changed man. It's clear that you're only doing it for appearances. You're going to have a much harder time trying to overcome the horrible reputation you've made for yourself."

And there it was. I told myself I was only trying to help him, offer him advice that any friend would offer. But I wasn't just any friend, not after what had happened here tonight. And I knew it. This was the true reason why I had said what I did. The pain it caused him would only be temporary. Wouldn't it? Then, we could get back to how we were. We were better suited there.

"I don't remember asking your opinion," he replied, his voice low and gritty.

"You didn't," I agreed. "But you need to hear it. It's the truth." My last words carried meaning beyond what we were actually discussing. He did need to hear me, because I had only ever told him the truth. And I was telling him the truth now. Our friendship was just that. It would never be more. Max was too chaotic, too wild, too electrifying to spend a lifetime with. He would drain me of my energy and leave me empty and broken. He was a risk that I wouldn't gamble my happiness on.

"I don't need to hear anything from you," he growled, his eyes blazing into mine. "The only thing I need is for you to do what a booty call is supposed to do: get me off and then go the hell home."

My body screeched to a halt, suspending all movement. My face fell for just an instant, the hurt rising, before I quashed it. Quickly, I put on a calm, impassive facade, turned, and dropped the towel. Now wasn't the time for weak insecurities. It was a time for strength.

I started for the stairs, looking for bits of clothes as I descended. Max remained in the bathroom but emerged as I began slipping from view, hastening my retreat down the stairs.

"Lily, I . . ."

I held up my hand to silence him. "Have a good night, Mr. Samson." I never turned toward him, never slowed my pace. I finished dressing quickly and walked steadily to my car. It wasn't until I turned the corner, effectively erasing his house from view, that I began to unravel.

I smacked my hand on the steering wheel as tears filled my eyes. But I refused to let them fall. I would not shed a single tear over that asshole. I took a few deep breaths and tried to relax. I tried to tell myself that his comment had simply caught me off guard. My reaction was a typical emotional response to a cruel comment that had been completely unwarranted.

*But who was I kidding?*

Max hadn't been the only one who had been cruel tonight, and I knew it. But I hadn't deserved that. My mind flashed back to the movie theater last week. I hadn't deserved that rebuke either. *What was it with men?* Granted, I had pulled away from Max tonight, but not in this way. I hadn't abandoned him as a friend. If anything, I had done it to save our friendship. It was he who fractured it, split it in a way that would prevent it from ever again growing back as strong as it once was.

He had treated me like I was trash and, even worse, had made me feel like maybe that's exactly what I was. And perhaps he was right. He had asked for me to show him more, but I had proved incapable. Instead, I had demonstrated that I was only after one thing. I was a vapid bloodhound, just like the rest of them.

I drove the rest of the way, lost in my thoughts and trying to tread water in my own murky truth. Only one thing could possibly free me from this torment, though I'm not sure it was a practical option.

*Am I too far into my life to become a lesbian?*

# chapter twenty-two

Saturday night had finally arrived and, thankfully my nerves wouldn't allow me to dwell on what had happened between Max and me last night. Instead, I focused solely on what might await me during the night ahead. I had absolutely no idea what to expect. I made every effort to try not to guess what Adam was planning. In addition to wondering where we would be going, I also had no idea what our conversation would be like. I knew tonight Adam would tell me how he felt about me, but until today I hadn't considered the possibility that I would have to reciprocate that same honesty.

Since I had no idea where we would be going, I did the best I could with planning what to wear. *"Dress formally,"* he had said. After a record-breaking number of outfit changes, I settled on a tight burgundy dress, which left no room for any type of undergarment whatsoever. I curled my hair in beachy waves and went light on the makeup, hoping for a more natural look. I didn't want to overdo it for whatever he had planned.

At just before seven o'clock, Adam arrived in a black Lamborghini. I knew he didn't own one, so he must have rented it just for tonight. As always, he looked delicious. His trendy, slender-fitting black suit hugged his perfectly firm body. And with his white shirt and thin black tie, he looked stylish but simple.

Despite the fact that I had been nervous for this date, being with Adam actually relaxed me. He emitted a kind of powerful calmness, like he could soothe my worries with his presence alone.

For the first time, I found myself just enjoying being near him without the constant thought of ravaging him. Although I still couldn't avoid the occasional image of his hand wandering off of the stick shift to find its place up my dress instead. But thankfully my thoughts were not consumed by those visions, as they had been during the movie. I was still capable of holding a normal conversation.

"So, when do I get to find out where we're going?" I asked.

"When we get there," he responded teasingly. "I'm pretty sure you'll like it, though. So don't worry."

From the moment this date had been arranged, I had promised myself that I would let him take the lead tonight. He would direct our conversation, even though I was dying to know the answer to the question I had asked when we talked in the parking lot Monday after school. *How did Adam Carter feel about me?* But I had to be patient with all things. Besides, I would find out tonight.

"We're going to Fleming's Steakhouse for dinner," he said excitedly. "I'll tell you that much. Have you ever been there?" He turned, his green eyes focused directly on me.

"No, but as long as I can eat something that was mooing a few hours ago, I'm in!"

He grinned proudly. "That's my girl!"

Though I was sure I was reading into it too deeply, I couldn't help but smile internally at his proclamation.

We arrived at the restaurant, which had a masculine feel with its wooden walls and dim amber lighting. The hostess led us to a section of tables a few steps up from the main dining area on the left. I was thankful for the privacy that our table in the corner granted us.

Adam ordered us sparkling water and wine from their interactive wine menu on an iPad. *At least this time I know we'll be sharing it.*

"So," he began when we were alone, "I guess now is finally the right time to talk." He settled back into his chair, relaxing a bit.

I braced myself for what this conversation might sound like. I had no idea where he would begin or what we were really even going to discuss. So I waited patiently for him to continue.

"I think we left each other with some unanswered questions after the movie, so I figured we could talk about them tonight." He was calm and direct, obviously not as embarrassed by this conversation as I was going to be. "I'm guessing you'd like to know why I reacted the way I did in the theater."

"Yeah, I didn't mean to—"

"I know you didn't mean to make me uncomfortable," he interrupted, saving me further mortification. "And I didn't mean to make you feel like I didn't want you. I do. Physically, emotionally. I want you." He lowered his voice a little further. "Just not in a movie theater," he said, smiling sweetly.

His voice was soft, seductive even. And as I looked into his clear green eyes and felt the warmth of his skin against mine when he took my hand, I knew I wanted him in the same way. "I understand" was all I could manage in return.

"What you were going to do . . . that's not how it should

be." He traced his fingers up and down my arm lightly, and my skin tingled. Our wine arrived, but he never took his eyes off me to look up when the waiter asked if we were ready to order. Adam simply gave him a polite, "I think we need a few more minutes."

"I want that to mean something," he continued. "I want *us* to mean something. To be honest, I'm not sure what that *something* is yet, but I know it's worth more than what that would have been." He paused for a moment. "Now I believe it's my turn to ask a few questions."

I realized then that I hadn't actually asked any questions of my own. Adam just knew what I had been thinking and had taken it upon himself to answer. There was a bit of comfort in the realization that he knew me so well. Most guys have trouble distinguishing women's feelings even after they tell them, but Adam had an intuition that was lacking in many men.

"How do you feel about me? About us?" he asked.

And there I waited, in this interminable limbo of mere seconds, for him to continue so that I wouldn't have to answer immediately.

"I guess I am just cautious about where I go in relationships. Chalk it up to having a twelve-year-old daughter, I guess. I'm just protective of *my* feelings as well as hers. I'm not looking to sleep with as many women as possible." Glancing at his hands folded on the table, he seemed to be choosing his next words carefully. "I'm looking for the right person, and if I didn't think that you could possibly be her, I wouldn't be here right now having this conversation. I just want to make sure you feel the same way before we take this any further." He exhaled as if a burden he'd been carrying had suddenly been lifted. Regardless of what my reaction would be, he seemed lighter having confessed this.

I took a deep breath before responding, "I'm not sure I love you yet, if that's what you're asking. But I definitely feel something when I'm around you. Something more than I would feel for some guy I just wanted to use for sex. That's not what this is, regardless of how it may have seemed the other night." I was surprised at how defensive I sounded suddenly.

"No, no. I would never think that. I don't think you're the type of person who would just screw some guy for the hell of it. Sorry if that's how it came off."

If he only knew just how right he was. I would *absolutely* screw some guy just for the hell of it. That guy just wasn't Adam Carter.

"Are you seeing anyone else?" he asked, more directly than I would have expected. *Jesus, had he infiltrated my brain tonight without my knowing it?*

"No," I said without even considering my answer, somehow managing to maintain eye contact. He didn't need to know about Max, especially after our fight yesterday. "No, just you," I repeated.

And I meant it. Max fulfilled a sexual need. That was all. And if that need could be filled by Adam—and his hopefully gigantic penis—I had no need for Max Samson anymore. He would just complicate things.

Adam smiled at my response. It had apparently appeased him, because he motioned to the waiter that he could now take our order. I breathed a sigh of relief that that conversation was finally out of the way.

The remainder of our dinner passed easily. We discussed Adam's plans to go to his shore house over Eva's spring break in a few weeks. It would be too cold to swim, but I couldn't stop myself from picturing Adam in a bathing suit, sun glistening off his wet chest.

I was reminded of some of the vacations I'd taken, and Adam seemed genuinely interested as I shared the details of my childhood trips to my parents' house on Lake Michigan. "The last time I was there was when my roommate Amanda and I went with some college friends. My parents had no idea we were even there. It was a crazy week: drinking on my dad's boat, cookouts, and ladder ball in the yard . . ."

I stopped short, suddenly self-conscious of how immature that made me look. Would he think I had acted like a teenager? Drinking, playing games, sneaking into a house without permission.

Instead, he just looked at me with a sincere smile. "Sounds like fun. I'd love to get a boat eventually. So," he asked with a subtle hint of seduction in his voice, "you ready for dessert?"

❤

Adam got out his valet ticket to give to the waiter, even though the Lamborghini was probably parked right out front where they kept all of the expensive cars. As we walked toward the front of the restaurant, I excused myself to go to the bathroom and told Adam I would meet him outside. I touched up my lipstick and ran my fingers through my hair before heading out to meet him.

I arrived outside to find Adam leaning against the car with the passenger door open for me. He extended a hand to help me in and then closed the door gently. As he slid into the driver's seat, I wanted so badly to ask where we were going, what he had planned for the night ahead, but I reminded myself that all things about Adam were worth waiting for, and this date was no exception.

Luckily, I didn't have to wait long as Adam parked in the lot for the Radnor Hotel, which was adjacent to the restaurant. *More drinks?* I wondered as we entered the lobby. I was at their bar once before when I stayed there for a wedding. I hadn't had much wine at dinner because I had been so nervous, but now that I was more relaxed, I didn't mind the thought of having a drink or two.

But to my surprise, Adam led me quickly past the bar and into an open elevator. *Holy shit! Had he gotten us a room?* It was so unexpected. So thoughtful. So... Adam.

Alone with him in the elevator, I was nervous. This was not the quickie on my lunch break that I'd become so accustomed to lately. This was planned. Intentional.

The elevator doors began to close, but they quickly opened again to let three more people on. Adam backed into the sidewall of the elevator, grabbing hold of my tightened stomach and pulling me against him. I felt his breath against the back of my neck, and my skin prickled in response.

As I let my ass press against him, I could feel his dick stiffen almost immediately, slowly growing and pulsing against me steadily. The position felt strangely familiar to what I'd experienced with Max only yesterday, but the meaning couldn't have been more different.

I tightened with the need to feel him inside me. But the emptiness I felt in return was nearly unbearable. I could see his intense gaze reflecting back at me in the mirror on the opposite wall.

Despite our company, his piercing stare and his strong hand pressed firmly against my pelvis created a feeling so intimate that I felt as if we were alone. I was reminded of my decision not to wear panties when I felt the creamy wetness make its way to the top of my thighs. As my heartbeat quickened, I struggled to control my breathing. I wanted to push against him, to feel him grind into the crack of my ass through the soft fabric of my dress. But I didn't dare move.

The elevator stopped at the fifth floor, allowing the other passengers to exit. To my surprise and pleasure, Adam did not release me from his solid grasp. Instead, he swept my hair to the side, planting soft kisses down my shoulder, eventually lifting my arm up above my head to tickle the inside of my elbow with his wet lips.

The elevator went up a few more floors before again coming to a stop, this time on the eighth floor. "This is us," Adam whispered, stroking my earlobe with his teeth. He took my hand and led me down the hall until we arrived at the room. *Our* room. As he took the key out of his pocket and opened the door for me, I filled with excitement.

It was then that I stepped into the sweetest thing anyone had ever done for me.

Elegant white-striped wallpaper covered the walls. The room was furnished with classic wooden furniture and a gold-and-red upholstered armless chair in one corner. But my eyes were immediately drawn to the king-size bed in the center of the room. Sprinkled across the floor and on the blue-and-gold-paisley comforter were pink rose petals that reminded me of the flower Adam had given me on our first date. The bed held a tray with a bottle of champagne on ice.

I pressed my hands together over my mouth and nose, my thumbs supporting my chin. I was in awe. "God, Adam . . . this is . . . it's beautiful." I turned around to see him propping the door open with his strong shoulder as he leaned, confident and relaxed. "I don't know what to say."

The corners of his mouth rose slightly to reveal a subtle smile. "Then don't say *anything.*" He let the door close behind him as he stepped to me, his bright eyes fixed as his soft thumb stroked my cheek. "I told you how it *shouldn't* be. Now let me show you how it *should.*"

*Dear God, just when I thought I couldn't get any wetter.*

Of all the sexually obscene comments that I had heard recently, I never would have guessed that hearing something so innocent, something so true, could have such an immediate effect on me. My legs weakened. But this time it was not from a sexual need. It was as if my chest suddenly filled with the presence of something I wasn't sure had ever existed in me before now.

Adam expressed true feeling without the vulgarity that I had become so used to. Emotionally, he had a hold on me that I couldn't escape, even if I'd wanted to. And I definitely didn't want to. Something told me that his physical grasp on me would be no less powerful. I was torn between whether to grab the back of his neck with both my hands and pull him in to kiss me or to just keep staring into his eyes until I was completely lost in him.

Lightly, he slid a hand up my back that sent chills undulating down my spine and pulled me slowly, effortlessly toward him. I leaned my head back as he supported it with his other hand and kissed me softly, letting his tongue linger in my mouth before he pulled out teasingly to nibble on my bottom lip. My back arched as he towered over me, consuming me fully.

He lay me back onto the bed and leaned over me, his weight supported by his forearms as he licked down the front of my neck and chest. I closed my eyes to let myself take in every touch. I concentrated on feeling his erection pressing into me as he slowly moved his hips back and forth on top of me, causing a muffled moan to escape my mouth into his neck.

But my need for this man went beyond a physical one. I wanted to stay like this, in this moment of anticipation. This moment of the unknown and the new. A moment I would never be able to get back after it passed.

Adam stood up in front of me and parted my legs just enough so he could position himself between them. I studied him closely as he loosened his tie, pulled it over his head, and let it drop to the floor a few feet away. He slipped his jacket down his arms slowly and tossed it to the chair in the corner without looking behind him. Then, one by one, he began to undo each button on his shirt.

*Holy shit! He's going to strip for me.*

Revealing more and more of his tanned, chiseled chest, he finally removed his shirt completely and tossed it onto the bed. As it landed, the scent of him wafted up, and I inhaled it deeply.

He grabbed ahold of his belt as he bit his bottom lip, seemingly unaware of how captivating he was to watch.

I savored him standing before me, slowly removing each piece of clothing. He was putting on a private show: an intimate strip tease for only me to enjoy. *Well, me and whoever else could see in the window since the curtains were still open.* With one swift motion, he pulled off his belt, creating a cracking sound as it went through the last loop.

I was so turned on. Adam had only kissed me, had barely even spoken, and wasn't even undressed. Yet I found it nearly impossible to hold myself back. I wanted him to touch me. Hell, I wanted to touch myself. I needed some kind of physical contact to complement this visual stimulation. I moved my hand along the inside of my thigh and felt a rush against my skin.

With his eyes cast upon me, Adam unbuttoned his pants, and I wanted him to keep going. To unzip them and finally let me see what I had been imagining for the past few weeks. But he didn't grant me that pleasure yet. Instead, he turned away from me, bending down, as he offered me a glimpse of his muscular back and flexed shoulders. Only Adam could make removing shoes and socks look sexy.

With his back toward me, I let my hand move up my thigh to stroke myself. I wondered why it had been so difficult for me to think of this man while I did this after our first date. Though I had always been clearly attracted to him, he hadn't been my fantasy. Until now.

*Thank the Lord for "now."*

He turned back around to look at me, and I moved my hand away, not wanting him to see how needy I was.

Moving to the edge of the bed, he squeezed the outside of my thighs and dragged me closer to him. Without speaking, he told me what he wanted, and I was eager to comply. I sat up to unzip his pants, pulling them down so he could step out of them. I gave myself time to admire the bulge pressing on the fabric of his black boxer briefs and ran my hands up his chest and down his abs to the soft light hair below his navel as he stood, powerfully, over me.

I couldn't wait any longer. With one aggressive motion, I pulled his boxers down, grabbing his firm ass on the way. I kissed his pelvis, licking my way down to his shaft. I was glad to see that what I had been envisioning was even more impressive in person. He groaned as I placed his balls in my hand and rubbed them gently. His cock swelled even more, turning a deeper red and pulsing slightly at my touch when I caressed its slick tip.

He eased me back softly onto the bed, and as he slid my dress up past my mouth and nose, he paused, obstructing my vision momentarily and pinning my hands above my head with the taut fabric. In the dim lighting, I was exposed. Wearing no bra or panties, every inch of me could be surveyed by him. But in contrast, I could see nothing.

I heard the champagne open and, within seconds, felt its cool bubbles run down my stomach, followed by an ice cube that he guided behind my ear and down my neck to my breasts. My flesh tingled, and my muscles tightened in shock. Then I felt his tongue glide across my skin, licking the champagne from me hungrily. His wet lips felt smooth, and I ached for him to go lower.

Then his hands were on me again, finally yanking my dress off completely. He lay next to me, his fingers tracing every inch of my body except the part I wanted him so desperately to find. My hips flexed to him, but he continued his slow seduction, armed with the self-control that I had never been able to possess.

My nipples lengthened between his fingers and teeth as he pulled and bit them, playfully, teasingly. If he continued to focus his attention here, I thought I might orgasm from that alone. I didn't know if that was even possible, but I was certainly willing to find out.

I was breathless and shaking: a mixture of wordless moans and unapologetic begging. I needed him inside me. To feel his fingers, that soft tongue, his hardness . . . I wanted all of him. Finally, his tongue wandered over every inch of my skin with increasing speed until it found its destination.

I tugged his hair between my fingers as I watched his face move back and forth between my legs, deliberately and carefully. He exuded a confidence that only served to highlight the vulnerability I felt surrendering myself physically and emotionally to this man. My feet pressed into the mattress, and as he twisted three fingers inside me, he moved his lips to suck forcefully on my clit. Part of me wanted him to keep going so I could feel myself convulse around his tongue, allowing him to drink every drop of the wetness he'd created.

But at the same time, another piece of me wanted to tell him to stop so he could spread me wide with his thickness and I could take him deep inside me, feel him against my skin as I came undone. Thankfully, Adam made my decision for me. He kissed up my stomach slowly until he reached my mouth, fully devouring me. He tasted sweet: an intoxicating combination of champagne and me.

As his mouth made his way down my shoulder blades, he rolled me to my left side, positioning himself behind me. His erection rubbed between my legs, and I pushed back, craving him inside me, silently pleading with him to take what he wanted and give me the same in return. He paused to let his tip rest at my slippery opening as he took my heavy, aching breasts in his large hands. He whispered into my ear, his breath warm, "Let me get a condom." As he began to push away from me, I grabbed his arm gently. "You don't need it," I assured him.

At last, he gave me what I needed: softly at first, and then, with steadily accelerating thrusts, he pushed into me. His hand moved to my throat, pulling my head back with a balance of tenderness and dominance that only Adam could elicit. I didn't know how long we'd been lost in that ecstasy, our sweaty bodies intertwined until they seemed to become one. Heavily, he breathed into my neck, whispering how close he was, how he couldn't wait much longer.

"Then don't," I breathed back. Just knowing that I could make him lose control was enough for me to do the same. With his arms pulling me even closer against him, I shook as the orgasm that had been building since the elevator ride rippled through me. Then Adam followed, filling me with every drop of pleasure he had, as he came in long bursts inside me.

Our only movement for what seemed like an eternity was our shallow breaths and pounding hearts. The feeling was foreign. I had become so used to hurrying. So used to focusing on a single goal with Max, that it felt odd to want to prolong anything. But with Adam, I didn't want any moment to end. I would kiss him until our tongues went numb and our arms tired from our embrace. I would hover on the brink of climax, in that sexual purgatory between pure frustration and fleeting bliss, just to feel connected to him for a moment longer.

The night passed with endless cries of pleasure and gentle kisses on soft flesh as we attempted to fulfill a need in each other that neither one of us could quite satiate.

Adam had been right. This was how it *should* be. And when I finally did rise the next morning, I felt as if I had found a piece of myself on that bed that I didn't know I had until that night.

# chapter twenty-three

Two weeks passed and I didn't talk to Max. He stopped coming down to eat lunch with us, made no visits to my classroom, and gave me a wide berth in the halls. On the rare occasions we did cross paths, I kept my eyes averted away from him, refusing to even acknowledge his existence.

Though, the silence wore on me. Despite my trying to shove the feelings deeply down inside myself, I couldn't truly deny them. I missed Max. Of course, I missed the sex. Who wouldn't? But ultimately, I missed our friendship. I still had Tina to help me pass the time, but that relationship wasn't the same. Or maybe *I* wasn't the same. It was hard to tell anymore.

Thank God for Adam. He kept me from slipping into sadness, always there like a bright light for me to find my way by. Our relationship had grown steadily since our night at the Radnor Hotel. Being with him made everything else slip away. And it also convinced me that I had done the right thing by distancing myself from Max. I couldn't jeopardize what I had with Adam. Max simply wasn't worth it.

As the days passed and winter began to fall away, I started to think of all the great things Adam and I could do this summer. We had both decided that it would be best to wait for the school year to end before telling Eva about our relationship. All she knew was that her dad had met someone he liked very much. I felt guilty for not telling her the full truth, but we felt it would be less awkward for Eva this way. *I mean, who wanted their dad to be banging their teacher?*

I sat at my desk during fifth period, replaying Adam's and my recent dates in my mind. We had gone to dinner a few times, a comedy show, rock climbing—*the image of Adam's muscles rippling beneath his shirt was enough to make me wet on the spot*—as well as spent some quiet nights at my apartment, watching movies or making love. It all screamed romantic comedy.

Our most recent date filled my mind, and I couldn't help but smile. Even though it was only mid-March, we had experienced an unusual bout of warm weather last week. Adam had decided that we needed an adventure, and since his weekends were usually spent with Eva, we'd conspired to play hooky from work last Friday and take advantage of the mild weather.

He hadn't told me where we were going, and since that had worked out so well for me the last time he had surprised me, I'd jumped at the chance to let him try it again. He'd told me to dress warmly, jeans and a sweatshirt were fine, and he'd pick me up after dropping Eva off at school.

We sat in an easy silence for most of the ride to our destination. Adam and I often didn't need words. It was enough to just be in each other's presence to feel content. He reached over at one point and grabbed my hand, holding it tightly for the rest of the drive. It was a sweet gesture, so like Adam.

After we had driven for a little over an hour, Adam pulled his Yukon onto a dirt road. As we drove into the woods, I couldn't help but get a little morbid. *This would be a great place to dump a body. I'd have to keep it in mind the next time Max pissed me off.*

The dirt road was brought to an abrupt end after about eight hundred meters by a thick rope-chain barrier.

"Gonna have to walk from here," Adam said quietly as he turned off the ignition and jumped out of the truck.

I followed suit, and Adam grabbed my hand as we ducked under the barricade and continued down the road.

It was beautiful. Trees surrounded us on both sides of the road. Huge trees that had probably been growing for thousands of years. If girls could be Boy Scouts, I may have been able to tell what kind of trees they were. Instead, all I had ever learned to do was hustle an old lady out of her spare change so she could buy some cookies.

We walked about three minutes down the road before coming to a clearing that overlooked a small lake. Five boarded-up houses lined one side of the lake, while trees surrounded it on all others. I instantly felt my imagination run away with me. I could see myself as a child, running along the banks of this lake, splashing with other children, having the kind of carefree summer only experienced by those under the age of twelve. This had been a great place once. I could feel it in the air.

"Where are we?" I asked, nearly in a whisper, as if I were afraid to disturb the serenity of this place.

"My family's old lake house," he replied in a low tone, paying the same reverence to this place that I had.

I started forward, wanting to explore. As I approached the houses, I realized that they weren't just boarded up. They were dilapidated. "Doesn't anyone come up here anymore?" I questioned, disbelieving that no one would want to spend their summer here.

"Not that I know of. There's a bigger house up beyond that hill," Adam responded as he pointed beyond the row of wooden houses. "I think they own a good bit of this land now. Though the lake is public property."

"How long has it been since you were here last?" I inspected the houses closely, with their small decks and chipped paint.

"God, seventeen years ago now. We spent our last summer here when I was fifteen. I loved coming here. There was always something different to explore. My brother and I would go out into the woods for hours and then come home and cool off in the lake. Those were such great times."

I was taken aback by how much there was to still learn about this man. I hadn't even known he had a brother. Adam had never mentioned him when we discussed our families. I wondered why.

Adam took a deep breath. Something settled over him, a density that he hadn't had a moment before.

"Why did you guys stop coming up here?"

Adam let out the breath he had been holding. He stared out into the lake, as if weighing his reply before he actually spoke it.

"I haven't been back here since our last summer in this house." He turned toward me for a moment before looking back to the lake. "I wanted to bring you here because a huge part of me revolves around this place. Some of my greatest memories took place here. It's almost as if those memories have a life all their own at this lake. I feel such a thrill being back, like I'm a kid all over again." He smiled faintly, the kind of smile you would give to someone you haven't seen in a long time and who lives only in the recesses of your memory.

"But my worst memory lives here, too. And it explains why I'm so protective of the people I love. Why I'm so careful when it comes to Eva. You can't really understand me, Lily, without knowing what took place here."

I grew anxious, not sure what to do or say in this moment. So, I did and said nothing. I just gave him space and time.

When he was ready, he continued, "My brother and I swam like fish. We grew up in this lake, played in it together every day. But when I hit thirteen, I decided that it wasn't cool to hang around with my little brother. See, there was a girl my age who lived in that house there." Adam pointed to the second house from the end. "I wanted to hang out with her, so I told my brother to beat it. He was only ten and wasn't interested in girls yet, so he didn't understand why I would want to go into the woods with her instead of going swimming with him."

Adam smiled, broader this time, more sincere. He turned toward me again. "I got my first kiss in the woods that day." As Adam turned back to face the lake, his smile faded. "When she and I were walking back, we heard voices yelling. So we started to run. When we reached the clearing, I scanned the crowd of people and saw my mother. And as my knees hit the dirt, my mind registered what was happening. She was sobbing, holding my brother in her arms. But he wasn't moving."

At this, Adam squatted down, resting both forearms on his thighs. "He got tangled in the weeds on the bottom of the lake. He wasn't even in water that deep. Maybe four feet. But he got tangled and trapped beneath the surface. If I had been there, Lily, I could have . . ." The words dropped from him, unable to face the light of day.

I strode to him, hunched beside him, one arm resting on his strong, capable shoulders and the other touching his forearm, giving balance to us both.

"I should have been there, Lily. I should have been, but I wasn't. I swore to myself that, from that point on, I would always be there. Others would be able to count on me, even though he couldn't."

As I gazed into his eyes that stared out over the serene water, I noticed the tears begin to well. And as a single tear fell down his face, my heart broke for him.

"We didn't come back the next summer. It was too soon, the loss too fresh. We returned for the last time the following year. We lasted two weeks before we realized that it would always be too soon, the loss would always be too fresh. The lake lost its magic. We boarded up the house and never looked back."

My hand moved from his shoulders to his back, circling it softly. "What was his name?" I asked. I immediately regretted asking this question, not wanting to pull even more pain into this moment. But as Adam looked at me, a smile returning to his face, I knew that it was all right.

"Seth," he replied as he stood, putting his arm around me. "His name was Seth."

Adam and I then wandered around the lake for a while, taking in the calmness that we found ourselves in the midst of. When we finally left, I felt a sudden, unexplainable welling of sadness. It was as if I had also lost something out on the lake. We walked in silence, Adam's arm wrapped around my shoulders. I climbed back into the Yukon as Adam settled in beside me.

As he put the key in the ignition, he stopped short. "Thanks for being here with me, Lily."

"I wouldn't want to be anywhere else."

He smiled at this, turned the key, and started for home.

We'd stopped at a diner on the way, eating sandwiches in between light, casual conversation. There had been enough depth for one day. Most of all, we had just enjoyed the company the other supplied. And what I had told Adam had been the truth. There wasn't a single other place on this planet I would have rather been than in that diner with him.

And this was the memory I was wrapped in as I sat at my desk smiling. Our relationship was what I had been waiting for. This was the happily ever after of my dreams. But the problem with dreams was that they could quickly disappear once you woke up. And this is exactly how I felt sometimes after my dates with Adam. Once he left and I was left alone with reality, the feelings I experienced while we were together started to fade. I couldn't even begin to sift through what this meant. I didn't even know where to start.

"Ahem."

I didn't have to turn to know who was standing in my doorway. So I didn't. I stared straight ahead, my head resting on my palms, propped up by my elbows.

"Lily? You have a minute?"

I dropped my arms to my desk and let out a heavy sigh, demonstrating annoyance I didn't really feel. "Sure."

"Listen, Lily, I . . . I don't quite know what to say."

"Then why are you here?" I didn't say this out of anger; it was a genuine question, and my face conveyed it.

"I'm here because it's driving me crazy not to be. I was a dick, Lily. I didn't mean that shit I said. I just felt like you were putting me down, and I overreacted. *Big*-time overreacted. I'm . . ." Max hesitated, lowering his voice, "I'm so sorry, Lily."

I took in his apology, trying to sort out the best course of action. Should I let Max walk away? Say that I didn't forgive him and hope the sadness wore off soon? Or did I jump back in but on different terms this time? A selfless person would have understood that Max wanted more than I could offer. That I would only hurt him if I stepped back into his life.

"I'm sorry too, Max." I couldn't feign virtue where there was none. I had been selfish since I first met Max, and I didn't have it in me to change now. "I was unnecessarily harsh. I genuinely just wanted to help you, but I went about it all wrong."

"Forgiven," Max said, smiling broadly. I had to laugh as he bound toward my desk, plopping himself on top of it. "So, what have you been up to?"

I settled back in my chair, putting my hands behind my head. I didn't know what to say to that, so I shrugged and hoped he wouldn't press me further.

"Yeah, me neither," he responded. "So, do you really forgive me?"

I shrugged again, but this time I smiled, letting him know that I was teasing him.

"Good, because I have a favor to ask."

*Of course you do.* I eyed him suspiciously. "What?" I asked.

"Well, I thought about what you said, and maybe you were right. I do have to do more to improve my image. So, I thought you might like to help me with that."

"What would I have to do exactly?" I couldn't think of a single way anything I had helped Max with since we met could *help* his image.

"Come away with me."

"What?" I nearly yelled, sitting up straighter.

"I have an appearance on Sunday in Atlantic City. A few of us were invited to an autograph signing at the Tropicana. There's going to be press there, maybe even some important people who could help me give my career a jump start. The other guys are all getting there Saturday, so I was going to head down Saturday morning."

"And I need to be there because . . . ?"

"You'd be a real image boost. First of all, you're a teacher, which already gets me points. But you're also a teacher at the school I'm working at. The press loves workplace romances. You're wholesome, beautiful, have no felony convictions . . . It'd be great for me to be seen with you."

"Is the fact that you're now banging your coworkers really going to garner you points? Because usually, that kind of behavior is frowned upon, even prohibited."

"Not here. I already checked," he replied eagerly.

I shook my head at this. Of course he had checked. That was just the sort of creepy thing Max would ask someone. *So, how is your day going? By the way, can I fuck coworkers?*"

Though, I guess he technically wasn't an employee anyway, so it didn't really matter. *Wait, what was I thinking? I should tell him no. Hell no.* But I didn't. I was intrigued by his proposal. And maybe this would be a good way for me to make it up to him after being such a bitch. *But what about Adam? How would I ever explain this to him?*

"Max, this is crazy. People will be there to get an autograph. They won't care who you're with."

"Totally untrue. My agent expects a ton of media attention at this thing. The NHL is promoting it as the best players of the past ten years all in one room. The papers will be all over us."

"Oh, Max, I don't know. Media whore was never really a

label I aspired to. The whole thing will be so . . . awkward."

"Come on, Lil. I need your help." He sounded so genuine and contrite, I knew I was a goner. But I also needed something to be clear.

"Okay, I'll do it," I said sourly, like I hadn't been intending to help him from the moment he asked. A girl had to add a little flair for the dramatic whenever she could. "However, what you have proposed is a business arrangement. Nothing more. I will help you because you're my friend, but the physical relationship is over. Deal?"

Max looked at me like I was speaking a foreign language. I could see his brain trying to process the contrasting information. Yes, I would accept him back as my friend, but no, I would not accept him back as a fuck buddy?

"Max? Do we have a deal or not?"

"So . . . ?" He still wasn't comprehending what I was getting at.

"No sex, Max. None. Never again." I threw in some nice hand gestures to make my point clear.

Max looked at me, bewildered. "Really?" he asked.

"Really," I said, my resolve firm.

After some deliberation and a couple cursory glances at me as my arms stayed folded across my chest, he finally relented. "Okay, deal." He reached out to shake my hand, and I accepted, smiling. Maybe this would be fun. Or hell. It could very possibly be hell. But whatever it was going to be, I'd find out soon enough.

"Thanks a ton, Lil. I appreciate this more than I could ever say."

"It's all right, Max. I'm glad to help."

Max half turned toward the door. "Okay, then, well, I'll

call you or stop by tomorrow and let you know what time I'll pick you up."

I nodded to him, signaling that that would be fine.

He nodded back and started toward the door. He began to leave when he stopped himself, put both hands on either side of the doorframe, and leaned back into my classroom. "Oh, one more thing."

I raised my eyebrows, prompting him to continue.

"You can never say never, doll." And with that, he left.

*And hell it was.*

# *chapter twenty-four*

Agreeing to go to Atlantic City with Max was actually the easy part. Explaining the arrangement to Adam was going to be a different story. I knew that Adam had nothing to worry about. The sexual relationship between Max and me was over. I had made that clear to Max and to myself.

But how do you tell your boyfriend that you're going on a trip with another man to *pretend* that you are *his* girlfriend? How could I possibly convince Adam that there was nothing more at play here? I just had to hope that he trusted me enough to believe me.

I felt that this was probably a conversation best had in person, but Adam and I hadn't made any plans to see each other this week yet. And it was already Wednesday; I didn't want to prolong telling him too long. I decided to send him a text and see if he was available to get together later.

> *Hey, babe. How's your day going? I*
> *wanted to see if you were around later.*
> *Maybe we could get together for a bit?*

I put my phone down on my desk and hoped for a speedy reply. Thankfully, I heard my phone vibrate not two minutes later.

*Hi, gorgeous. Eva has dance class at
6:30. I could swing by for a bit after I
drop her off. Does that work?*

I quickly typed my reply as the bell signaling the end of fifth period rang.

*That's perfect! See you then.*

I threw my phone into my purse, closed both in my desk drawer, and stood to greet my students. And as I stood there smiling at all the innocent faces before me, all I could think about was how telling Adam was really going to blow.

❤

I heard a knock on my door at six forty-five. *Adam.* I was no more clear about what I was going to say to him than I had been earlier today. I was just going to have to wing it.

I opened my door to find him there, bright eyes and smiling. *My Adam.* My body responded to the sight of him immediately. It was like I forgot how hot he was when he wasn't directly in front of me. "Hi, beautiful," he said as he stepped toward me, leaning in to give me a brief, sweet kiss before walking past me and into my apartment.

"So, how was your day?" he asked me as he plopped down onto my couch.

I sat down beside him. "Interesting," I replied.

"Oh, yeah? How so?" He spoke with an easiness that was befitting a person who was completely comfortable in his surroundings. *Boy, was I about to ruin that.*

"Max came to see me."

"Max?"

I had never mentioned my friendship with Max before, especially since there hadn't been anything to tell as of late. I took a deep breath.

"Yeah, Max Samson. The hockey player starting up a team at our school."

"Oh, yeah. Eva was telling me about him. What did he want to see you about?"

I experienced a brief moment of panic when Adam said that Eva had mentioned Max. Had Eva mentioned how often Max and I were together? He did stop by frequently after her class, knowing that I had second period free. At least he had before our fight. But since Adam didn't seem to know who I was talking about initially, my anxiety slightly abated. *Slightly.*

"He needed to ask me a question. See, he has been trying to improve his image. I never followed hockey, but I guess he was a difficult person to play with. So he's been trying to change the impression people have of him. Hence the school hockey team and all that. Well . . ." I struggled to swallow, as my mouth had suddenly become completely dry. "He has an autograph signing this weekend in Atlantic City, and he thought that if I went with him, it might help people see him more positively." As I expelled the last sentence in a single breath, I became aware of how stupid it sounded. *How would taking a girl to Atlantic City help someone's image?* He had made it sound so convincing at the time.

"Wait . . . what?" Adam sat up, instantly tensing.

"He just asked me as a friend. He figured that, since the press would be there, they would see him with just your average, everyday girl and think that he was becoming more stable." I immediately realized what I had said and hoped that Adam hadn't picked up on it. *Your* average, everyday girl. That was what the major problem was, wasn't it? I was Adam's girl. Not Max's. Though, this wasn't what Adam homed in on.

"So, you're saying he's not stable? I don't...I don't understand any of this. Why you? Did you tell him you'd go?" The questions poured out of Adam like flood water. I immediately regretted telling Max I'd go. But Max had been the one who had saved me from the bar that night, and he had been there for me on numerous other occasions. It felt wrong not to be there for him now.

"No, he is stable. He just has a reputation for not being that way. I don't know why me"—*Lily, you fucking liar*—"other than we're friends and he needs my help. I thought that it would be wrong not to help him." My voice grew meeker as I spoke, losing its conviction.

"So, you're going to go away with him? To Atlantic City? And pretend to be his girlfriend? And I'm supposed to do what, give you guys a ride?" He stood abruptly, running his hand through his hair as he paced wildly around my living room. "You're my girlfriend, Lily. Did you think I'd really be okay with some other guy taking *my girlfriend* on vacation and passing her off as his? Did you even care how this would make me feel?"

I stood quickly to intercept him, stopping him from continuing. I didn't want to hear any more, especially since it wasn't going to change anything. I was going to go with or without Adam's support. But I didn't want him to hurt either. I needed to make him understand that this was no big deal. He had nothing to worry about.

"Adam, stop. Please." I grabbed his arms with my hands

and pulled him back down beside me on the couch. "Adam, I wouldn't go if I thought this was anything more than one friend helping another. And as far as appearances go, no one even really knows you and I are seeing each other. I need you to trust me. I won't hurt you, Adam. Please believe that."

Adam exhaled and his shoulders drooped. I recognized his body language. It was defeat. "I do trust you, Lily. I just don't trust him." He hesitated, clearly unsure of what to say next. He lowered his head but lifted his eyes to gaze at me. "But you're a grown woman and you make your own decisions. You're asking for my trust, and you have it."

I threw my arms around him, kissing him deeply and making my affection for him plain.

I explained that I'd fill him in on the details once I got them all from Max. Pretty soon, it was time for Adam to leave and pick up Eva. As I walked him to the door, he pulled me firmly to him, embracing me and looking into my eyes.

"Lily, I just have to say one more thing."

I let my silence prompt him to continue.

"If he touches you, I'll fucking kill him." He planted a quick kiss on my lips before disengaging from me and leaving, pulling the door closed behind him.

I stayed there, staring at the door, not able to believe that I had just made Adam curse.

*Fuck me, that was hot.*

# chapter twenty-five

In the limo, I had taken a seat across from Max only because that seemed preferable to sitting next to him. As I thought back to our flight from Aspen, I congratulated myself on a wise decision. Sitting next to him could be risky. But when I'd chosen a seat across from him, I hadn't anticipated that I'd have to look at him, into his captivating eyes and gorgeous white smile.

I watched Max pour some Scotch into a glass for himself. He downed it quickly before refilling it and sipping it slowly. The air between us was tense, but I didn't know why. And since he'd picked me up fifteen minutes ago, neither of us had said anything except for a terse hello to one another.

Despite the fact that I had become comfortable with Max after I had accepted our new arrangement, there was an undeniable awkwardness between us now. Like we didn't know what to do if we weren't having sex. I had made it clear that I was done with that, and he seemed to understand. Although I guess he really had no choice.

But even I was starting to wonder if we could really stay friends with the absence of what we knew best. From the moment we had met, we had some sort of compulsory chemistry—an indisputable attraction that defied all reason.

The sex without strings was easy. It was the friendship without sex that would be difficult. But right now Max needed a friend to help him, and I felt as if I owed our friendship at least that much, no matter how uncomfortable this weekend might be.

I was pulled out of my own thoughts by Max.

"Would you like a drink?" He gave the bar an unnecessary cursory glance before continuing. "I don't think I can make you any redheaded sluts, but I doubt you'll want to drink those for a while anyway." He grinned broadly in a way that left me wondering whether he had brought that up to remind me of how stupid I looked that night or just to get me to crack a smile.

I thought for a moment before answering. "I'll take a vodka and cranberry." It was only ten in the morning, but I knew it would be a long ride to Atlantic City—both literally and emotionally—so an exception seemed warranted. Alcohol with some fruit juice felt like a reasonable balance between genuine need and time appropriateness.

As I reached to take the cold glass, my fingers grazed his. The touch was accidental but in no way less thrilling. "So what is it we're doing?" I asked, taking a gulp of my drink. Max hadn't even really told me the specifics of our agenda before I'd agreed to come along.

"I'm not sure. I mean, I'm still confused myself. I know we both said things that hurt the other when we were at my house. We discussed that. I said I was sorry. I guess I just don't see why things need to change." He leaned closer to take my hand. "We had a good thing going." The urgency at which the words left his beautiful lips made me think that this had been weighing on him since our conversation.

It was too late to correct him by saying that I had only been asking about the weekend's plans. "Max," I sighed, "we can't. Let's just leave it at that, okay?" I pulled my hand away much too abruptly for either one of us.

"Seems to me, doll, that may be one of the only things we *can* do. At least the only thing we can do right anyway." He cast his eyes to the floor as he sat back into the leather.

"Don't do that..." I exhaled with as much conviction as I could force through my lungs. "Don't call me 'doll.'" I ran my fingers through my hair as I gazed out at the highway.

"What's going on?" he asked, genuinely concerned.

"Max," I said, forcing my eyes to meet his for the first time, "I'm seeing someone. I mean... I've been seeing someone for a little while." I took a moment to collect my thoughts and drain my drink. "It's gotten serious recently. I can't do this anymore. I can't do this to *him*." I crossed my legs to firm my resolve.

"What's his name?"

"What? What does it matter?" I asked, shaking my head, confused. "Adam. Why?"

"Do you love him?" he asked flatly. "Adam. Are you in love with him?"

I swallowed hard. I had always been honest with Max, and this conversation would be no different. "No." But for some reason I felt as if that answer wasn't what he had hoped to hear. As if Max would think I had no reason to end things with him if I was not in love with Adam. It felt wrong. Like I had no excuse for shutting Max out like I had for someone I didn't even love yet. "No, I don't," I reiterated.

As the words hovered in the air between us, I heard them myself for the first time. I *didn't* love Adam. Since our first "date" to the coffeehouse, I had felt like I could love him one day. But over two months later, I was still waiting for "one day" to arrive. Now, for the first time, I was really starting to think that maybe what I'd been feeling lately was not that I *could* love him, but rather that I *should*. And I couldn't help but admit to myself that the thought that it hadn't happened yet scared me a little. Adam was kindhearted, protective, generous, and a fucking demon in the sack. What was there not to love?

Max let out a subtle laugh through his nostrils at my confession and shook his head before pouring himself another Scotch. "Fuck, Lily, when were you gonna tell me this?"

"Whenever you asked, I guess." Why did he seem so angry? So upset? He could probably sleep with any woman he wanted. Christ, he could take the pick of the litter of those bloodhounds at the bar. *What was the big fucking deal?*

"Whenever I asked? Why the fuck would I ask something like that with the arrangement we had? We were just fucking around, right?"

I managed to say, "Yeah, you're right," before shifting in my seat uncomfortably.

The rest of the ride passed without so much as a word between us. I didn't think either of us knew what to say, so we were better off saying nothing. I busied myself with my phone, checking Facebook and texting every so often so I wouldn't have to make eye contact with Max. I was hoping when we got to the hotel and were able to get some space from one another, the tension would be alleviated. I told myself that Max's reaction probably just came from the initial shock of realizing that I was serious about ending things with him.

♥

I waited in the lobby as Max checked us in. From a distance, I could hear him explaining to the frumpy woman at the counter that we would need two rooms instead, preferably next to one another. *Ugh, he had seriously booked one room initially, even though I had broken things off with him already?* He really could be a presumptuous asshole sometimes.

Max handed me my key and grabbed both our bags, motioning for me to follow him to the elevators.

"I think I'm gonna relax for a bit in my room," I said. "Take a nap or something. What's the plan for tonight? Do I need to be anywhere at a certain time or anything?"

"You don't need to do anything you don't want to do." He was sincere when he said it, but I could tell there was a hint of disappointment deeper down. "But no, there really isn't any type of schedule for tonight. I told some of the other guys I'd meet them for drinks around two thirty at one of the bars downstairs. But I was thinking the two of us could grab dinner at Il Verdi. I made a reservation for seven o'clock. It's a good Italian place, but I wasn't sure if you'd still be up for it."

I thought for a moment. He seemed to be trying to keep things as normal as possible, despite our earlier conversation. "Sure, why not."

"Great!" He seemed genuinely surprised at my response. "I'll meet you at the restaurant a little before seven, then."

"Okay, see you then," I said as I slid my key into the door and he did the same to his. It was a little after noon. That gave me plenty of time to relax before I had to get ready to go back out.

I thought back to the last time I had even stayed in a hotel. It was when Adam had taken me to the Radnor. But something told me that tonight definitely wouldn't be as memorable as my night with Adam had been.

I set my bag on the chair and unpacked some of my things.

After ordering some fruit and a turkey club from room service, I managed to get a second wind and decided to head down to the gym. I needed to relieve a little tension, and since I knew my normal form of stress relief was out of the question, I hoped that forty-five minutes on the treadmill would do the trick.

♥

Feeling more energized after my workout and a shower, I was much more positive about the night ahead. Max seemed excited to have dinner with me, and I knew this weekend was important to his career—and our friendship. I had come here to support him, and that's exactly what I intended to do. I spoke to Adam briefly before getting ready for dinner because I wanted to reaffirm my promise that nothing was really going on between Max and me.

"We're having dinner in a bit," I said and then suddenly felt the need to justify it. "Just for image purposes. I'm guessing we'll probably get a few pictures taken. No major appearances until tomorrow morning, though."

"Lily, I trust you. I told you that before. You said he's your friend, and I can understand that." I thought I could hear him smiling on the other end of the phone. "You *are* staying in separate rooms, though, right?"

"Of course," I blurted out quickly. *Thank God for the last-minute room availability.*

"Okay, just checking. I mean, remember what I did to that guy at the concert who was all over you? I don't have to fight for you twice, do I?" He laughed, but I could hear his protective sincerity.

"I promise you. You have nothing to worry about. I have to

go get ready, but enjoy the rest of your night. I'll text you before I go to bed," I assured him.

"Okay, sounds like a plan. Have a good night."

After saying goodbye to Adam, I focused my attention on looking camera-ready for any photo opportunities that might present themselves throughout the course of the night. I had packed one formal outfit—a black strapless dress that I paired with the only designer shoes I owned: three-inch red Manolo Blahniks for a splash of color. My eye shadow was a dark, smoky gray, and my lips matched my shoes. I had even remembered to pack some nice earrings, despite the fact that I rarely wore jewelry. As I finished straightening my last section of hair, I silently congratulated myself. I looked hot. And I hoped Max would think so too.

Just before seven, I grabbed my clutch and headed downstairs to meet Max for dinner. I couldn't help but wonder what he'd look like. *Gorgeous obviously.* But I had never seen him dressed up before, and I was looking forward to devouring him with my eyes throughout dinner. What was the saying people always used to describe not being able to act on their desires? *It doesn't hurt to look at the menu as long as you don't order?* Yeah, something like that. Something told me that seeing Max, looking so dapper, would probably leave me pretty "hungry" by the end of the weekend, though.

I arrived a few minutes early and checked in with the hostess, who seated me at a table against the beige wall. I ordered a glass of Pinot Grigio and looked over the menu while I waited for Max to arrive. After waiting fifteen minutes, I decided he must have gotten held up taking some pictures with fans or something.

Two glasses of wine and almost forty minutes later, I

decided I'd been stood up. How could he have forgotten about this? He had been the one who'd made the reservation. As I left the restaurant, I took out my phone. *Nasty voicemail, here I come.* Maybe I'd say something about how he hadn't been kidding when he told me that day at the bar what an arrogant fucking prick he really was. Or perhaps I'd mention how he was a selfish bastard who only did things on his terms.

But to my surprise, he picked up on the first ring. "Lily, get over here!"

"You've got some fucking nerve. You stand me up, and then you think you can order me around? Fuck you!"

"Wait, wait, wait . . . don't hang up. I'm at the craps table. I just rolled for almost an hour. It was fucking awesome! They won't let you make a phone call if you're the one shooting. My turn just ended. We were all making a shitload of money. I didn't forget about dinner. Come meet me here. I need to cash out, and then we'll eat. I promise." His speech told me he'd been drinking for most of the day, and I thought he heard me hesitate. "I didn't forget. I'm dressed for dinner," he added, clearly hoping to persuade me.

I could hear people screaming with excitement in the background. "I'm almost there anyway. I'll come by. Then we're going to dinner." I hung up quickly without saying goodbye, hoping he could tell that I was annoyed with him, though I was secretly cursing at myself for not standing my ground.

I spotted him from across the casino. There was a crowd around the table, and Max's deep voice boomed when he saw me. "Lil, over here!" He motioned for me to come closer. "They all passed on their turns to roll because they want me to shoot again. This table's hot because of me."

One glance at him, and there was no denying that

places always seemed hotter with Max there: planes, bars, auditoriums, cars…casinos. He wore a slim, dark-gray suit with a black shirt and no tie. He threw the dice to the other end of the table, and the people cheered. I wondered how many of them were watching because he was playing well and how many of them just wanted to watch hockey great Max Samson look like a drunken fool.

When I arrived at the table, I could barely squeeze in, but he pulled me to him. Once wedged under his arm, it became clear why there was a crowd around him. I had to admit that there was a certain thrill that came with being Max Samson's "girlfriend" for the weekend. Not only was he good-looking, but Max was the life of the party.

Chips shifted across the table at a rapid pace as people yelled out numbers. I had no idea what was happening. "Pick one of those," he said, pointing to the five numbers near the dealers. "Not four, though. That's what's called the point."

I had no idea what he was talking about, but I chose nine. Max yelled, "Nine," and tossed a hundred-dollar chip on the table toward the dealer. "And press the ten," he said, dropping another hundred-dollar chip down.

"Are you crazy? That's a ton of money. What if you don't win?"

"I always win," he replied with a wink as he threw the dice to the other end of the table again.

They bounced around, knocking over a stack of chips before the dealer yelled out, "Six. Came hard."

Other people seemed to be winning, but I still didn't know what was happening, and Max was too busy chatting with the people beside him and throwing chips around to explain anything.

A bell dinged as Max threw down a fifty-dollar chip to give to the dealers as a tip. "Thank you, Mr. Samson. Good luck," said the pretty blonde as she pushed the dice to him with a stick.

He rolled again, and this time I knew what had happened, as all the chips on the table were scooped into the hole. "Seven out. Seven out," the dealer called.

"Guess you don't win *every* time," I pointed out. "Now, let's go."

Some bystanders waved some encouraging gestures for Max to stay.

"You only lose if you stop trying, Lil. Just one more. It's getting good." He clapped his hands loudly and tossed down a chip on the pass line as the woman to his left received the dice.

I rolled my eyes.

Max took another drink off the waitress's tray and replaced it with the empty glass in his hand. "Thanks, sweetheart," he said with a charming smile and a flirtatious wink as he handed her a twenty-five-dollar tip.

I'd had enough. "Max, I'm going to bed," I said, turning around to push through the crowd, when I felt a strong hand on my arm.

"Lily, stay."

"Fuck you, Max. I'm done. Enjoy your game." This time I didn't let him stop me. And before long, I heard his slurred cheers again in the distance.

❤

Back at my room, I ordered room service again because I hadn't eaten since lunch. Then I took a long bath, got into bed, and texted Adam good night sometime around eleven thirty.

I still had to be up fairly early for the autograph signing, and in spite of Max's behavior, I still planned to put on a facade—which was getting increasingly difficult—to help him. Besides, the sooner he got a broadcasting job, the sooner I wouldn't have to deal with any of this anymore.

I must have fallen asleep at some point because I awoke around two thirty to loud voices in the hall. One of them I recognized instantly, and the other two sounded like they probably came from female versions of Max: sloppy drunks with no consideration for the people around them. I heard Max shushing them loudly as the door to his room shut behind them. But within minutes, there was music playing through the wall, accompanied by flirtatious, high-pitched laughter.

I put my pillow over my ears and turned the TV on, hoping to drown out the cackling. God only knew what noises I would hear next. These could be tame compared to what was to come. And it wouldn't help that our beds shared a wall.

After about a half hour, I'd had it. I banged on the wall, and when they made no effort to be quieter, I marched out of my room to give him a piece of my mind. I slammed on his door with my open palm until it opened and my hand collided with some slut's face.

"Ow, what the fuck?"

"Um, 'what the fuck?' How about shutting the hell up?" I pushed past the two scantily clad pieces of trash to get to Max. "Can you turn your fucking dance party down? Some of us are trying to get some sleep so we can be ready for tomorrow."

Max was lying on the couch with his shirt unbuttoned and a bottle of vodka from the mini bar in his hand when I barged in, but he rose to counter me. "We're just having a good time. Calm down."

I couldn't help but drink in the sight of him, even in these circumstances. His muscular frame, his pants low on his waist. His boxers peeking above the top of them. Christ. Boxers? He really *had* gotten dressed up!

"No, Max. *You* need to calm down. You're here to improve your image, and you're acting like an out-of-control asshat." I was practically screaming. "What the hell am I here for if you're gonna pull this shit?" I shook my head in disbelief as I looked around at the empty bottles of liquor scattered around the room. The girls had already started grabbing their things, when I thought I would give them a few words of encouragement. "Closing time, skanks. Get the fuck out!"

As the ho train left, Max's eyes grew wide with amusement. But his enjoyment of my comment disappeared as suddenly as it had arrived, and he took on a defensive tone. "You're gonna call me out of control? You?"

"What the hell's that supposed to mean? I'm *nothing* like you!"

"No? Let's take a little inventory of your previous transgressions, shall we?" He was practically yelling. "Hmm... let's see. You let me fuck you in an airport hours after we met. So there's *that*. You've been using a middle school as your own private bedroom for the last two fucking months..." He raised his eyebrows, clearly proud of his accusations. "You called me in the middle of the night to get you from a nightclub because you were one shot away from needing your stomach pumped like a fucking teenager." His voice softened. "And you don't tell me about whatever the hell his name is...Andy or Adam or whatever until today. So don't stand here and act like you're some fucking saint or something. You're no better than I am."

My head spun. Max was so passionate, so reckless, so

unconcerned with what others thought of him. He was himself. Take it or leave it. And though I'd never admit it to him, Max was right. I did act like I was better than him. But clearly my actions didn't support that claim. So I wanted to avoid that part of the conversation altogether. "What are you bringing Adam into this for?" was all I could think to say.

"It wasn't me who brought him into this. It was you, remember?" He stepped closer to me, minimizing the already small gap between us. "You brought him into this without my knowledge."

"Oh, I'm sorry. I'm fucking twenty-seven years old. I didn't know I needed to ask your permission before I slept with someone. You and I weren't *anything*." The words left my lips before I could filter them, and I immediately regretted it. Of all the hurtful things I could have said, I had chosen the worst.

"Yeah, I'm starting to get that now." His face dropped, and he ran a hand through his thick, dark hair. "What are you and this Adam guy, then? You don't love him. You said so yourself."

"I don't know, Max. It doesn't matter. Just like it doesn't matter what you were doing with those classless hussies who were just here."

"You don't know *what* the hell I was doing in here. You don't know shit. We were just having fun without worrying what other people thought. You should try it sometime."

"I'm done," I conceded, rubbing my temples. "I don't have it in me to fight with you at three in the morning. We can talk about what a selfish dick you are some other time."

I stormed toward the door, but as I opened it, a hand reached above me to push it shut again. I smelled the alcohol when his breath tickled my neck as he spoke. "Can he make you wet with just the sound of his voice?"

*Oh, shit.*

He paused to let me absorb what he had just said before continuing. "You're gonna miss this. You know that?" I could feel his presence behind me, but we hadn't touched. "The way I talk to you. How fucking wild I am. You're gonna miss it when I'm gone." He removed his hand away from the door and stepped back a few feet to let me open it. "But I'm here now. It's your choice."

I'd been looking at the menu long enough, and Max had just asked to take my order.

My eyes remained fixed on the door. I was scared that if I turned around, my decision would be made the second I gazed into his bright blue eyes. I'd been a fool to think that Max wouldn't have this effect on me.

How had I expected to go away with him for a night and think that I could resist his advances? I guess part of me had hoped that he wouldn't even offer. But another, more primal part of me knew what he said was true. And as I felt a deep throb low in my stomach, I was reminded that, on more than one occasion, Max had brought me to the verge of orgasm with his words alone.

He was so rugged. So bold. So hedonistic. And in that moment I realized why it had always been so difficult for me to refuse him. I saw a part of myself in him that I rarely let scratch the surface. I either had to let that part of myself go completely or learn to embrace it without Max. But for now, I needed one last time with him. I hadn't known that day at Max's house would be it for us. I needed closure. I needed to say goodbye to him. To this.

At last, I let myself turn around, but I kept my back against the door for a moment. Max stood confident, one hand in his pocket and the other high against the wall. He looked so powerful. I expected him to say something seductive or come toward me, but he waited for me to make the first move.

Without saying a word, I stepped toward him, needing to feel his skin against my own. I pulled his head toward mine, rubbing his hair as our lips met. In seconds, I was tugging at his shirt, needing to see his strong shoulders and squeeze the muscles of his biceps.

We slid our hands up and down each other's bodies, removing pieces of clothing with reckless speed. The barriers of time and fabric seemed too much for us to bear. He groaned into my neck as I grabbed ahold of his bulging erection beneath his boxers and pulled them down. "We need a fucking condom. Now!" I practically yelled.

I clung to Max as he staggered toward the bag on his bed, neither one of us willing to let the other go. He stumbled clumsily and we both ended up in a heap on the bed. The thrill of how needy we were coursed through my veins like a drug. I fumbled urgently with his belt buckle and kissed his chest, sliding my hands all over his body while his . . . remained . . . by his side?

*What?*

Passed-out asshole.

I waited for my heart to relax and my breath to slow before climbing off him. I inspected the room, picking my clothes up slowly, one by one. I turned my head over my shoulder to look at him sprawled on the bed.

"That was the last time," I uttered calmly as I made my way to the door, "even though you missed it." As I gripped the handle, I stopped, seemingly speaking my next words to the panel before me. "This time I mean it."

♥

Surprisingly, I wasn't too tired when I awoke the next morning. Unfortunately, the same could not be said for Max, who was barely alive when I knocked on his door with coffee and a cranberry muffin for him. He opened his door and invited me in, but I wasn't falling for that. *Morning After Max* looked just as fuckable as he did any other time.

"It's nine fifteen, Max. You have to be downstairs in forty-five minutes. Get in the shower. You smell like you just took a bath in Jack Daniels." I hoped that despite my blunt description, he would see I cared. "And put something in your stomach," I added, handing him breakfast.

"Thanks," he said, rubbing his eyes before he took the coffee. "Keep the muffin, though. I don't think I can eat anything now. I'll meet you downstairs in a little bit."

Shockingly enough, Max managed to get himself somewhat together and make it to the autograph signing on time. He did a decent job of smiling for the cameras and making small talk with the press and some fans. But by the time we got into the limo a few hours later, he was wiped out. He sipped slowly on ginger ale and kept his sunglasses on for most of the ride.

"Max, you should try to get some rest," I urged, actually feeling somewhat sorry for him. He was clearly more hungover than I'd ever remembered being in my life.

But Max didn't try to sleep. Instead, he made an effort to talk to me. "Did you have a fun time?" he asked with a smirk.

I couldn't be sure if he was just being friendly or hitting on me again. "It was ... uh, interesting. What about you? How do you think your appearance went?"

"Would have been better if I didn't feel like such shit. But I think I did okay, considering." He relaxed into the seat and let out an audible sigh through his nose. "Hey," he said, perking up a bit, "I've been meaning to ask you. Have you ever been to a hockey game?"

I never considered myself a sports nut by any means, but I found it weird that I had been banging a hockey player but had never been to an actual game. "Not a professional one."

"Well, we should definitely try to get to a Flyers game sometime. It's what friends would do, right? Go to a game or something?" He grinned for what seemed like the first time all weekend. "If you wanna start small, though, you should come to one of the games I coach. Some of those little fuckers can actually play." He really had a way with words.

The rest of the ride was easy. We talked of work, spring break, and even discussed our families. Max was trying. He was making a clear effort to accept our current status, and I appreciated that. Maybe he had just needed a night to get it out of his system. And as I exited the limo and stole one last fleeting glance at Max's strong features and gorgeous smile, I was hoping the same was true for me.

# chapter twenty-six

After the trip to Atlantic City, Adam didn't mention Max, and I was grateful. The entire trip had passed with his simple question of "How was it?" and my reply of, "Fine. Nothing special." It scared me how readily the lie left my lips. As if remorse was only necessary if the truth were uncovered. *I was becoming a real bitch.*

Since Adam had seemed content to pretend that Max didn't exist, I was shocked when he asked me to go to Swift Middle School's first hockey game. Many of the students were going, and Eva had asked Adam to take her, though she would inevitably ditch him as soon as they arrived. Of course, the circumstances under which we would go would be delusive. We would act like we just both happened to be there and just happened to be sitting next to each other. But I agreed because I thought my refusal may seem suspicious. Also, I was clearly a glutton for punishment.

I wasn't sure how I felt about Adam and Max being in the same building. Sitting there in close proximity to the two of them may send me right over the sexual edge. I was getting turned on just thinking about it.

The game started at seven o'clock the Friday after our Atlantic City trip. I hadn't spoken much to Max since Sunday, and I was hoping I wouldn't run into him tonight. I wasn't up for awkward conversation, especially in front of Adam. But my body clearly hadn't gotten the message, because as soon as I walked into the ice rink, my eyes found him immediately. He was on ice skates, watching his team warm up. And though I kept moving and intentionally averting my gaze, my eyes kept darting back to him, as if they needed him as a focal point in order to clearly focus on anything else.

Adam and I agreed to meet in the stands, close to center ice. I scanned for him inconspicuously. When I finally spotted him, I drank in the sight of him in his Drexel University sweatshirt and loose-fitting jeans. *Christ, the man looked gorgeous in everything.* I was suddenly very thankful that I had worn underwear. I needed the extra barrier to soak up the wetness that had been steadily building to a puddle since I walked in the building. I climbed the stairs and felt his eyes on me, watching me move toward him in his periphery. As I reached his row, he turned fully toward me.

"Miss Hamilton, how nice to see you." His mouth was serious, but his eyes were aglow with amusement. "Would you like to sit down?" He pointed to the open seat next to him.

I turned on my best *I love teaching* smile. "Mr. Carter, nice to see you as well. Sure, I'll sit." This charade made me feel ridiculous. What were we going to talk about all night with parents and teachers all around us? My smile faded as I sat down beside Adam, feeling ill at ease. He slumped down lower in his chair.

"So, how was your day?" he asked in a low voice.

"It was okay. Yours?"

"Well, it's definitely better now that you're here." I didn't have to look at him to know he was smiling. His words helped defrost some of the ice that had begun to build on my nerves. My body relaxed, and I settled more comfortably into my chair.

"So, how the hell do you play this game?" I asked.

He chuckled softly beside me. "Well, you hit that little black thing—it's called a puck—into that big white thing, called a net."

I bit on my tongue a little, crossing my arms over my chest. I adored playful Adam. "You forgot to explain what those stick things they all have are," I challenged.

"Hmm, well, oddly enough, they *are* called sticks, so you got that much right. They're used to hit the little black thing into the big white thing."

"Ooooh, it all makes sense now. Thank you so much for sharing some of your sports knowledge with me, Mr. Carter."

"My pleasure, Miss Hamilton." As usual, my filthy mind focused on the word *pleasure*. I would love to share other things for his pleasure later. Unfortunately, that wasn't going to happen. He would need to take Eva home after the game, and I thought it would probably be inappropriate to give her father a blow job while she was in the back seat. *Excuse me, honey, do you mind closing your eyes while I tongue your dad's balls?* Yup, totally inappropriate.

This wasn't the first time I had contemplated the difficulties that would exist in dating a man with a teenage daughter. And it wasn't just because it interfered with my sexual depravity. It was because of everything. I worried what it could mean for our relationship if Eva didn't like me. We got along well in a student-teacher capacity, but that wasn't a good indicator of how it would be on a more personal level.

I blew out a breath and repositioned myself in my seat, shifting my weight slightly. There was no sense worrying about something that I didn't even know was going to be an issue. I had enough things going on that actually were issues. The foremost being how to stop myself from stuffing my hand down my pants and relieving all of this sexual tension I was feeling.

Then, as if on cue, Max skated toward me. He must have seen me at some point, because his path was clearly directed at me. He smiled broadly and waved. He yelled something that was difficult to hear over the cheering throng of spectators. But I had heard him.

"Thanks for coming, doll."

As he skated back toward Swift's bench, I felt my skin grow hot. I knew I was blushing. My fucking body was betraying me again, branding me a liar without my uttering a single syllable. I could only hope that Adam hadn't heard Max. I sneaked a peek at Adam out of the corner of my eye. He sat motionless, staring straight ahead at the ice. *He'd heard all right.*

I didn't know what to do. Did I explain that "doll" was just a pet name? Did I pretend like he had misheard? Did I act angry that Max would so presumptuously call me that? Did I pretend that I hadn't just nearly turned purple and that one of the sexiest men alive hadn't just singled me out in a crowd of at least a hundred? *Ding, ding, ding!*

"So, want to place any bets on how bad the Swift kids are?" I asked jovially.

"No, thanks." Adam's reply was clipped and authoritative. Much like how I envisioned he would be in a meeting of wealthy men trying to throw their weight around. This was another side to Adam. The detached businessman. But I knew him too well, despite our short time together. I knew that the truth always lay in his eyes. And today, those bright-green orbs were blazing. As I contemplated the best way to proceed, I couldn't help but wonder where my own truth lay.

♥

Adam pretended to be absorbed in the game, clapping and cheering for the Swift boys, who, to my dismay, were pretty good. It would've been much more cathartic to watch them fall flat on their faces. Much like I had. But Max had been right. There was definite talent skating on the ice.

As the buzzer sounded to mark the end of the first period, Adam rubbed his open palms on the thighs of his jeans. "You want to get some air?" he asked me finally.

"Sure," I replied.

We rose, and I briefly wondered if we should be seen walking out of the building together. But the people around me weren't my primary concern. It wasn't *their* judgment I feared. My anxiety grew with every step as I tried to act casual and think happy thoughts. *Maybe he just wants to fuck me in the parking lot*, I thought hopefully. But ultimately, I knew better.

I followed Adam outside and around the left side of the building. This side of the rink faced sparse woods, and my mind took me back to our trip to the lake. The trees there had witnessed a beautiful exchange between Adam and me. I had a feeling these trees would not have the same privilege.

Adam walked ahead of me and then turned abruptly and took two sharp steps back toward me so that we stood nearly nose to nose. "Is there something that I need to know?" His voice was even, but there was a strain in it, like he was trying very hard not to show his anger. And maybe something more. His pain.

"About what, Adam?" I asked innocently. *I'm going straight to hell.*

"Come on, Lily. I saw the way he looked at you. Not to

mention his calling you 'doll.' And then you got all awkward and flushed. Just tell me the truth. Please. Is there something going on between you two?"

I took a deep breath. This was my chance. I could come clean here and maybe salvage things with Adam. I knew that if I lied now and he ever found out about it, that could be too much for us to overcome. I took a deep breath.

"No, Adam. We're just friends. I told you that."

I had been selfish for quite some time, but now I was, to the very core of my being, a liar as well. And I assumed that role while being stoic and resolute, letting nothing show on my face except a tinge of annoyance. Annoyance that he hadn't believed me when I had told him this very thing last week. I knew as well as anyone that the best defense was a good offense.

I crossed my arms in front of my chest and looked straight into Adam's eyes. Let him search all he wanted. He wouldn't find the truth. I buried it too deeply, right next to my sense of right and wrong.

"Lily, I want to believe that. I really do." He dropped his eyes for a moment, as if he couldn't face me and say what was next. "But I asked Eva about Max when you got back from Atlantic City. And without my even having to ask if she ever sees you two together, she told me that she sees him with you all the time. That he comes to your classroom frequently and that you two are in the halls together all the time. What am I supposed to think when I hear things like that?"

He looked at me expectantly, his eyes pleading with me to make it better. To assuage his feelings of betrayal and disappointment. And I would, for him and for me.

"First of all," I began, my tone intentionally slow and patient, "the last time Max came to my classroom was last week when he asked me to go to Atlantic City with him. I don't think he had been to my classroom for weeks prior to that, and he hasn't been there since. When he first came to Swift, Principal Murdock asked me to show him around. So in the beginning, he did come and see me often because I was the only person he knew in the building. Since then, however, I don't feel that his visits have been frequent by any means. We are friends, which you already know. Therefore, I don't find it odd that she has seen us walking together in the halls. Max is in the school daily, and he eats the same period lunch that I do, again because I was who he knew from the beginning so he started eating lunch with me. I wouldn't be surprised if she was seeing us at this time, since the gym and my classroom are in the same general direction and we often walk that way together." I paused, trying to gauge whether or not he was buying any of this. Most of it was actually the truth, which made me feel a little better. Though it shouldn't have. I didn't deserve for anything to make me feel better.

But I also knew that I couldn't lose Adam. He was too good for me, but still, I clung to him. I recognized that I had been weak from the very beginning when it came to Max, for reasons that I couldn't even begin to dissect or examine. I was drawn to Max like a moth to light, but that attraction was shallow. The moth doesn't need the light to survive; he just finds it hard to resist.

But I was attracted to Adam for different, deeper reasons. Adam was my sun. He could help me to grow and live a life that would be fruitful. One that I could be proud of. I needed that. I didn't deserve it, but I still had to have it. It was this thought that enabled me to justify the next lie that would leave my lips.

"I love you, Adam. Please believe me."

And as his face softened, I knew that I had lost myself. He

pulled me to him, enveloping me in those strong arms that I craved so much. And as he whispered, "I love you, too, Lily," my eyes filled with tears.

# chapter twenty-seven

I hibernated for the rest of the weekend. Adam called a couple of times, and I tried to sound as upbeat and positive as I could muster. But sadness was the prevailing emotion. I wasn't sure how I had gotten to this place. I was a total disaster.

As my alarm sounded Monday morning, I contemplated calling out sick. But as I lay there debating it, I decided that nothing accompanied misery better than a classroom full of seventh graders. So I took a shower, got dressed, and headed out the door. I'd have to do without coffee today because I didn't have time to brew any, and I sure as shit wasn't stopping at the coffeehouse.

Once my school day got underway, I was happy I had come in. My students forced my focus off my problems and into them learning how to properly conduct research. I had never been so thankful for needy kids in my life.

As the end of the day approached, my sadness returned. The last bell rang, and the students filtered excitedly out of my room, leaving me alone to become reabsorbed in my own problems. I stood up, needing to get out of this room. I scooped some papers off my desk and headed out to make copies.

I exited my room and turned right, when I saw Max. I couldn't stop myself from rolling my eyes and turning the other way, hoping that just once, he would take the goddamn hint. He didn't.

"Hey, Lily! Wait. Where are you going?"

I kept walking. I didn't want to talk to Max. I didn't want to talk to anybody. I quickened my pace, but it didn't matter. I didn't make it five steps before a strong hand gently gripped my bicep.

"Lily, wait. What's wrong?"

I didn't turn around. I couldn't. My emotions were on shaky ground as it was. "Nothing, Max. Just let me go."

"No way. Not until you tell me what's wrong, Did I do something?"

His ignorance fueled another emotion that had been simmering since Friday. Anger. "You bet your ass you did something!" I didn't care who heard me in that moment. My anger had turned to rage, and I turned to face its target. "Where the hell do you get off calling me 'doll' in front of the entire rink? Have you lost your friggin' mind? Do you have any idea how much damage that could've done?"

Max stood there, dumbstruck. "I-I'm sorry, Lily. I didn't even realize I called you 'doll.' It's just habit. Did you get in trouble or something?"

*Or something.* As I glared at Max, I felt my anger fading. He looked genuinely concerned and contrite. His goal hadn't been to hurt me. I had overreacted.

"It's fine, Max. No worries. I'll see you later." I again turned away from him, needing distance. I would only bring him down.

"Wait, no way." He took two long, gliding steps and positioned himself in front of me, preventing me from walking any farther. "There's something else wrong, isn't there? What is it?"

"I don't want to talk about it. Please, Max. I'm just having a bad day." I kept my eyes cast down, frightened of what he would see if he were to look into them. He was the one person I knew would be able to find the truth there. Max took a step forward and put his arm around me, pulling me sideways so that I stood beside him.

"I know just what you need." Just as I was about to say no, that was exactly what I didn't need, he added, "Let's get a drink."

I sighed. A drink may be exactly what I did need. Or maybe two drinks. Or five.

"Okay," I said quietly. "You want me to meet you at Flanagan's?"

"Nah, I know of a better place. It's only about ten minutes from here. I'll drive and then bring you back to pick up your car later."

I pulled away slightly. "You aren't taking me to your house, are you?" I asked, a wry smile forming on my lips.

"Ha, there's my girl. No, I'm not taking you to my house. Unless, of course, that's where you want to go. In that case, no objections here." Max was smiling mischievously.

"Why would I want to go back there? So you can call me names again?" My voice was light and sarcastic, but Max's face clouded at my comment. "Oh, relax, you big baby. I'm just joking around," I added, hoping to erase the unease my comment had created.

"Good one," he said dryly. But a smile quickly crept to his lips. "Meet you at my car in ten minutes." He released me and walked down the hall, never looking back. *He is such a cocky prick*, I thought, smiling. I went back into my classroom and started collecting my things. I knew this was probably a bad idea. I should distance myself from Max, not spend more time alone with him. But I couldn't help it. In times like this, what a girl really needs is a good friend.

❤

Max drove toward a part of town I hadn't really ever been to. It was largely residential and affluent, so I never had any reason to visit before. Just as I was beginning to think that this was a really weird place for a bar, he pulled into a driveway that led to a large white house with dark-red shutters. I looked quizzically at Max.

"I just have to pick something up. It'll only take a second. Come on." He motioned for me to follow him, but I resisted. I didn't feel like being forced into an awkward social situation, especially when he just had to pick something up quickly. Max walked around to my door and opened it. "Come on," he urged.

"Why can't I stay here? You're just going to be a minute, aren't you?"

"You really want to be that weird girl who sits in someone's driveway acting all antisocial and shit? Just come in."

I blew out a deep breath, making my annoyance clear. I had a strong urge to stomp my feet up the stone walkway, but I was thankfully able to resist the temptation.

When we reached the door, Max surprised me by turning the knob and just walking in. Whoever lived here, he must know them well. As Max stepped inside, he yelled to the inhabitants, but it took me a moment to register what he had said.

"Mom? Dad? I'm home. I brought someone with me." *Did he just say Mom and Dad?* I closed my eyes, trying to wish it all away. I reeled back and punched Max between the shoulder blades as hard as I could.

"You fucking asshole! Is this your parents' house?" I whispered through gritted teeth.

Max opened his mouth to reply when I heard a soft, smooth voice float toward us.

"Oh, Max, I'm glad you're here. Dad is burning the chicken on the grill again. Who did you bring with you?" As she turned the corner, a beautiful older woman with short brown hair and smooth, flawless skin stopped suddenly but quickly regained her composure and resumed walking again. She examined me with kind eyes, and I thought I saw her smile broaden.

"Hi, Mom," Max said as he leaned in to give her a kiss on the cheek. "This is my friend, Lily. She's an English teacher at Swift."

"A teacher, God bless you," she said, offering a soft chuckle.

"My mom used to be a teacher," Max added.

"Yes, I did, a long time ago. I taught history, though. It's a pleasure to meet you, Lily. Please, please, come in."

*Jesus Christ, this is really happening?* "Thank you, Mrs. Samson. It's a pleasure to meet you as well. Your home is lovely." And it was. I had only made it halfway into the foyer, and I could tell that the house was beautiful. Dark hardwood floors spanned the hallway and seemed to continue into the adjoining rooms. The walls were painted teal, which complimented the floor beautifully.

"Thank you. I love this house. We've lived here almost thirty years, and it took me twenty-five of those years to get Max's father to fix it up the way I wanted it. Slow as molasses, that man. And please, call me Marjory."

I nodded and followed her and Max into the house. We walked past a formal dining room, which could have easily seated twenty people. The teal walls continued into here, but the crown molding gave the room a wealthy feel. As did the hutch filled with fine china that probably cost more than I would make in a year.

Past the dining room was the kitchen, which was gigantic. It had all stainless-steel appliances, two stoves, marble countertops, and white cupboards. I tried to take it all in as we continued to walk around the white kitchen table and through French doors that led outside. I stepped out onto stone pavers that formed a beautiful back patio. The Samsons lived on at least two acres of land. And in the middle of their perfectly manicured lawn was an in-ground pool that instantly made me jealous of them. I continued to follow them to the patio table that was beautifully set with floral print plates and linen napkins. Beyond us was a man hovering over a grill.

"We thought we'd take advantage of the nice weather and eat outside. I'll just set another place," Marjory said kindly.

"Please don't go to any trouble," I said apologetically.

"No, no, it's no trouble at all. We're happy to have you." She smiled quickly at Max before heading back the way we had just come.

I took advantage of this brief moment alone to quietly give Max the bitching out he deserved. "Max, what the hell were you thinking? You fucking knew we were coming here. Why didn't you tell me?"

"First of all, there is no cursing in the Samson home." *God I wanted to hit him.* "Second, if I had told you, you wouldn't have come." Max said it simply, as if his reasons should have been obvious.

"You're damn right I wouldn't have come. What should that have told you?"

"You were visibly upset. I didn't want to just leave you like that, but I knew that I was having dinner with my parents. So, I told a little white lie so that you'd join me. It's no big deal. Come meet my dad." As Max spoke, he began to walk away from me, preventing any further argument.

The man at the grill, clearly Max's dad, had yet to register that he had guests, since he was clearly absorbed in whatever he was cooking. Max strode over to him and put his hand on the back of his dad's neck, digging in with his thumb and index finger. His dad turned, surprised, and then engulfed Max in a warm hug.

"How ya doin', buddy?" Max's dad asked. As he released his son, Max motioned to me, effectively redirecting his father's attention.

"Dad, this is Lily. We work together at Swift."

Max's dad turned in my direction and extended his hand. He looked a lot like Max. Tall, thin, and well built, with the same piercing blue eyes as his son and short silver hair. "Nice to meet you, Lily. I'm glad you could join us."

"Thank you so much for having me, Mr. Samson. I'm sorry to intrude."

"Call me Bill. And you're no intrusion at all. We love company. Especially company Max brings home."

Bill winked at his son as Max replied, "Subtle, Dad." Max turned to me and explained, "I don't bring people over very often."

"Ever," his dad corrected. "He doesn't bring people over ever."

"Thanks for clarifying, Dad," Max interjected sarcastically.

Bill turned back to the grill, muttering something about just telling the truth. I giggled at their exchange. It was refreshing to watch, and I began to feel my emotions brighten.

"So, what are you doing to this poor chicken?" Max asked his dad.

"I'm cooking it. What does it look like?"

"It looks like you're torturing it. The poor thing already had to experience one death. Do you have to put it through this too?"

"Very funny, very funny. You just take this pretty young lady over and sit down. I have this under control."

"All right, but if you cook it much longer, my team is going to be able to use it as a puck."

"Just"— Bill scooted Max with his hands—"just get away from here. I've been grilling longer than you've been alive. Go on."

Max laughed as he guided me back to the table.

"So, these are your parents," I said as we sat down.

"Yup, these are them."

"They're not what I pictured."

He looked at me questioningly. "What did you picture?"

"Hmm." I thought for a moment. "People who dressed in all black and had afternoon tea in the drawing room."

"You thought my parents were British?"

I laughed loudly. "No, but I thought they'd be, I don't know, pretentious or something."

"Glad to see you think so highly of me, doll. Oh, I'm sorry. Lily." Max was smiling, but his eyes didn't carry it. What I had said bothered him.

"I don't mind you calling me doll. I just didn't like it out there so publicly. And I didn't mean to insult you. I just meant that…" I paused, trying to find the right words. "You're so confident and have that I-don't-give-a-fuck-attitude. I just expected you to have parents who had their heads halfway lodged up your ass." I smiled at my last statement, hoping that it would bring us back to friendlier ground.

"I understand why you said what you did. My arrogance doesn't reflect how I was raised. I think my behavior has embarrassed them on more than one occasion." Max stared at his dad's back as he spoke and then cast his eyes to the ground.

"What do they do for a living? This house is incredible."

"It is nice, isn't it?" said an airy voice behind me. I turned to see Max's mom behind me with another place setting and a tray of drinks. Max rose to take them from her, and she sat down beside me. "Well, I taught for ten years before staying home to raise Max. Bill was the CEO of a large investment firm in the city before he retired three years ago. Now he stays around the house, driving me crazy." She said this in a serious tone, but I could tell from the way she gazed at her husband while she said it that she loved him dearly.

"So," she continued, "is your family from around here?"

"No, I'm originally from Chicago. I came out here to go to Penn for college and ended up loving the area and wanting to stay."

"Are your parents still in Chicago?" she asked.

"Yes, they still live out there. My dad's a district attorney, and my mom was also a stay-at-home mom."

"Oh, they must miss you terribly. I used to hate when Max was traveling. I sometimes wouldn't get to see him for months. That's why I make him come over at least once a week now that he's back in town. I'm just not built to go long periods of time without seeing my baby." She looked at Max the way I wished my parents would look at me. Their eyes always held so much judgment. But Marjory's just held pure, unconditional love.

"Do you see them often?"

I was caught off guard, immersed in my own moment. "I'm sorry, who?"

"Your parents. Do you see them often?"

"No, not really. I saw them at Christmas, but not since."

"That's a shame. You should call and invite them to come out here and see you. I bet they'd love it."

Sensing my discomfort, Max swooped in and changed the subject. "Mom, you may want to check on Dad. He's starting to pace and change grilling utensils a lot."

"Dear Lord, give me strength. Bill, what are you doing to that chicken?"

"Don't you worry, doll. I got it all under control." My breath caught at Bill's words. Max's dad called his wife "doll." I quickly looked at Max. He was staring straight at me, into me, with the blazing desire I had come to know so well.

Max had called me "doll" from the moment he met me, a term that he had heard his dad lovingly call his mom probably throughout his life. I looked at him, and it came flooding back. The night at his house. The realizations I had made there about Max's feelings for me. They were all true and so much deeper than I had imagined. I thought that I could end it that night with my harshness. That I could effectively sever any romantic feelings he may have for me if I made it clear that I wasn't receptive to them.

I was wrong.

I suddenly felt like I was suffocating. "Marjory, may I use your restroom?"

"Sure, dear. Go back through the kitchen and down the hall. You'll see it on the right."

I stood slowly, my eyes still locked with Max's. It was like we were having a deep conversation that no one else could hear. But I didn't want to talk anymore. I looked away and walked quickly to the kitchen. Once inside, I practically ran down the hall, easily finding the bathroom and locking myself inside.

I lowered the toilet lid and sat down. *What the fuck was happening?* I had been having such a good time, and now it was all shot to shit. What was I supposed to do now? Why the hell hadn't I driven my own car? Now I was trapped here in this beautifully constructed nightmare.

I forced myself to take a few deep breaths so that I could better evaluate the situation. So Max called me a pet name that his dad called his mom. What did that really even mean? It's a name he's comfortable with. He'd probably called dozens of girls "doll." *Ugh.* I lowered my face into my hands. I was totally overreacting. This was no big deal. *Get a friggin grip, Lily.*

When I finally raised my head, I found myself face-to-face with the bathroom mirror. As I stared at it, I realized that I didn't know this girl. The girl staring back at me was blinded by the haze of things she wanted to see and hear. She wanted Max to be an asshole. She wanted him to be someone who fucked around a lot and never caught feelings. Someone who would watch her be happy with another man and still stick around and be her friend. All of these things would allow her to convince herself that he didn't deserve her.

But the real Lily knew that this wasn't the real Max. Both reflections were facades, masks that allowed them to do bad things and stay free of blame. It was time to start being ourselves.

The real Max came from a good family. He was kind and thoughtful. He was a good man. His feelings for her were strong and unwavering, deeply rooted in his very essence. And the real Lily damn well knew it.

I tried to be completely truthful with myself in that bathroom. What were my feelings for Max? Just as I was trying to get it sorted out, there was a knock on the door.

"Lily? You okay?" It was Max. Of course it was Max. I'd probably been gone ten minutes.

"Yeah, I'm fine," I replied slowly. I rose and gave myself one more look in the mirror. *Okay, Lily, tonight you try to stay real.* Then I unlocked the door and stepped out.

Max was waiting for me, leaning against the opposite wall. He looked at me cautiously, as though he was afraid I may bolt for the front door. We stood there a moment, just looking at one another, neither of us sure of what to say.

"Dinner's about ready," Max said, breaking our silence.

"Guess we better get back out there, then."

Max nodded, and we walked back out to the porch and took our seats.

"Here ya go, Lily. I carved you a nice piece of white meat here," Bill said as I settled into my chair and put my napkin on my lap.

"Dad, no part of that bird is white anymore," Max said, shaking his head.

"What are you talking about? This chicken's done perfectly," Bill declared.

"Done perfectly! Are you nuts, old man? That thing has suffered twice, and now we're all going to suffer trying to eat it." It was becoming clear to me that this banter was a normal part of the routine in the Samson household. My shoulders relaxed and my lips began to turn up into a smile as the two men continued bickering.

"Now you listen to me, hotshot. You may be a big deal hockey player, but you're no... uh... what's that 'Bam!' guy's name, doll? Uh..."

"Emeril Lagasse?" Marjory offered.

"Yeah, that's him. Emeril Lagasse. When you're him, you can judge my cooking. Until then, zip it."

"Really, Dad? Emeril? That's the best you could think of? Really?"

"Okay, thank you for the vaudeville act, you two. Can we eat now, or would the two of you like to arm wrestle to prove who's manlier?" Max's mom's eyes twinkled, and it was obvious: she loved every second of this. And the real Lily had to admit, she sort of loved it, too.

❤

The rest of dinner flew by. I was so wrapped up in the lively exchange between my three hosts that I lost all track of time. Finally, Bill rose.

"Come on, you two. I just bought a brand-new fishing pole. State of the art. Let's go out to the garage and I'll show it to you."

Max stood, dropping his napkin on his plate. He looked to me, and I was just about to stand as well when Marjory intervened.

"Bill, you act like you have a wooly mammoth fossil in there. Who wants to see a fishing pole?"

"Who *wouldn't* want to see a fishing pole? I swear, sometimes I don't know how we made it thirty-five years when we have so little in common," Bill huffed but quickly broke into a wide smile.

"I don't know either, with as crazy as you make me. All right, go show them your fishing pole," Marjory said with exaggerated excitement, "I'll just straighten up a little."

"Okay, kids. Let's go," Bill declared as he made his way around the table, gave his wife a quick peck on the cheek, and started walking.

"I think I'll help clean up," I interrupted. Max turned to look at me, as if to ask me if I was okay. "I'm fine. I'll meet up with you guys in a bit."

"Suit yourself. Let's go, Max. These women don't appreciate fine art."

Marjory scoffed at Bill's comment as Max held my gaze a second longer before turning to follow his dad.

Marjory began collecting plates, so I did the same. I followed her into the kitchen and set them down on the counter by the sink.

"I just have to rinse them and put them into the dishwasher, so you can just keep me company if that's all right with you."

"Sure," I replied. I was both intrigued and nervous. I wanted to know more about this woman who raised Max, but I wasn't sure I wanted her knowing very much about me. For some reason, I knew it would bother me if she didn't like me, even though I doubted that I would ever see her again.

"So, Lily, you and Max are just friends?" Marjory asked, clearly trying to subtly ascertain particular bits of information.

"Yup, just friends," I replied, sounding more upbeat than I felt.

"Hmm, that's quite a shame." Marjory didn't expand on this statement, and I knew that I should drop it. That this was better left alone. But I couldn't resist.

"Why?" It was a simple question, but I had a feeling the

answer would be more complicated.

Marjory continued rinsing dishes and placing them in the dishwasher, giving herself time to carefully construct her response. Then, once she had worked it out in her mind, she wiped her hands on the dish towel and turned toward me.

"You know how my son feels about you, don't you?"

I quaked slightly at her words. Had Max talked to her about me? How did she know how he felt? *Maybe the same way I knew.* I nodded, embracing what I had promised myself in the bathroom. *Stay real, Lily.*

"He would never talk to me about it, of course," she said, answering my unspoken question. "But no one knows that man better than I do. And I have a feeling that only two other people are even close to knowing him as well as me. One is Bill, and I suspect that the other is you. Do you think that's true, Lily?" Her question was kind and genuine. She obviously loved her son very much, and her curiosity was based completely on ensuring his happiness.

"I don't know much about Max's personal life, in terms of friends . . . I don't know if anyone knows him better." My words rocked me. I really didn't know much about Max. Granted, there were some things I was intimately knowledgeable of, but nothing that truly mattered. And here was his mother, thinking that I knew him better than anyone except for his parents.

"It doesn't surprise me that you don't know any of Max's friends. He cut a lot of them loose when his career started declining. He spent time with a lot of hangers-on and good-time Charlies. Once he really stopped and took a look around, he realized that he was essentially alone, except for Bill and me. It changed him. Made him more guarded and detached. But then, he shows up here today with you"—she smiled at me—"and I just hoped..." She paused in an attempt to quell the rising emotions. Her eyes glistened as she turned her head and looked out the window that was above the sink. "No mother wants their child to be lonely, Lily."

"I don't want him to be lonely either," I admitted quietly. No matter how confused my feelings were for Max, I knew this for absolute certainty. "But I can only help him in that regard as his friend. It isn't any more than that between us." I needed to say this almost as much as I wanted her to hear it. I didn't want to give her hope for something I couldn't promise. And I had to remind myself that I couldn't promise anything.

"I'm glad he has such a good friend," she said, looking back at me.

I wanted to correct her. Tell her that, really, I was a pretty horrible friend. He was much better to me than I was to him. But I didn't have the courage to tell any more of the truth to her. "I'm going to go see what the guys are up to," I said meekly, beginning to walk toward the doors. As I was about to step through, I heard her again.

"Lily?"

I turned to face her.

"Just promise me..." Her voice was an octave higher than normal, hopeful. She exhaled slightly before finishing her sentence, effectively lowering her register, "Just promise that you'll be good to him."

I nodded slightly and then stepped through the doors. I could tell that she wanted me to give Max a chance, but taking a chance on him could cost me a lot. And as I made my way toward the garage, I wondered if some things were worth the gamble.

♥

Max and I left a short time later. His parents hugged us both, and as we climbed into the Range Rover, Bill yelled that Max had better "bring his girl back for a visit." Marjory answered that with a sharp elbow to Bill's ribs.

"They're really great," I told Max.

"Yeah, they are," he said as he pulled out of their driveway and started down the street, offering one last wave to his parents as he left.

We drove the rest of the way back to school in silence, both of us milling the evening over in our heads. It was dark now, and the darkness brought some winter chill back into the air. I shivered slightly, and Max reached over and turned on the heat. When we pulled into the Swift parking lot, Max parked next to my car.

I wasn't quite sure what to say. Things felt awkward, and I didn't know how to fix them. "Thanks for tonight," I said finally. "It was a lot of fun hanging out with you and your parents. Definitely improved my mood."

He looked thoughtful for a minute, as if gaining courage for what he would say next. "Why were you upset earlier?" He lowered his head and pulled his hands from the steering wheel and onto his lap. "Was it because of him?" Max looked over at me, his eyes pleading with me to confide in him.

"It was a lot of things. I feel like..." I sighed. "I feel like every time I try to make things better, I end up making them worse. I don't know up from down anymore. It's so... complicated. And I hate complicated. It's like I can't tell right from wrong." I looked out the passenger window, unable to let Max see my face as I asked my next question. "Max, am I a bad person?"

He didn't answer right away, which forced me to look at him to try to see what he was thinking. He smiled weakly at me and said, "I don't think one bad person can always identify another."

This wasn't the answer I was expecting, but it was the answer I needed. It was honest. Max was never going to be that person who told me the sun shined out of my ass just because it's what I wanted to hear. He knew that my actions had been questionable since I met him, and he wasn't going to try to convince me otherwise. Instead, he let me know it wasn't him I needed to convince. He was in no place to judge me. If I had to ask whether or not I was a bad person, then I probably already knew my answer.

Maybe that's why I had always been drawn to Max. The darker, baser parts of me found a kindred spirit in his demons. I could be whoever I wanted to be with Max. He would like me anyway. Suddenly, I needed to touch him. I needed to feel the electric pulsing that ran through his veins when our skin connected. I needed to feel loved.

I stretched out my arm toward him, allowing my fingertips to graze his jawbone. And as my fingers made contact, I felt it. The warmth and acceptance radiated into my hand as he leaned slightly into my touch. But then it was severed as he pulled away from me sharply.

I let me hand drop into my lap as I stared at him, unsure of what had just transpired. He averted his gaze out the windshield, putting one hand on the ignition to turn the engine over and the other atop the steering wheel.

"There is one thing I do know. Sometimes, doll, in our attempt to have everything, we find ourselves left with nothing." He then turned the ignition, signaling that the conversation was over.

I pulled the handle and climbed out of the car. He waited for me to remove my keys from my purse before he drove off.

I watched him go, leaning back against my driver's-side door. And for the first time in a long time, I cried.

# chapter twenty-eight

By the middle of the day on Tuesday, I had no choice but to vent to Tina about the predicament I'd been facing lately. Even if she didn't have any solid advice to offer, I still needed to hear myself say aloud what I'd been contemplating silently for so long, even if it would be difficult.

So when the bell rang for our lunch, I peeked my head into her room and told her we were going out for lunch, my treat. I owed Tina a lunch anyway. We'd made a bet about how many mandatory faculty meetings we'd have in February. *Never take the under*, I reminded myself.

"Yes, can't wait!" Tina looked more excited than she probably should at the prospect of getting a slice of pizza, and I suspected it was because she figured I had some juicy details of my Max escapades to share since we hadn't gotten a chance to catch up lately. We strolled silently out of the building, but as soon as we were out of earshot of young, impressionable minds, Tina wasted no time. "So, what do you have for me? Let's hear it. Tell me you sucked him off in the parking lot or something."

"No." I couldn't help but laugh, even in my despondent state. "I think we were actually off of school grounds when that happened. Though it *was* during school hours." I shook my head and let my posture reveal what I struggled to expose through words. And despite Tina's typically lighthearted comments, she knew when to be serious.

"Lil, what's wrong?"

"I don't even know where to begin." I was thankful for the time and the privacy that walking to lunch provided me because I felt like I might start to cry again as soon as I spoke. "Things with Max . . . they're complicated. It's so hard to explain. I haven't told you about everything."

Tina raised her eyebrows to prompt me to continue.

"Or I guess I should really say every*one*." I paused for a few moments to let my words sink into Tina's brain.

As we cut across the field like high schoolers, Tina stopped in her tracks. I could see my words had clicked. "Wait, what? There's someone else?"

I knew normally Tina would congratulate me on such a fine accomplishment, but she was considerate, careful of how her reaction might press a button in me that she knew I didn't want pushed. "Yeah, I'll start from the beginning, I guess." I began walking again slowly toward the hill, and Tina followed. I did my best to explain the fucked-up timeline of events and emotions that had transpired over the course of the last few months. I had been right; hearing myself say what I'd done was tough to swallow. But somehow I managed to hold my composure.

"Why didn't you tell me about this before?" Her tone was not accusatory. She was clearly concerned.

"I guess a couple reasons, really. The first is probably that I didn't want to seem like a whore. I mean, I was worried that fucking Max would make me seem like a one. But Christ, what would I look like if I was fucking Max *and* someone else?" I breathed in deeply and expelled a loud sigh, preparing for what I was about to say next. "The second reason is that the other guy is Adam *Carter.*"

I could tell by Tina's puzzled expression that she had no idea who that was.

"Eva Carter's father. She's in my first-period class." I pulled my phone out to show her a picture.

Tina did her best to temper her reaction, but her body language revealed her true shock. "He's hot. Seriously?"

"Seriously."

We arrived at Lupi's, ordered a few slices and fries to split, and then quickly sat down to resume our conversation.

"So what are you going to do?" Tina asked. "I mean, you said that the time in Atlantic City was your last time with Max, right? And you told Adam you loved him. So that's who you're picking?"

Her last question lingered in the air like a dense fog, making it difficult for me to see straight. Somehow, during all of this, I had never thought I was making a choice. I had never considered that this was actually a voluntary decision that I had control over.

So much of what I'd done had been based off deeper feelings: reflex, sexual desire, fear. I had told Adam I'd loved him because I was afraid he'd leave if I didn't. That he'd see me for who I really was: an indecisively selfish and promiscuous fraud. And I'd reached out to Max again because I didn't know how *not* to. He was an addiction I just couldn't get over.

"I don't know. That's who I *should* pick. He'd give me a wonderful life, full of family dinners and flowers and...God, sex like I've never experienced before. He's so loving and so commanding at the same time. But I can't see myself without

Max. I try, and I just can't. He's a temptation I can't resist."

Tina listened carefully before constructing her response. "If you want my opinion, and I don't even know if you do—"

"Yeah, any opinion could help right now," I interrupted.

"This may seem like a surprise coming from me, but you can't pick a good lay over a good life."

Something inside me battled with her last line, and I couldn't help but get defensive. For the first time, I understood what Max had come to realize weeks ago. "The thing with Max—it's more than just a good lay." I put my pizza down, needing all my energy to process my new epiphany. "It's like, I can't give up our friendship because it'll leave me with no part of him at all. But if we stay friends, I have this undeniable attraction for him that goes beyond something physical. I saw that yesterday at his house. There was something more, and I am just now starting to let myself acknowledge it."

Tina studied my expression, and I thought her own probably mirrored mine. "Wow, I had no idea your feelings for Max went that deep. And I obviously had no idea about Adam at all. You have to do what is best for you. You have to do what *you* can live with."

"I'm just so conflicted. Max is really no good for me. He's impulsive. And wild. I know that. But he brings out a side of me that I feel I need to hide from Adam. And Adam is . . . he's just so good. He makes me a better version of myself. He's everything I should love. But somehow I can't seem to love him. At least not yet." Finally, I let a tear stream down my cheek before wiping it away. "And if I keep doing this, I'm gonna fuck everything up—with both of them."

"I think you need to see what things can really be like with Max. Let yourself open up to him a little now that you realize it could be something more. You owe yourself that. And truthfully, maybe you owe it to him too." Tina's eyes welled before she was able to conjure up her innate sarcasm. "Love whoever it is you're gonna love. I mean, do you really think I planned to fall in love with a two-hundred-and-fifty-pound insurance salesman whose idea of adventure is eating Indian food from the new place down the street? No." Tina shook her head and laughed quietly before making her tone more serious again. "My point is that even though you may feel torn, you should take comfort in the fact that this isn't really your decision at all. Love finds *you*. It's not the other way around. The only choice you really have is whether or not you want to be found."

# chapter twenty-nine

I returned from lunch feeling a little better. Tina was right. If love was in the cards for me with one of these men, then let it find me. I just had to make sure I was paying attention.

As eighth period ended and the dismissal bell rang, I thought back to what Max had said. I knew I was going to have to find a balance between Tina's and Max's advice. I wanted to open myself up but not lose everything in the process. *Being a girl really sucked sometimes.*

I looked at the clock on my computer. Eleven more minutes and I could leave, maybe go for a run to help clear my head. I scrolled through my iPhone to pick out a playlist for my workout. I needed to make sure I was properly motivated.

"Hi, doll."

I had been wondering if he would stop by today. Last night had been intense for both of us, and I wasn't sure whether we needed space, a discussion, or to pretend it hadn't happened. Clearly, the correct answer was not space.

"Hi," I replied, not wanting to offer too much.

"So, are we good?" He got right to the point, motioning to the distance between us with his hand.

"Yup."

"Okay, good." He breathed a heavy sigh of relief. "What are you doing Thursday?"

*Guess we were pretending it hadn't happened.* "Umm, nothing that I know of. Why?" My head was facing him, but my body was still turned toward my desk. I didn't want to open my body up to him. At least not right now.

"Remember when I said we should go to a Flyers game? We should do that Thursday."

"Oh, we should, should we? And why should we do that?" I couldn't resist teasing him.

"Because we're friends and friends hang out."

I stared at him, knowing that this couldn't be the entire explanation.

"Although it's not actually a game. It's more of a fundraiser that I need a date to," he spat out guiltily.

*This man had no couth.* "Oh, no you don't, Max. Don't even ask. I'm not reliving Atlantic City. Forget about it."

"I can't forget about it. Listen, my agent called and said that he got a lot of positive feedback about how well I handled myself at the autograph signing. He also said that numerous people, important people, made comments about how great it was to see that I had fallen for such a nice, down-to-earth girl. I can't look like I booted her to the curb two weeks later." His voice was pleading, but that isn't what I focused on.

"Why would they think *you* booted *me*? Why wouldn't they think that *I* dumped *you*?" I sounded pouty and I knew it. But it was insulting that people would assume that this asshat had dumped me. I could dump people. Did I look desperate or something?

"I don't know, doll. I think the point I'm trying to make is that we can avoid the dumping altogether if you agree to go with me. How about it?"

I eyed him suspiciously. Was this just a way to get me out

with him again? Or did he really want my help? It was a fifty-fifty split.

"We don't even have to stay over anywhere this time," he continued. "We'll have a blast, and I'll totally behave. The only negative I can see is that you may be a little tired at work the next day. Otherwise, it'll be great."

Maybe that was the only negative he could see, but I saw plenty of others. The one foremost on my brain was how Adam would react to this. He was going to completely lose his shit. If I were going to go, I definitely couldn't tell Adam. I would just have to hope that he didn't find out.

*But should I go?* I wasn't so sure. I had vowed to give Max a chance, and here was my opportunity.

I sighed deeply before putting my elbows on my desk and plopping my head down onto my hands. I didn't even try to disguise the irritation that filled my voice. "What should I wear?"

❤

Max was picking me up at five thirty, which meant that I had very little time to get home, get showered, and get dressed. Thankfully I had chosen my outfit the night before. I had decided on a deep red strapless cocktail dress that stopped at my knee. The material was satin, and it managed to be elegant and simple at the same time. Paired with some black heels and a diamond pendant necklace my parents gave me for my college graduation, I had to admit, I looked pretty damn good.

I looked out my window about a hundred times between five fifteen and the time Max arrived. He was picking me up in a limo because he said it was important to arrive at these types of things in style. But I was paranoid. I hadn't told Adam I was going with Max. What if Adam decided to drop by? What if he was in the area and drove past? As unlikely as these things were, I still felt like I was inevitably going to get caught.

The limo pulled up out front at five twenty-five. I grabbed my clutch and booked it out of my apartment and down the stairs. Just as Max was getting out of the car, I was hustling toward him down the sidewalk.

"Ready?" I asked.

"Uh, yeeesss." He dragged the word out, clearly trying to figure out why the hell I was practically sprinting toward him.

"Okay, great. Let's go." I pushed past him and got into the limo.

"Lily . . . ?" he asked.

"Yeah?" I poked my head out of the door to look at him.

He ran his hand through his hair. "Nothing." He got into the car, and the driver closed the door behind him. We sat beside each other this time, each of us next to a door.

I glanced over at him. He was in a black tux, with his hair gelled so that it framed his face perfectly. *God, he was gorgeous.* In an attempt to shake from my mind the thoughts of sitting on his face, I started talking. "Well, you sure clean up well." I smiled warmly at him in an effort to let him know that I wanted us to have a good time tonight. No petty bickering, no angry words, and no complicated sex. I just wanted to enjoy his company and see if I could get any clarity on our relationship.

"Thanks, doll. You don't look too shabby yourself," he replied with a sly grin.

He really knew how to flatter a girl.

♥

The rest of the ride passed in easy conversation. We were back to how we had been two months ago, before his house and the fiasco in Atlantic City. It felt good. It felt right.

We pulled up in front of the Wells Fargo Center behind a line of other limos and expensive cars. As we waited to get closer to the entrance, I realized that I didn't even know what this fundraiser was for. "What charity are the Flyers supporting with this fundraiser?"

"March of Dimes," Max replied.

I nodded my head and stared out of the window. Finally, the door on Max's side was yanked open and he helped me out of the car. My mind flashed back to when I had been here with Adam for the Sixers game. Guilt swept through me. I shouldn't be here. But I had known that when I said yes. Why did I keep doing all the wrong things? Max slid his hand to the small of my back to escort me into the arena, which sent shivers down my spine. *Oh yeah. That's why.*

His firm hand fit perfectly into the crook just above my ass. I found myself pushing back a bit, trying to feel more of his hand through the material of my dress. I did love this man's hands on my body. The way he explored me, caressed me, rubbed me. It was intoxicating.

Max led me onto the main concourse and through a curtained opening to the arena seats. When I passed the curtains, I couldn't help but gasp. The floor where the basketball and hockey games were held had been completely transformed into a gala befitting the wealthy who were in attendance. The floor was covered with a thin navy-blue carpet, more likely to protect the floor beneath than for the comfort of the guests. There were tables with beautiful orchid arrangements atop white tablecloths, surrounded by chairs covered with white linen and finished off with black bows. A band played as service staff trolled the crowd with hors d'oeuvres. It was beautiful.

Max reached for my hand and cupped it gently in his. "You good?" he asked.

"Yeah, I'm good," I replied, beaming.

He walked slowly down the stairs to the court so that I could keep up with him in my heels. Once down, we were immediately met with a photographer who had clearly been hired to take pictures of all of the guests. Max quickly pulled me to him before I could protest, holding me much closer than I would have liked, considering it was going to be documented on film.

Once the photographer looked up to signal that he had gotten the shot, Max and I turned and were immediately met with people. Max seemed to know most of them and talked in warm, casual conversation. I was impressed. Max was a natural charmer and was able to instantly win over those he spoke with. However, this left me wondering how such a charismatic person could be thought of as a total dick by so many people.

Though, I guess I knew that answer. I had seen destructive Max on more than one occasion. What really didn't make sense was why I was more sexually attracted to that Max than the one standing before me now. I guess there was just always something appealing about a bad boy.

Max finally managed to escape the throng that surrounded him, and he led me toward an open space. He smiled at me. "Having fun?"

"It's definitely interesting. I've never been to something like this before."

A waitress approached us with a tray full of champagne. "Can I offer you something to drink?"

"Yes, thank you," Max said as he lifted two champagne flutes off her tray and handed one to me.

"Thank you," I repeated as I took a sip. I wasn't a big fan of champagne, but I also didn't want to stand out and ask for something else.

"Ready to mingle?" Max asked.

"This is your show. I'm just along for the ride." I immediately regretted my word choice. My horny brain instantly flashed to images of the times I had ridden Max. I felt a pulsing low in my body, a yearning building from the memories alone. The slight smirk on his face told me that he was reliving the same experiences. "Ready when you are." *Jesus Christ, Lily, just stop talking.*

"Okay, let's start in a corner and work our way around." Max said this seriously, but he was still smirking and there was a decided crinkling of his eyes. I hated that filthy minds so often thought alike.

The fundraiser ended up being more fun than I had initially anticipated. Max stayed by my side, pulling me into conversation to ensure that I didn't get bored. The only real issue I ran into was that I really hated having to hold on to a glass. With having to secure my clutch with one hand, I despised not having my other hand free. Therefore, I quickly downed my champagne. But those disciples of evil, also known as the serving staff, kept coming over and offering me more. And every time, just as I lifted my hand to decline, someone would say, "Yes, thank you," and hand me another flute. *I need to slow the hell down.*

As we were engaged in conversation with a former teammate of Max's, the emcee asked for our attention.

"Ladies and gentlemen, I would like to first say thank you

to all of you for attending this year's Flyers Fundraiser for the March of Dimes."

A round of applause broke out around us as I leaned slightly into Max, trying to get my balance. *Damn champagne.*

"I would also like to take this opportunity to recognize some of our generous contributors," the emcee continued. Impeccably dressed in a black tuxedo, he was an older man, maybe about sixty. He donned a pair of black rimmed reading glasses and began rattling off the names of people who had donated exorbitant amounts of money to the March of Dimes.

I completely tuned him out until I heard a name that nearly made me made me faint on the spot.

"Lily Hamilton, with a donation of fifteen thousand dollars."

*What the fuck?*

I immediately stood up straighter and looked around. Had I heard him correctly? There had to be some mistake. Some people who had met me earlier in the evening looked approvingly at me, nodding their heads in my direction.

"Relax," Max whispered in my ear.

"But I didn't donate any money. What is he talking about?" I was concerned. It was one thing to pretend you loved your boyfriend. It was another to pretend like you had given a ton of money to sick babies. If I hadn't been convinced that my place in hell had already been reserved with a velvet rope, I would have really panicked.

"Calm down, doll. I made the donation."

I looked at Max, stunned. "Why would you do that? Why didn't you make it in your own name?"

Max looked up at the emcee and took a sip of his champagne. Then he turned and looked down at me. "Because you *are* a good person, Lily. It means more coming from you."

I wanted to disagree. Remind him that we were here to fix his image, not mine. This was too much for me to process. I began to pull away from him, disengage.

But he quickly put his arm around me, preventing me from pushing him away. "You are a good person, doll. I should have told you that Monday, but I was afraid."

I looked up at him, leaning back against him. "Afraid of what?"

He sighed and returned my gaze. The heat radiated between us so much, it was nearly visible. "Afraid that if you knew you were too good for me that you'd pull away."

I didn't know what to say. So I let my actions speak for me.

I reached my hands up around Max's neck and pulled myself up to my tiptoes so that I could give him a kiss on the cheek. It was meant to be a simple thank-you, a gesture that marked the strength of our friendship. But as my lips grazed his cool, soft skin, I let them linger there decidedly longer than a friend would have. And I didn't care.

❤

Max and I stayed close to one another for the remainder of the night, finding reasons to touch each other more than we should have. As the fundraiser began to wind down, Max asked me if I was ready to leave. Though I really wasn't, I nodded, still tipsy from the champagne. And as he led me back up the stadium stairs, onto the main concourse, and out of the building, I thought about how much I didn't want this night to end. I knew that there had been magic for us tonight in this place. But all magic comes with a price, and I knew that I would pay mine.

The limo ride home was a little awkward, as the real world started to pull us apart again. For the first time in hours, I thought of Adam and how he would feel if he saw me nuzzled into Max's side. And how unfair it was for all of the mixed signals I sent to Max, though I wasn't sure how not to send them. I was as mixed up as the messages were, and I just couldn't get my emotions in order. So when we arrived back at my apartment, I found myself inviting Max upstairs, even though I knew it was the wrong thing to do. Or was it the right thing? *Goddamn!*

He hesitated, but when I told him that I would drop him off at his place in the morning before school, my eyes twinkling and a coy smirk on my face, he relented.

He followed me up the stairs and leaned against the wall while I unlocked my door. He chuckled as I fumbled with my keys, and my mind went back to the night he brought me home from the bar. *Ah, memories.*

"You want something to drink?" I asked as I swung the door open.

"Sure. Whatever you're having."

I walked into the kitchen to take inventory of what we had.

"Is your roommate here?" Max yelled from the living room.

"She's never here. I forget I even have a roommate half the time." I grabbed a bottle of wine and two glasses and then returned to join Max. He was sitting on the couch, his forearms resting on his thighs. I plopped down beside him.

"This is all I have."

"That'll work," he replied, taking the bottle from me and filling our glasses.

I settled back against the couch. We were both silent,

neither of us sure of how to get a conversation going.

"What should we do now?" I asked.

"I dunno. You wanna get naked and have a romp in your bed?" Max replied, his smile broad.

"Uh, no thank you," I replied, rolling my eyes slightly.

"Just checking."

Silence settled over us again, and I was beginning to wonder if I should offer to let him take my car home and pick me up in the morning. The distance between us was growing again, and I didn't like the way it made me feel. Like I was losing something very dear to me.

Max put his glass down on my coffee table and looked at me, his eyes serious.

*Fuck.* I braced myself for whatever words would leave his mouth next.

"How about now?" he said, his face still serious.

I thought a moment. *How about now, what?* He raised an eyebrow, and it dawned on me. The romp in my bed. Once he saw the light bulb go off in my head, he started laughing, and I joined him. I blamed it on my slightly inebriated state, but once I started laughing, I couldn't stop. Eventually, my ribs started to hurt and I was forced to rein it back in.

That exchange was exactly the kick-start we needed to get us back to who we were. Max and Lily, the most fucked-up friends on the planet. Two hours later, I looked at the clock. One thirty. *Christ, I was never getting up tomorrow.*

Somewhere along the way, we had turned on the radio and had begun dancing hysterically. We had just begun imitating how the kids dance at the school-sponsored dances when a slower song came on. It was Bruno Mars's "When I Was Your Man."

Max and I looked at each other a moment before he pulled me to him and we swayed to the music, my arms wrapped around his neck and my head on his chest, his cheek nuzzled against the top of my head as his hands went to my waist. In this moment, we were perfect, our closeness evident in every way. And as I listened to the words, I thought about how they related to us in ways that gave me a pang of sadness that coated my other feelings.

I lifted my head and looked at him briefly before reaching up and kissing him on the cheek. I pulled away and then leaned in again, kissing his cheek once more, but this time, closer to his mouth. Again, I pulled away, slightly this time, pausing in front of his lips, making it clear what I intended to do next, giving him time to pull away. But he didn't. And as my lips made contact with his, the wild passion returned. The yearning low in my body was back, and I started to grind against him, knowing that I couldn't stop myself now. But I didn't have to.

Max suddenly pulled away from my lips, moving down to kiss my cheek and neck. Then, he pulled back farther, as far as he could while still maintaining our embrace.

"Lily, I . . . I want this more than you'll ever know. But I can't do it. Not like this."

I looked at him curiously, wanting him to explain what "not like this" meant. It could mean any host of things, and I wanted, needed, him to be clear.

"I want you to want this sober, too. I don't want to be a drunk mistake."

I continued to just stare at him. I took him in, this man who constantly surprised me. He had taken off his tuxedo jacket a long time ago, but he was still wearing his white dress shirt, which had the top three buttons undone. His bowtie hung untied around his neck. He was even sexier like this than he had been at the fundraiser.

"You're never a mistake, Max," I whispered.

"Thanks, doll," he said as he leaned in one last time and gave me a sweet kiss on my shoulder. "We should take a picture," he declared suddenly, detaching from me completely.

"A picture?" I asked, confused.

"Yeah, I need a more current one for my wall." He winked. He fished his phone from his pocket and stood closer to me, positioning it in front of us. He grinned widely as he draped his arm over my shoulders.

I smiled as well. But, at the last minute, I lifted myself higher, closed my eyes, and kissed Max on the cheek. *May as well make it good.*

After he snapped the picture, he lowered his phone so we could both look at it. I had to admit, we looked great together. "Can you text that to me?" I asked as I rested my head on his chest.

"Sure, doll. Anything for you."

❤

I woke up the next morning in my bed, still fully clothed from the night before. *I must have been drunker than I thought.* I went into the bathroom and splashed some water on my face before wandering out into the living room to find Max.

The previous night replayed in my mind as I walked down the hallway. I wasn't sure where my feelings stood for Max. It was frustrating. Despite my feelings not being what I wanted them to be for Adam, I still knew what they were. I was a tangled mess when it came to Max.

When I reached the living room, I saw that Max wasn't there. And as I wandered into the kitchen, I was surprised not to find him there either. But what was there, lying on the counter, was a note. I scooped it up as my breath caught in my chest. Why would he leave? Had I said something I didn't remember?

*Hey, doll. I figured you were going to be pressed for time this morning, so I called a cab. I also went out and got you some coffee—it's in the microwave. See you later.*

*Max*

I reread the note as I walked to the other side of the kitchen. *He really could be sweet sometimes.* I opened the microwave door and took a step back. There, in front of the cup of coffee, was a copy of the picture Max had taken last night.
*Definitely sweet.*

# chapter thirty

Seeing Max interact with his family earlier in the week had surprisingly touched some nerve in me I didn't even know I had, and this had only been intensified by our evening together at the fundraiser. But all of this was just too confusing, and with my birthday coming up, I craved the familiar.

For this reason, I was glad that I had invited my parents out to celebrate with me. It had definitely been short notice, but I figured it was worth a shot. And when I called my parents, they actually agreed to come out for a few nights the weekend of my birthday to visit. Of course they were going to be staying at a hotel. I had to draw the line somewhere.

And with my parents' arrival quickly approaching, I thought it might be a good time to let Adam know that they'd be in town. I'd let myself see how things might be with Max, but I felt like if my relationship with Adam were going to progress further, he would have to meet my parents at some point.

"It'll be casual," I said when I called him last week to invite him to dinner at my apartment. "Nothing fancy. I'm just cooking dinner at my house. I didn't want to go out because of what happened when we were at the restaurant in Colorado." Though I hadn't told Adam that much about my parents, he knew our general relationship was far from perfect. I thought he might actually decline my invitation so my parents and I would have some time to spend alone without the new boyfriend, but Adam agreed that it would be a good idea for him to meet them.

His exact words were actually, "Sure, what dad *doesn't* want to meet the guy who's screwing his daughter?"

I laughed at his unexpected response. Sometimes he could say things that were so "non-Adam." But he clearly knew what a big step this was for me.

With careful planning, I had tried to delicately maneuver their arrivals so that I'd be able to acclimate gradually. I didn't need everyone getting there at once, and I certainly didn't need anyone seeing Amanda wander around the apartment in her bra while she ironed a shirt. She had a date with some new guy she'd been seeing, and she planned to be out of the house by five thirty.

Adam was scheduled to arrive around six o'clock, and my parents planned to get there around six thirty—which I was hoping would be when the turkey would be done. That way I wouldn't have to talk to them for any lengthy amount of time. We could eat dinner, cut the cake Adam planned to bring, and my parents could get the hell out.

But I should have known nothing would go as planned. At five forty, I heard, "Fucking wire popped through another bra! These are both new. I got a white one and a nude one. I need to find something to keep these puppies up," Amanda said, cupping her D-cup breasts and lifting them toward her neck. "Can you help me find another light bra? I'm wearing a pink shirt, and you'll be able to see through it if my bra's too dark."

*Who cares if you can see your bra through your shirt? Your date'll probably have it off in a few hours anyway.* "You can borrow one of mine." *Anything to get her out of the apartment.*

With Amanda out the door, I took a moment to check on the turkey. But as soon as I opened the oven door, I knew I had a major problem. I had never cooked a turkey before—or really anything for that matter—but I was pretty sure it shouldn't smell like burning plastic.

I cursed aloud to no one as I removed the pan and placed it on the stove. With one quick examination, I knew immediately what was wrong. I had left some sort of plastic package inside the turkey. Some parts of the carcass or gravy or something. With the plastic melted, I had to move on to plan B. So I called Adam, hoping he had time to pick something up before my parents arrived.

"Yeah, hon. No problem. I'll figure something out. Be there soon."

"Hurry," I urged, fearing my parents' arrival before Adam got here with the food.

I used the time before Adam got to my apartment to open some windows and light a candle to mask the smell.

Adam appeared at my door about twenty-five minutes later. "Happy birthday," he said. He held up two Boston Market bags, smiling. "Chicken, mashed potatoes, steamed vegetables, and cornbread. We'll put these in some pans and throw them in the oven. Your parents will never know where it's from."

*No argument here.* I was pretty sure Boston Market was well below my parents' dining echelon.

Adam immediately took command of the kitchen, keeping the food warm and taking out serving dishes as he prepared for my parents. He was alarmingly calm for someone who was about to meet his girlfriend's pretentious parents for the first time and serve them fast food.

The doorbell rang, and Adam continued our charade in the kitchen as I answered the door, plastering on my best *so glad to see you* face. "Mom. Dad." I smiled. "I'm so happy you're here." The truth was that I *was* happy they were here. My nerves were just on overdrive.

"Happy birthday, sweetheart," my mom said, hugging me formally. As always, she was well put together. In a crisp, bright-patterned skirt paired with a cream silk blouse and not one of her shoulder-length, light-brown hairs out of place, she stood the epitome of perfection. Combined with my father, who wore black pants and a light-blue dress shirt, they were clearly overdressed for the occasion. *Or maybe we are underdressed,* I thought as I looked down at my casual pastel green dress from Express and thought of Adam in his jeans and untucked red polo.

As I greeted my parents for the first time since their arrival last night, I couldn't help but remember how we had parted in Aspen. I'd left on such bad terms, and we had only spoken a few times since. They knew about Adam, but they didn't know much.

As if on cue, he emerged from the kitchen, extending a solid hand to my father and a polite peck on the cheek to my mother. He smiled broadly when my dad said, "You must be Adam."

"I must be," Adam replied jovially, obviously unaware of the effect my dad's innocuous choice in words had on me. My being seen with one man or another lately clearly had no real correlation to who I was actually dating.

"I'm Howard. This is my wife, Lynn."

"It's a pleasure to finally meet both of you." Adam took my mom's coat and offered my parents a drink. *Thank God for*

*Adam, because I didn't think to do either one of those things.*
You would have thought that all of the parties my parents
threw when I was a child would have instilled better hosting
skills in their offspring. Apparently not.

But Adam was a pro. He and my dad talked about beer
over Yuenglings—a Pennsylvanian lager my dad hadn't tried
until tonight—and some golf tournament that was coming up
in June. It was at a course nearby. And as I listened to them
discuss the tournament, all I could think was what a bitch my
drive home would be during my last week of the school year.
I was already anticipating having to flip off about fifteen old
people just to get home each afternoon.

"Traffic's gonna be horrendous around here that week,"
Adam added much more eloquently than I would have as he
moved on to discuss other hobbies. "Do you fish at all?" he
asked my father before casually turning his attention toward
my mother to be sure she was included in the conversation.
"Lily tells me you have a house on Lake Michigan. My family
spent a lot of time at a lake close to here."

"We don't really do much fishing," my mom said with a
polite smile. "We have a catamaran that we sail when we're
there."

I didn't have much to add to the conversation, so I busied
myself setting the table. Adam was fitting in so well with my
parents, and I didn't want to ruin that.

As we sat down to our Boston Market feast, my mom
complimented me—or at least she thought she did. "Lily, this
looks fabulous. Did you make all of this? You are really getting
to be quite the cook, dear." Then she turned toward Adam
before allowing me to answer. "Did you help her with all this?"

Adam slipped me a knowing glance and laughed silently

with his eyes as he patted my knee under the table. "Nope, not me. This was all Lily. She's the reason we're eating this delicious meal."

*What an ass.*

"Well, it's wonderful. Really, Lily. You've outdone yourself," my father added. He wiped his napkin across his graying beard before continuing. "So, Adam, Lily hasn't told us much about you. What do you do for a living?"

"Can you at least let him take his first bite before you start with the inquisition?"

"It's fine, Lily," Adam assured me as he put a comforting hand on my shoulder. "Your father has every right to know about the man who's dating his daughter." He focused his eyes back on my father to give him his undivided attention before answering. "I'm an architect. I work for a small firm in the city designing custom homes in the area."

My father relaxed a bit, clearly pleased with Adam's response. "An architect? That's impressive. I considered that myself before deciding to pursue a career in law. We were hoping Lily would follow in our footsteps, actually. I'm sure she's told you."

"Dad, can we not do this now?"

"I'm just saying, honey. I'm sure an architect would agree with me. You're smart enough to go to law school. You could even take a few classes in the summer to get started."

"He isn't *just* an architect. He's a person. For once, can't you just see someone for who they really are instead of making judgments based on what they do and where they come from?" I surprised myself when I looked to my mother's warm brown eyes for assistance. I hoped even she would realize that this was not the appropriate time for this.

But I was met with more attacks. "It's just that we want more for you, dear. That's all." She said it with a tone that I was sure she hoped would make her comment seem more innocent than she truly intended.

I put my fork down, suddenly losing my appetite. I sat back in my chair and crossed my arms over my chest, visibly fuming.

Adam had never seen me this angry, and for a brief moment I thought he might think I was overreacting. He had remained quiet until a question was finally directed at him, forcing him to respond. "Adam," my mother asked calmly, "don't you think Lily should do something better than teach?"

*Were they serious? They were actually hoping my boyfriend would take their side on this?* If they knew Adam like I did, they would know that would never happen. But the extent to which he came to my defense shocked even me.

"With all due respect, Mr. and Mrs. Hamilton," Adam began candidly.

"Howard and Lynn, please," my father encouraged.

"With all due respect, Howard ... Lynn ... you asked for my thoughts, so I'll give them to you." I studied Adam closely. His expression was stoic. "What Lily chooses to do with her life isn't for me to decide. And I'm certainly not going to judge her for it. Lily loves teaching. And she's good at it."

Adam turned his head to face me, casting his clear green eyes seemingly inside me. "I love your daughter. And I don't love her despite what she chooses to do for a career. I love her because she's kindhearted. And accepting. And because of so many other reasons that I can't even put into words." Adam took my hand in his as he spoke, maintaining our connection while returning his focus to my parents. "I've found that it's much easier to love people for who they really are instead of who you feel they *should* be."

*Hot damn! Take that, fuckers!*

I felt as if I had been drinking all night. My head was fuzzy, and Adam had somehow managed to become even more attractive than he already was. He had already saved me from my dinner disaster, and now he had come to my rescue again. Not only did he completely accept me for who I was, but I could count on him to defend me when other people didn't. And like that, it hit me. This was what had been missing with Adam: this feeling of complete acceptance that I'd always craved.

I kept my eyes fixed on him, unable to look away as my parents silently processed Adam's words.

My father finally spoke. "Thank you for your honesty, Adam. I respect that quality in a person. And I can see that you truly love my daughter," he said sincerely.

"I do" was all Adam said in return, letting his guard down a bit.

Gradually, the tension began to ease and the mood lightened. We relaxed as we realized that any residual awkwardness had finally evaporated. My parents still asked Adam about himself. But when he spoke of Eva, they didn't press him for information about her mother, though I knew they probably wanted to. Instead, they seemed to focus on the positive, and I could tell they really understood how much he cared for those he loved.

When we finished eating, Adam rose to clear the dishes. "Who's up for dessert?" he asked. "I'll admit, I bought it at the store on my way, so it isn't nearly as good as the home-cooked meal you just enjoyed, but it wouldn't be a birthday without a cake. Lynn, would you like to light the candles?"

♥

The second the door closed behind my parents, I plopped down on the couch, too exhausted to move. I had been dreading having Adam meet them. There was enough tension between my parents and me without the added component of a new boyfriend in the mix. But Adam had handled it with grace and dignity, effectively answering my father's probing questions while simultaneously putting him in his place.

Regardless of the fact that the night had ended on a high note, Adam knew that tonight had been both physically and emotionally draining on me, so he took a seat next to me on the sofa. I moved toward the edge of the couch as he leaned over to massage my shoulders. "You did well," he said. "You worry too much about what people think of you," he said softly. "Just relax and be yourself. Let people love you for you."

Then, tilting my head up to meet his, Adam took my tongue into his mouth, claiming me. He stroked the back of my head, letting his fingers tangle in my hair in a way that sent immediate goose bumps across my skin. I let myself melt into him and taste the sweetness on his hot lips.

My stomach tightened as he slid a hand down the front of my throat and chest before finally allowing his smooth fingers to graze my nipple with delicate desire. I was restless with a familiar ache between my thighs, and I felt the slippery anticipatory wetness as my muscles clenched inside me.

I clutched his neck, curling his messy hair around my fingers as he traced soft kisses down my skin to my collarbone. *God, I love that mouth.* My hands tugged his shirt up, searching for his sculpted chest and rigid core. He pulled away for a brief moment to remove his shirt, his emerald eyes blazing into me as he seated himself again.

I didn't dare look away from him. Holding his gaze, I rose to unzip my dress, and Adam watched it fall softly to my feet as I stood before him. "God, you're beautiful. I don't tell you that enough," he whispered against my stomach, caressing me with wet lips. He reached behind me to unclasp my lace bra and slide it off each shoulder delicately. "I mean, really beautiful."

His fingers dug into the flesh of my ass before he clenched my panties between his teeth and fingertips and slowly pulled them down. I stood posed: a naked, unyielding statue designed for his admiration. I wanted him to study me. To take in every inch of flesh, every imperfection as his eyes drank me in.

He hugged me against him, cradling me as he let me fall to my back against the plush cushions of the couch. His weight pressing against me was a welcome sensation, and I raked my fingers against his back and hard ass, willing him to take me. My only interruption was my own urgent searching for his belt and zipper.

"Speaking of beautiful," I said between labored breaths as he climbed off me to fully undress. I reciprocated his earlier examination and allowed myself the pleasure of gazing boldly at this perfectly built specimen standing before me. His sinewy biceps extended from broad shoulders. And his rigid chest narrowed toward his lean abdomen.

As my eyes worked their way down the definition of his abs, they focused on the length of his already slick cock. Reaching up, I tugged steadily at him, feeling his thickness grow between my fingers as they curled around him. He thrust forcefully toward me, allowing a groan to vibrate against his throat before escaping his lips.

I wrapped my mouth around him and pulled him deeper as my nails bore ardently into the stiff muscles of his ass. At this moment, towering over me with his hands twisting in my tousled hair, he possessed me completely. His moans were raw, raspy, and unfiltered until he reluctantly pulled away, his dick pulsating on the verge of climax.

Then he moved to kneel beside me, brushing his fingertips tenderly against my sensitive flesh. And my skin tingled in response. His every touch worshiped me with a reverence so honest. So generous. My hips flexed involuntarily toward him, silently willing him to give me what I craved.

"What do you want me to do?" he asked, stroking my nipple with the perfect amount of pressure.

I slid my tongue across my dry lips before answering. "I want to watch you put your fingers inside me." My legs fell open as a quiet invitation, and his thumb entered me. He kneaded my ass eagerly with his palm and fingers, pulling my pelvis up toward him while he pressed his thumb forcefully against the inside of me. The pressure of his thumb pushing toward the back of me and his hand surging me upward was an indescribable combination.

I writhed in response, my muscles straining from the pleasure. He parted my lips with his warm tongue and bit my own playfully. Then, tilting my head to the side, he nibbled at my ear and sucked hungrily at the top of my neck, sending soft chills down my skin.

I examined his hand pressing against me before he pulled out and left me wanting for a passing moment. His palm faced up now, and he slid his fingers deep inside me, twisting and massaging my insides while his thumb now worked expertly against my throbbing clit. He leaned in to bite delicately at my nipples, elongating them with his teeth.

"Please . . . oh, God . . . please, Adam. This feels incredible,"

I managed to exhale between shaky breaths. "I want you." I was so truthful, so exposed. Yet, for the first time with Adam, I felt anything but vulnerable.

He continued his seduction, bringing me closer to orgasm with each stroke of his fingers until he knew if he kept going, I'd lose complete control of my body. But as heavenly as that would feel, I wanted him inside me. I needed his body pressed against mine as he moved in and out of me with soft precision.

Adam pulled out of me, leaving his fingertips resting at the edge of my drenched opening for a moment before climbing onto me, his thickness invading me at last. I wrapped my quivering calves around his thighs, urging him deeper. I wasn't going to last long. With his powerful hands, he pinned my arms to the couch, leaving me prey to his provocative movements.

I couldn't wait any longer, and the intensity of the orgasm tore through me. He pumped into me faster, moaning his release, both of us shaking against the other. And for the first time with Adam, I did not censor myself. I let every deliciously vulgar phrase I could think of spill from my lips without concern for how he might perceive me.

That's when I finally realized that, for so long, my own self-worth had come from others' opinions of me. But with Adam it was different. He showed me that it was my opinion of myself that really mattered. So for the first time, I said the most truthful, uncensored sentence I had ever spoken to this man. "I love you," I breathed into him. "I really love you."

# chapter thirty-one

For the first time in months, my mind felt clear. The doubt and uncertainty I'd become so accustomed to had been replaced with a strong sense of commitment. Of course I felt commitment to Adam. But more importantly, I was finally committed to myself. I had told Adam I loved him, and for the first time, I didn't regret it. I didn't second-guess my decision. Love had found me, and I was never planning to let it go.

Saturday night had been the last time I'd seen Adam because he left to go to the shore for Eva's spring break the next morning. We had spoken a few times since he'd left, but with Eva there, it was easier to exchange texts.

Wednesday night I texted him just to let him know I was thinking of him.

> *Hope you're having a fun time at*
> *the shore! Just wanted to let you know*
> *I miss you. Xoxo.*

He responded almost instantly.

> *Are there any parts of me*
> *you miss specifically???*

Hmm, this could be interesting. I hadn't seen this side of Adam before, but I definitely wanted to fuck it.

> *I can think of a few . . . your*
> *mouth . . . your firm ass.*

*I miss your mouth and ass too.*
*Anything else?*

> *Well, there is one part of you that I can't*
> *seem to get enough of . . . Wait, should we*
> *be doing this? Is Eva around?*

I suddenly had to remind myself that he was on vacation with his daughter—who also happened to be one of my students.

*Eva's out on the deck. I'm in my room. I*
*can't call you in case she comes inside, but*
*keep texting . . . That part of me you can't*
*get enough of . . . it's pretty hard right now.*

I couldn't believe it. Adam Carter was sexting me. And it seemed like he was going to be pretty fucking good at it too. *Lily, you lucky bitch!* I locked my bedroom door and made myself comfortable on my bed.

> *You're turning me on too. I wish you*
> *could feel how wet I am for you already.*

Max may have been able to make me wet with his voice,

but Adam could apparently do it with just written words. Before he replied, I sent another text, no longer bashful with this man.

> *I wish I were there. My tongue would make you even harder.*

I couldn't stop myself from thinking of how tight the front of his jeans must feel with his erection pressed up against them. I wished I were there to unzip them and take him in my mouth. Then another text came through.

> *God, Lily. I wish you were with me too. Touch yourself and tell me how wet you are. Pretend I'm there.*

Jesus Christ! Where was this Adam before now?

If only he knew I was one step ahead of him. I had already slid my hand down to massage myself gently. Slowly. Pretending it was Adam's hand on me as I remembered how he worshiped me with his fingers Saturday night on my couch. I thought about how far we'd come since our first date, when I had wanted Adam so badly but couldn't do this while I thought of him. So much had changed. Adam was so sexual to me now.

> *God, Adam, my fingers are so slippery. I'm imagining they're yours moving against me.*

I wrote back. I wanted to know he was doing the same

thing and picturing me. I imagined him lying relaxed with a pillow against his headboard. One hand texting me and the other gripped tightly around himself, pulling steadily. I pressed my hand in soft circles over my clit for a few moments before sending another text.

> *You're not gonna make me*
> *do this alone, are you?*

*Oh, believe me. You're not doing this alone. And it feels even better when I touch myself, knowing you're doing the same thing.*

> *Pretend it's my hand stroking you...*
> *getting you closer with every pull.*

I pictured his hand increasing its speed until he couldn't wait any longer.

*Yes, Lily... you are getting me closer. I wish you could see me when I finish.*

That line pushed me over the edge, causing my body to clench tightly around my own fingers as I thought of Adam making himself come for me. When I was able to regain my composure, I texted him.

> *Wow, you just got me off from an hour*
> *and a half away. That's pretty impressive.*
> *I hope I have the same effect on you. Are*
> *you coming for me yet?*

*Yes! Lily. Oh, God. I wish my hand was*
*your mouth instead so you could lick off*
*all the evidence of my pleasure.*

The thought of Adam slick with come got me revved up again.

*Wow, Adam. I want you even more than*
*I did a few minutes ago, if that's even*
*possible. Can't wait till you're home!*

*I miss you too. I guess I didn't*
*say that earlier, lol.*

*I liked what you said better ; ) This was*
*definitely fun. Although, it looks like I*
*missed a perfectly good opportunity to try*
*out FaceTime on my iPad.*

*Haha, yes. FaceTime would have been*
*even better. p.s. Are you talking about*
*your teacher iPad? Isn't that for work use*
*only?*

I couldn't help but laugh out loud as I typed my next response.

*Lmao! Yes . . . but you are a parent of one*
*of my students. That counts, right?*

*Well played, lol. Have a good*
*night. Love you.*

*Love you too!*

❤

Adam wasn't the only one who texted me that week. I guess it was to be expected that I would receive a text or two from Max, especially after our night at the Flyers fundraiser. We had experienced a closeness that was not prompted by sex. It had meant something to him, and it had meant something to me as well. However, now my feelings for both men were different. Now I loved Adam, and my resolve was clearer than ever.

So when Max texted to see how my break was going, I just gave him short, to-the-point answers. And when he asked if I wanted to grab a drink on Thursday night, I simply told him I had other plans. I didn't want to be rude, but I couldn't lead him on either.

However, I'd be an idiot to think that I could avoid an encounter with Max forever. I would see him at work soon enough, and I was sure a conversation about what happened between us at my apartment was inevitable.

So when the Tuesday after Easter rolled around, I wasn't surprised to see Max appear in my doorway after first period. It had become our tradition. "Hey, doll," he said cheerily as he strolled confidently into my classroom, closing the door behind him. "I missed you over break. I was hoping we could have gotten together."

"Sorry," I replied sincerely, for more reasons than one. As I gazed into his honest sky-blue eyes, I couldn't help but feel bad for how I had treated Max without even realizing it. For so long my concern had been for my own feelings. And for Adam's. But never for Max's.

Max brushed his dark hair out of his face with his fingers.

He still looked beautiful in his casual attire: a dark-green Swift Hockey T-shirt and khaki cargo shorts, which hung low on his hips. "It's fine, Lil," he said with a grin that revealed dimples I somehow hadn't noticed until now. "We can make up for lost time. What do you say we head out to the announcer's booth? Old time's sake?" he asked with a sly tilt of his head as he plopped himself down on the edge of my desk to face me.

I took in the sight of him from my chair. He leaned with one hand comfortably on my desk as he sat, legs open and relaxed. I was surprised at my ability to sit directly in front of his waist, knowing what awaited me under those shorts, and still resist him—especially after I hadn't had sex in over a week. That realization only served to further confirm my commitment to Adam.

I looked up at him as he sat powerfully above me, awaiting my answer. "Max, I can't."

"I know you're probably busy the day after break and all, but I have a feeling I can convince you," he said with that seductive rasp in his voice as he rose to stand behind me. Before I could find the right words to reply, he bent down, sweeping my hair away from my neck and planting soft kisses across my skin.

"Max, don't!" I immediately felt remorse for how direct, how harsh I sounded as I pulled away.

"What's wrong? After the fundraiser, you wanted this. What did I do?" he asked, concern in his voice. He moved to the side to face me, his eyes apologizing for something he hadn't even done. That only made what I was about to tell him more difficult.

"Nothing, Max. I'm sorry. You didn't do anything wrong." I chose my words and tone carefully this time. "My feelings have changed. *I've* changed."

He looked at me curiously, unsure of what I was trying to say. "Your feelings about who? About me? About Adam?"

"It's hard to explain, Max. I love you as a friend, but we can never be more. I told you before that I didn't love Adam." I averted my eyes toward the floor, unable to hold eye contact with him. "That was true when I said it, but something changed last weekend. I'm in love with him now." I closed my eyes for a second, ashamed of how indecisive I must have sounded. "We can't do this."

He remained silent for a few seconds. When I sensed his disappointment, I forced myself to look up.

His face had dropped, and he looked genuinely confused. I could see him attempting to mask his sadness with anger. "You're serious?" His voice was loud, harsh. "Jesus, Lily. Make up your fucking mind already."

"I have," I said quietly.

He shook his head, and I watched him turn and move quickly toward the door.

Pausing briefly with his hand on the doorknob, he seemed as though he had something more to say but was deciding whether he should. "Yeah? Well you're making the wrong fucking choice," he said sternly. Without turning around, he reached into his pocket, pulled out a small wrapped box, and placed it gently onto the student desk closest to the door. "Happy birthday," he said sadly. His last words mingled with the slamming of the door after he left.

I sat, unmoving, for a few minutes before standing to get the gift Max had left. I returned to my chair, knowing I'd probably want to be sitting as I unwrapped it. The red paper was covered in airplanes, and I couldn't help but let out a subtle laugh, despite my mood. Inside the box was a note.

*We look good together. Wish I could see you every morning like this. Happy birthday, doll.*

*Love, Max*

I lifted the soft white cotton from the jewelry box to remove a silver locket. The chain was solid: the type that wouldn't get tangled, no matter how much it moved on itself. I knew it had probably been an extra purchase, and the thoughtful touch was not lost on me. I ran my fingers along the intricately engraved metal before opening the clasp. Inside was a picture I didn't know Max had even taken. It must have been the morning after the fundraiser. I was asleep in my bed, my head resting peacefully on Max's shoulder as he was stretching his other arm up to snap the picture. His grin was wide. He looked happier than I ever remember seeing him as he held me safely in his arm.

Collapsing my head into my hands, I felt my eyes well instantly. But I wasn't the one who had the right to be crying. I had hurt Max. Not the other way around. Until now, Max had seemed this solid, unstoppable force. A stone wall incapable of breaking. But somehow, with little more than a sentence, I had managed to crush him. I couldn't help but think back to the fundraiser, when Max had displayed such a grand gesture to assure me that I was a good person. He'd been wrong.

# chapter thirty-two

The rest of the day passed with a slowness that should only be experienced by tortoises and snails. There was something tragic in finding out that, despite having one of the best things in the world happen to you, it was still tainted. Adam loved me. I loved Adam. But that love wasn't built of rainbows and butterflies like it was supposed to be. It was built from dark clouds and grisly shadows. And I had no one to blame but myself.

Not only was I to blame for our relationship resting on a craggy foundation, mortared with half truths and dishonest actions, but I had also devastated Max. I had led him on, strung him along, and then left him hanging. *I was such a fucking bitch.*

But I couldn't fix things with Max. Our relationship would never be what he wanted it to be. And I felt that, on the whole, I had been honest with him about it. With the exception of the fundraiser—*that fucking fundraiser*—and that brief incident in his car after dinner with his parents, I had always told him that he wasn't my choice. But I *had* given mixed messages, and I was surely going to burn in hell for it. Actually, I welcomed hell. It was currently preferable to my reality.

Though, that wasn't entirely true. I had Adam. The one bright spot in my murky life. And despite the fact that I ultimately didn't deserve him, I sure as fuck wasn't going to tell him that. Everything would be okay as long as I had him. I just knew it.

As I drove home, I willed my eyes to pay attention to the road while my mind focused on other things. I should have felt relieved. I had finally resisted Max, told him that our sexual relationship was over, and what's more, I had actually meant it this time. This freed me up to give myself a hundred percent to Adam. But I wasn't relieved. What I was, was fundamentally unhappy.

And I stayed that way for the rest of the evening. I put on a chipper facade when I talked with Adam on the phone, discussing how our days were—I was a little less than truthful during that part of the conversation—and when I could see him.

"Tomorrow night?" he suggested. "Eva has dance class from six to nine because they're preparing for a recital, which is going to be ungodly. I really wish she would show interest in an activity that required more clothing. Anyway, I can pick up some takeout and we can relax at your place."

"Sounds perfect," I said as I closed my eyes. The image of Adam lazing on my couch was delicious and instantly brightened my mood.

"Good. See you then, babe."

"See you then." I smiled into the phone.

I hung up, thankful to Adam for putting me in the best mood I had been in all day.

❤

I woke up late on Wednesday morning, still groggy from a night of restless sleep and bad dreams. The most vivid dream I could recall was one in which I was a snake and I swallowed the head of a lion whole. Now that was some fucked-up shit.

I eyed the coffeehouse, but as I drove past it, my mouth turned into a pout. I had run out of coffee at home, and stopping was out of the question. I would have been obnoxiously late for work if I had, even by *my* standards. I pulled my car into my parking space in the Swift faculty lot and power walked to the entrance of the building, my head bent as I tried to find my work keys in my purse.

I raised my head just in time to see Adam's Yukon parked in front of the building. A smile developed as I scampered to the open driver's-side window.

"Well, aren't you a sight for sore eyes?" I said flirtily.

"I could say the same about you, beautiful. Here, I got you this." He passed me a cup of coffee through the window. "I stopped on my way and thought you might like one."

*God, how I loved this man.* "You are a truly amazing human being. I ran out of coffee this morning, and I didn't have time to stop. Clearly," I said as I looked down at my watch. "I better get going. But I'm still seeing your sweet ass tonight, right?" I asked with a sly smile.

"Count on it," he said gruffly, his voice deep with desire.

"Great. Have a good day. Build stuff," I said as I straightened and turned toward the school. But as my head swiveled toward the building entrance, I halted abruptly. *I guess I'm not the only one running late today.* Max was walking toward the front doors, anger showing in his eyes before he looked away from me dismissively.

"You okay?" Adam asked, leaning slightly out the window.

"Yeah," I said, recovering quickly. "I just wanted to wait

until he went inside."

"Why?" Adam asked in a concerned voice.

"So I could do this," I replied as I leaned up into the window, meeting Adam's soft lips.

I quickly straightened and left Adam smiling broadly in his car as I made my way into school. I hoped that I wouldn't see Max in the main office as I signed in, and thankfully, I didn't. Wherever he had gone, he had gone there fast. I silently prayed that things wouldn't always remain this way between Max and me. I still wanted his friendship, but I wasn't sure he would be able to give it. And I couldn't blame him. As I hurried down the hallway to my classroom, I tried to push my problems with Max from my mind. And when I walked into my room and my gaze locked on Eva, I managed to find more positive things to think about.

❤

By the time fifth period arrived, I was starving. I grabbed my bottle of water and headed down to see what disgusting muck they were serving for lunch today. When I arrived at the faculty lunchroom, I was relieved to see that Max wasn't present.

Even though I didn't want him to feel like he needed to change his routine because of me, I really wasn't up for dealing with him right now. My day had been going pretty well, I was going to see Adam later, and I didn't want to ruin all of that with high school drama. Well, maybe not *high school* drama. I didn't remember anyone in my high school fucking a random guy in an airport and then pursuing some wild sexcapades with him while also banging the boy who would've probably been voted "most likely to succeed" by his peers. No, this was definitely Lily drama.

Our lunch bunch played Jeopardy and gossiped tirelessly about the other teachers in the building. With about ten minutes left in the period, I stood and dumped my trash, telling the others that I needed to head up early and prep some things for my next class. As I walked down the hall to my classroom, I was stopped by one of our guidance counselors, who wanted to discuss one of my students with me. As we talked, I felt a shadow fall over my right shoulder. I turned to see Max standing beside me.

"Hey, Lily, can we talk a minute?" he asked.

"Not right now, Max. I'm in the middle of something." My voice sounded more annoyed than I meant for it to. I really could not have cared less about his interrupting this conversation. But I also didn't want to give him mixed signals about our relationship. And the only way I knew how to do that was to avoid him like the plague until this awkward tension passed. Though, I wasn't sure it ever could pass if I kept refusing to talk to him. *Oh, Jesus Christ, what was this chick saying?*

"Okay, well, I guess let me know if the call home doesn't work," the counselor said.

*Wait, had I said I was calling home?* "Will do. Have a good one," I replied.

I turned to my left and continued walking toward my classroom. But I was suddenly stopped short by a large, firm hand on my bicep.

"Wait, where are you going? I need to talk to you." Max's voice was exasperated.

"Max, I really don't think this is the time or place for us to talk," I sighed, eyeing my surroundings for people who may be able to hear our conversation.

"Fine, then, let's go out after work. I have some things I want to say."

"I can't. I have plans," I explained.

"With him?" I felt Max's anger build, could almost hear it rumble just beneath his skin.

"Yes, Max, with him." I said this flippantly, trying to end this conversation as quickly as possible.

"Whatever," Max grumbled as he turned on his heels and stormed off in the opposite direction.

Regret and sadness washed over me again as I watched him turn the corner and disappear from sight. I didn't know why I kept being such a bitch to Max. He hadn't done anything to deserve it. But I just didn't know how to be normal with him after everything that had transpired between us. Dread filled me as I realized that Max and I were probably not going to be friends after all of this.

# chapter thirty-three

Excitement began to fight its way into my body as the day drew to a close and my mini-date with Adam approached. When I got home, I quickly straightened up before jumping in the shower. Then I returned to my room, pulled on a pair of jeans that hugged my ass perfectly and a low-cut tank top that showed off the girls.

At five, I heard Amanda come home.

"Hey," I said as I walked into the kitchen, where she was grabbing a beer from the fridge.

"Hey," she replied as she chugged half of the beer.

"Rough day?" I asked with a smirk.

"What tipped you off?" she replied curtly as she finished off her beer. "I'm going to get changed and then head back to the office. My boss dumped this huge account on my desk this afternoon and said he wanted a list of all their assets from the past five years by tomorrow. He's such a fucking asshole. I'll see ya." Amanda stalked heavily from the room.

I felt bad for her. As fucked up as her moral compass could be, she was fucking brilliant and could definitely find employment with an accounting firm that valued the great work she did. She was really selling herself short.

I looked around for something to keep me occupied for

the next hour. Nothing jumped out at me, so I decided to pick up the phone and call my parents. On my birthday, I'd vowed to keep in better touch with them. It had meant a lot to me that they had come all the way out here for me, and I wanted to keep our relationship on an upswing.

My mom answered after the second ring.

"Hi, Mom."

"Oh, Lily, how are you doing, darling?"

"I'm doing well. How are you guys?"

"We're doing well, doing very well. Howard," my mom yelled for my dad, "pick up the other phone. It's Lily."

"Who?" I heard my father bellow.

"Lily. Just pick up the phone." She directed her attention back to me. "I swear, this man's going to drive me insane. So, what's new? Anything?"

"No, nothing really. I . . ."

"Hello?" my dad said loudly into the receiver.

"Hi, Dad."

"Lily, good to hear from you. What have you been up to?"

"I was just telling Mom, I haven't really been up to much. We just finished spring break, so now it's the home stretch until summer. What have you guys been doing?"

"Oh, nothing," my dad said absentmindedly, clearly wanting to discuss something else. "So, how's that fella of yours? Adam?"

"He's such a nice man, Lily. I'm so happy you found him," my mom interjected.

"Yeah, that one's a real keeper. You hang on to him. Listen to your old man. I know what I'm talking about. Some of the characters I see . . . you wouldn't even believe me if I told you. No, sir, you have a real good man there. He'll treat you the way you should be treated," my dad lectured.

"And what way is that, exactly?" I couldn't help but ask this question. My relationship with my parents had been so strained. I wanted to see how far we'd actually come.

"Why, like a princess, of course. That's what you are. My princess."

My dad's words brought stinging tears to my eyes. It had been years since he had called me his princess. And as they raved on about Adam, it made me supremely happy to know that they actually thought I deserved him. As our conversation came to a close, I promised to call them next week. I hung up, feeling happy.

Finally, there was a knock on my door around six fifteen. I pulled it open and was met with Adam's bright smile.

"Hey, handsome," I said as I grinned like a lovesick teenager. He wore gray sweatpants and a blue, Nike, long-sleeved T-shirt. Even dressed casually, this man oozed sex appeal.

"Hey, beautiful." He held up two bags of takeout. "Panera."

"Awesome," I replied as I stepped back from the door to allow Adam to enter.

He leaned in to give me a quick kiss before he walked through my living room and into my kitchen, plopping the bags down on the counter and moving toward the cupboards where I kept the paper plates. As I watched him move about my kitchen, knowing the location of every item he needed, I smiled, feeling totally turned on by how well he knew everything about me.

"Where are we eating?" he asked.

"Living room? We could watch a movie or something."

"Good call." Adam began piling items to carry to the living

room. I stepped in to grab the food bags as he carefully carried everything else and set it down on my coffee table. "What movie?"

"Uh, I don't know." I grabbed the remote and began scrolling through the guide.

"Ha, that one! We've gotta watch that one." Adam laughed loudly.

I knew exactly which one had caught his interest. *Bad Teacher.* I grinned at him sardonically as I clicked the OK button on the remote.

"You think you're a real riot, don't you?" I said as I sat down beside him and began reaching for food.

"I have my moments," he replied as he took a bite of his sandwich.

We ate quickly and quietly. Once we finished, I cleaned up our trash, and then we both settled into each other on the couch, his back against the arm of the couch and me nestled in front of him. I was amazed at how well my body fit into his, all of my curves finding their exact symmetrical place against this man's body. As if our bodies were really intended to be one.

"So, this is what you do all day. I want my tax money back," Adam joked in reference to the movie as he hugged me tighter.

"Hell, no. I need that money to support myself while I pursue my real career."

"And what would that be?"

"I'm going to write books that you can read for your book club."

"Are you now?" Adam moved slightly as he said this so that he could look at me, our faces inches apart. "What kind of books?" His tone had dropped a few decibels.

I felt his erection beneath me. My skin prickled and my

abdomen throbbed with expectation. I shifted slightly, causing my clit to rub against the seam of my jeans. Pleasure shot through me but was quickly replaced with the need for more.

"Erotic books," I replied, my voice deep and seductive.

Adam moved in one deft movement, wrapping himself around me so that now he hovered above me as I lay flat against the couch. "Oh, yeah? What are you going to draw inspiration from?"

I reached down with my hand and tucked it into Adam's sweatpants and beneath the elastic band of his boxer briefs. "I think this will give me all the inspiration I need," I whispered as I began to stroke him slowly. I briefly thought back to how he had pushed my hand away when I had tried to feel his length in the theater. I never imagined that I would be comfortable touching him again after that night. But I was. I touched Adam freely because I knew that he was mine to lick, and stroke, and do anything else that my heart desired. And I was his.

He groaned against my neck as I worked my hand up and down his shaft. He reached down with one hand and pushed his pants and boxers off as he bore his weight with the other arm. Then he moved to my jeans, undoing the button and slowly lowering the zipper before rolling off me so that he was kneeling beside the couch.

My hand felt cold at the loss of the pulsing warmth his cock had provided. He pulled my jeans down with both hands before his right reached behind him and pushed my coffee table away from us. He then urged me up to sit as he slowly traced his fingers along the smooth skin of my stomach, inching my shirt up as they moved. When my shirt was just below my breasts, he stopped and leaned in to kiss my navel.

I leaned back, giving him greater access. His kisses

trailed softly up my abdomen as his hands pushed my shirt up to my neck, revealing the see-through black lace bra I wore underneath. His breath caught as he saw my swollen breasts and taut nipples straining against the material. I caught the rest of my shirt and pulled it over my head as his tongue flicked at my nipples through the flimsy material.

He reached behind me and unclasped my bra, though it didn't fall. Instead, he slowly, one at a time, pulled the straps from my shoulders. I then let it fall to my lap, coming to rest atop the panties that matched it. He urgently pulled his shirt over his head, revealing his sinewy biceps, his flat, hard stomach, his smooth chest. He pulled me forward so that I sat straight up as he gently separated my legs so he could fit between them. He ran kisses all along my collarbone as he guided my legs around his hips, urging them to latch behind him. Then he lifted me effortlessly and lowered me to the floor. He snatched my bra from where it had fallen on my stomach before pulling my panties off.

Sitting back on his heels between my legs, he took his hard length in his hand and began massaging my swollen clit with it.

"I've thought about this all day," he whispered in a deep growl. "Ever since I saw you this morning, I've gotten hard just thinking about what I was going to do to you tonight."

I moaned at his words. I needed him to fill me. The stimulation of my clit wasn't enough. I needed all of Adam. I needed it now.

"Oh, Adam, I want you so badly," I groaned as my head rolled from side to side in this sexual bliss.

"I know you do, baby. I can feel how bad you want me. You're so wet. You feel so good."

"Please, Adam, please. Take me."

At my words, he pushed inside me, causing all of my nerve endings to shoot pleasure throughout my body. He stayed kneeling and placed the palm of his right hand onto my pelvis so his fingers could swirl euphorically around my clit. He applied gentle pressure downward with his palm so that the slight curve of his cock hit my G-spot with every thrust.

The pleasure was nearly unbearable. My hands flung out, searching for something to latch on to as an anchor, to hold me in this place of brutal ecstasy, but found nothing. Adam's free hand found my breast and circled my nipples, causing me to arch my back in bliss. This allowed him to palm a heavy breast in his large, rugged hand as his thumb stimulated my nipple.

For a moment, I felt guilty. Guilty because he couldn't possibly be feeling as sexually stimulated as I was. I wished that I could give him more, but he was spending my body in every way, leaving me with nothing more to give than my deep, passion-filled moans that reverberated low in my chest with every hard thrust of his cock. Every speck of my body was tensing in anticipation of the release that was building in my pelvis.

"I can't wait any longer. I'm going to come, Adam."

"Yeah, baby, come all over me. I want to feel you pulse around me. Let go for me. Let go."

His words sent me reeling. My body spasmed in response as he finally dropped his hands to either side of me and rested his weight on them as he pumped wildly into me. I cried out, unable to hold that much pleasure inside my body. Finally, he slowed, uttering out only a soft, "Lily," and my body relaxed. He put his right forearm onto the floor beside me and tilted my head toward him with his left. His lips enveloped mine in a passionate kiss that was slow but deep.

I didn't know how long we lay there, but it wasn't long enough. It would have never been long enough. When his lips finally left mine, they felt sore and swollen. He lowered his head and nipped at my ear.

"I love you so much," he whispered.

I brought my arms up and wrapped them around his neck. "I love you too, baby." I exhaled deeply, "I don't deserve you."

♥

We still had an hour before Adam needed to pick up Eva, so we decided to take a quick shower. I was sad to wash away the evidence of the fantastic lovemaking we had just had, but at least I got to see him naked a little while longer.

As he stepped into the steaming hot shower behind me, I turned to face him. And as I drank in his perfect form, I decided that it was time to return the favor. He had made love to me in a way that was clearly intended to please me first and foremost. Now, I was going to do the same for him.

I grabbed my loofah and poured my vanilla-scented soap onto it. Then I dragged it along his chest, leaving a thin film of white bubbles in its wake. I moved the sponge and my hand over his chest, spreading the soap. I worked it over his shoulders and then back down to his stomach. My eyes followed my hands on their journey until the sponge reached the crest of his hips. I stole a look up at him, and his eyes caught mine. His green eyes were blazing, and he held my gaze as my hands thoroughly cleaned the skin between his hips.

I finally pulled my eyes away and looked down to see if my hands had caused the desired effect. They had. His cock bulged again. I dropped the loofah and took him in my hand once more. The combination of soap and water allowed me to stroke him without any friction or resistance. I looked back up at him and brought my lips to his. I nipped at his bottom lip before pushing my tongue into his mouth, letting him know that I was going to do the taking this time.

"God, I've never gotten so hard this quickly after sex before," he murmured between kisses.

I smiled, taking pride in knowing that I turned him on so much. I pulled away from him and half turned, never taking my right hand from his cock but reaching with my left to turn the showerhead so that it pointed against the wall. Then I dropped to my knees in the tub, taking him into my mouth.

He released a guttural sound as he placed a hand against the shower wall for added support. This sound only prompted me to move my mouth faster, suck harder, and twist my hand around him tighter. My right stayed at the base of his cock, pulling gently to cover the area my mouth couldn't.

I pulled my mouth back so that my tongue could work the head as his hands tousled in my hair, applying a slight pressure that caused me to take all of him into my mouth again. My lips slid over him as my tongue worked to stimulate his cock.

"Oh, I'm gonna come. Oh, fuck." He gently tugged on my hair, trying to pull me back before he ejaculated.

But I would not pull back. I continued to suck him, wanting to feel the salty taste of his semen running down my throat. And as his cock pulsed and began to shoot come, I continued to milk him, drinking every drop that he expelled.

After he emptied into me, he pulled me to my feet and brought his body into mine, forcing me against the tiled wall that was warm thanks to the water spraying against it. He kissed me deeply again, taking back the control that I had briefly taken from him.

"Mmm, you feel so good," he breathed in between kisses. "I wish I could have my way with you all night."

"God, me too," I replied as I drew my arms around his neck. As his kisses quickened and began to spread to my neck, I thought that maybe we were about to have a round three. But as I rocked my body into his, I felt his cock only semi-erect. I felt a slight pang of disappointment until realization spread through me: I had fucked this man too well for him to be able to go a third time.

We finally pulled ourselves apart long enough to leave the shower. We wrapped ourselves in towels and then made our way out into the living room to retrieve our clothes.

Adam took my hands and gave them a simple tug that told me he wanted me to sit on the couch. So, I did. I sat there in my towel as he gathered his clothes and began to dress.

I glanced at the clock on my wall. Eight thirty-five. Sadness filled me. Adam would have to leave soon to get Eva by nine. But as he pulled his shirt over his head, he sat back down on the couch beside me. He then reached over and opened my towel, letting it drop so that my naked body was revealed. He moved closer to me and began running his fingers all over me.

"We're going to need a vacation soon so that I can touch you like this for an entire weekend," Adam said as his eyes roamed over my body. "Being away from you last week was torture. I need to make up for lost time. Thank God the studio is only five minutes away, because I plan to have my hands on you until I positively have to stop." He pushed me back gently and pulled my left leg up onto the couch. Then, he ran his finger against my clit and along the path that led to my slick opening. He thrust two fingers inside as his other hand drifted back and forth from my clit to my breasts.

My breathing quickened as his hands worked magic all over my body. Finally, as he dangled me precariously close to the edge, he thrust a third finger inside of me. And as all three swirled deliciously, he connected with my G-spot and flung me over the edge. I clenched around him as my body quaked in delicious release. As my orgasm ended, Adam withdrew his fingers but continued caressing my breasts until the clock told him it was time to leave.

I walked him toward the door, an emptiness already starting to form at the thought of being without him. He pulled the door open and then turned back to me, pulling me to him, our arms wrapping around each other.

"What's wrong?" he asked, noticing a change in my demeanor.

I hugged him tighter. "I hate that you have to go," I admitted.

"I know, beautiful, I hate it too." His hands began to circle my back as we stared into each other's eyes for a moment.

"All right, well, I guess I gotta let you go," I sighed as I started to withdraw my arms.

But he tightened his grip and brought his face close to mine. "You'll never have to let me go," he said softly. Then, he kissed me one last, wonderful time before he pulled away. "I'll call you tomorrow." He walked away from my apartment, descended the stairs, and was gone.

# chapter thirty-four

My sleep was deeper and more restful after my night with Adam. Everything was as it should be. As much as I hated to think this way, having Max out of the way would allow me to be the girlfriend Adam deserved. And this thought gave way to hope. Hope that our relationship would work out. That I could become a person worthy of such a great man.

I woke up rejuvenated and positive. And this mood carried me throughout the day, adding some much-needed pep to my step. I couldn't wait to talk to Adam, to see him again. Such thoughts consumed my day.

So when the final bell rang and I heard one of my students say, "Hi, Mr. Carter" as they all filed from my room, I nearly jumped out of my skin with excitement. I actually had to do a double take, his presence not registering the first time. He had never visited me at school before. *God, he must have really missed me.*

But as I analyzed him, my excitement dissipated. Instead of jumping out of my chair and running to him, I reclined farther back, grabbing the armrests of my chair as if bracing myself for impact. It quickly became clear that he wasn't here to resume our activities of the previous night. Only one thing could cause the look that Adam wore.

I sat there, not saying a word, instead just eyeing him cautiously, tears already starting to form in the corners of my eyes. He stood stoic, observing me with a cold, detached stare I had only seen once before: at the hockey game. This was wrong. All wrong.

He finally moved, approaching me slowly, as if it took everything he had in him to get any closer to me. A sick feeling took hold of my stomach as I realized that he didn't want to be anywhere near me. His eyes surveyed me as if they were truly seeing me for the first time. I wondered if how he saw me could be any worse than how I saw myself in this moment.

He reached my desk, and my eyes flickered to his hand, sensing movement. He had something in his palm, and he brought it toward me. He slid it to me across my desk, clearly not wanting to risk touching me. His phone.

"You want to explain that?" he asked, his voice even.

I looked down at it. My breath instantly caught in my throat. *How the hell had he gotten that?* Of course, I knew how. *Why* was the more pertinent question. But then, I knew that answer, too.

I closed my eyes, trying to will back the tears and collect myself before I responded. But when I opened them again, I was confronted with the same image. There, on Adam's phone, was the picture of Max and me in my bed the morning after the fundraiser. The same one Max had put in the locket he gave me.

I didn't know how to come back from this. There were no words that could undo what he now knew. And even if I told the truth: that nothing sexual had happened and that I hadn't even realized that Max was in bed with me when he took it, it wouldn't matter now. Funny how when you'd told nothing but lies for months, it was the truth that seemed the most unbelievable.

"Adam, I... I don't know what to say," I sighed. I looked up at him, into his bright-green eyes that always told me everything I needed to know. And what I found there made me hang my head in shame.

"How about you try the truth?" he growled, low and commanding.

"I don't know that you'll believe the truth," I said simply, honestly.

He scoffed, "You're probably right. It's hard to believe the truth from such a manipulator."

I winced. Was that what I was? A manipulator? I had lied to him. But I had done it because I was selfish. That, I could own. But a manipulator? The name didn't sit right.

"I don't think I'm manipulative, Adam," I started quietly, "I haven't been completely honest, and I've omitted truth in order to protect myself and my relationship with you. I've made stupid mistakes because I've been too blind and too wrapped up in my own needs that I couldn't see what was right in front of me. And even though I see it now, I know that it doesn't undo my misdeeds. And all of that may make me selfish and arrogant and impulsive. But I don't think that I am, by nature, a manipulator. I actually think that I'm capable of such brutal honesty and complete transparency it would amaze you."

I don't know why this point was so important to me. Maybe it was because I was finally realizing that underneath all of the slime and dirt I had covered myself in, there still did live a good person. And I wasn't going to wear a title that I hadn't earned. Not even for this beautiful man in front of me, who I still wanted desperately.

Adam stood there, his hands by his sides, his face expressionless.

*Okay, maybe my tirade had been ill-timed.* "Adam, please, please hear me out. I love you. That's the—"

"You love me?" He looked ready to explode. "You love me? Are you fucking kidding? You clearly don't know jack shit about love or how to properly show it. This"—he gestured to the phone—"this is supposed to be you loving me? This makes me sick. *You* make me sick." He snatched his phone from my desk and started toward the door.

I couldn't let him leave. I had to say or do something.

But I couldn't. I felt rooted to my chair, bound by some inexplicable force. So instead, I stayed seated, offering so little fight it was pathetic. "Adam, I swear it's over."

"You're right," he replied gruffly. "It is."

With that, he left, stalking out of my room and very possibly out of my life. And what had I done to stop him? Nothing. I guess I could add coward to my list of descriptors.

I plopped my head down onto my arms, which were resting on my desk. And misery settled over me. Just as I was about to work myself up into the kind of sobs that shake your whole body, Tina popped her head into my door.

"Yo, Lil, did . . . holy shit, are you okay?"

I motioned around me with my hands and then shrugged, unable to form coherent words.

"Did you and Adam Carter just have a huge fight over Max?"

"Yeah," I finally choked out. "How'd you know?" I asked, though I was sure my red, swollen eyes were probably a pretty good indicator.

"Because I was just outside for bus duty, and I saw Adam

walk calmly up to Max and punch him right in the face."

And I was proven wrong once again. I didn't have to welcome hell. I was already there.

# chapter thirty-five

"Wait, what? Back up." How could that have even happened? What were the chances that these two men, whom I so successfully kept away from one another for so long, found this moment to collide?

Tina relaxed a bit, contemplating her words carefully. "I was standing in front of the building when I saw Max get out of his car. My eyes locked on him immediately, for obvious reasons." I could tell she realized the inappropriateness of her last few words. "I'm sorry. I didn't mean..."

"It's fine. Just tell me what happened."

"So anyway, I watched Max walk toward the front door, and as I turned my head, I saw Adam leaving the building. I could tell he was already angry. His face was red, and he was in a hurry." Tina paused to see how I was responding to the story. I tried to remain calm, and she continued. "Then he saw Max. Adam snapped. He walked straight toward Max without saying a word and decked him. Max dropped to the pavement. He didn't even see it coming."

"Oh my God!" I remembered the times that Adam had mentioned fighting Max for me. I couldn't believe he had actually done it.

"I know. It was totally hot."

I shook my head, still in disbelief. "What did Max do?"

She tempered her excitement. "Absolutely nothing. He just stayed on the sidewalk holding his face as he watched Adam get into his car and leave."

Max didn't even retaliate. He had finally shown some sort of restraint. *Too little, too late.*

"Adam would obviously know what Max looks like, but do you think Max knew it was Adam who punched him?"

"I'm pretty sure he knows it was Adam who hit him. It wouldn't be too difficult to figure out. He deserved it." I took the locket from my desk and held it open for Tina's inspection. "Max gave me this after I ended things with him for good a few days ago. My friendship with Max has been strained since, to say the least. When he realized he'd lost me for good, he sent this picture to Adam. He took it like two weeks ago the morning after I went to a Flyers fundraiser with him. I didn't even know he'd taken it until he gave it to me in the locket."

"Did you sleep with him that night?"

"No, but I would have. We had a connection that went beyond something sexual. But we were both drinking. Max actually said he wouldn't sleep with me because he wanted to be my sober choice, not a drunken mistake." I shook my head as I played back my mixed signals in my mind. "I realized I loved Adam two nights later. Max came into my room Tuesday to pick up where we left off after the fundraiser. I broke him. I saw it in his eyes when he left." I could feel myself grow angrier. "But we're not in kindergarten. You don't sabotage somebody just because they don't want to be your friend anymore. He needs to grow the fuck up."

"Well, I'm sure Max is pretty embarrassed about the whole thing. It sounds like he put himself out there, and you rejected him. Then Adam knocked him to the ground in front of students, parents, and teachers."

I couldn't believe Tina was actually feeling sorry for that manipulative asshole right now. "What he did was dishonest, and he did it intentionally to ruin my relationship with Adam. Not to *start* a relationship with me. If he's trying to show me he cares, he went about it completely the wrong way. No matter how badly he felt, there's no excuse for what he did. He had no right to do that." As I thought about what he'd done, I could feel my guilt for how I had treated Max quickly getting replaced by anger when I realized he hadn't sent the picture impulsively. He had thought about it for days.

Tina eyed me curiously, waiting for me to continue. When I didn't, she broke the silence. "What about Adam? What are you going to say to him?"

My eyes grew puffy with tears I was trying to hold in. "He won't even talk to me. He's so mad."

She could see how spent I was. "You have to try. You can't just let him walk away. Look, Max fought to get you. Granted, he went about it the wrong way, but he still *fought*. And Adam fought for you too." She looked at me to make sure I was listening to her next words as she handed me a tissue. "Now it's *your* turn to fight."

# chapter thirty-six

When I left the school building, I noticed that Max's truck was gone. I hoped that he had gone directly home, because that's where I was headed. As I pulled into his driveway, my anger had grown exponentially. By the time I knocked on his door, I was ready to rip his head off.

But when he opened the door, I thawed a bit. He looked terrible. He was shirtless, and his ribs showed a scrape from where he'd hit the sidewalk. His cheekbone wore a fresh, red bruise. I was almost at the point of feeling slightly bad for him, when he smiled at me.

"Can I come in?" I asked coldly.

"Sure thing, doll," he replied as he stepped back from the door to let me enter.

I cringed at his calling me "doll." I used to enjoy the nickname, take pride in it even. *What a difference a day can make.* "Don't call me 'doll,' Max."

The tone of my voice effectively removed the smile from his lips. He cleared his throat, closed the door, and then turned toward me, stuffing his hands in his pockets.

I took a step toward him, my rage renewed, "You are the biggest fucking asshole I have ever met. What would ever possess you to send that picture to Adam? How did you even get his number? Are you completely insane?"

"Which question do you want me to answer first?" he asked, trying to restore camaraderie that no longer existed between us.

I just glared at him. I was completely over him in this moment. This bastard had ruined my life and now had the gall to make light of it. Any endearing qualities I had ever seen in Max had disappeared. I now saw why teams didn't want him. This was Max. And he was ugly.

"I work at the school too. It's not hard to get a phone number. I don't know why you're so upset," he started sincerely. "I did you a favor."

I shook my head as if I had misheard him. A favor! He was certifiable. "What?" I yelled.

"He's not right for you, Lily." Max shifted his weight, squaring himself up for what he would say next. "I get that he looks good on paper, but not for the long haul. A relationship built on a lie will never last. Besides, he doesn't get you the way I do. You can't be yourself with him."

I was seething. "How do you know how I am with him? You know nothing about us."

"Right," he replied, laughing sarcastically, "because people always lie and withhold things from people they can be themselves with. You're delusional."

"Fuck you, Max." My emotions were chaotic, but my voice was calm. I wanted him to hear me, to know that I meant what I was saying. "When did I ever intimate that I would ever be in a relationship with you? When? After the fundraiser? When I was drunk?" I was being cruel, and I didn't care. How dare this prick act like he did this for me? It's never been about me. He was only capable of caring about himself. "You said you wanted to be my sober choice. Well, this is me sober. And I don't choose you."

I watched Max's face drop as I spoke, every word hitting him like a Mack truck. But I wasn't done. "I know that I've done some horrible things since I've known you, but that doesn't make us the same. My actions were horrible, but your horribleness stems from your very core. It's who you are."

I extinguished the final bit of air that was in my lungs. I hadn't thought it possible for us to ever get to this point. But here we were, looking at each other with a detachment that was characteristic of complete strangers.

When it became clear that he had no response, I pushed past him and opened the door.

That was when he found his voice. "You never gave me a chance, you know? To be what he is to you. I could've been that. For you, I could've been anything."

I wavered slightly but caught myself. He did this every time. Sucked me back in when I had finally firmed my resolve. It wouldn't happen this time. I reached into my purse and pulled out the box with the locket inside. I set it down on a table next to his front door.

"Goodbye, Max" was all I uttered as I left, pulling the door closed behind me.

# chapter thirty-seven

Tina had told me to fight. But for so long, I fought to keep these two men apart. I had fought to resist Max. I had fought to try to love Adam. And I had even fought to try to love myself. When I arrived at home that afternoon, I felt as if I didn't have any fight left in me. I needed to take a day to collect my thoughts. Plus, I still had some hope that once Adam calmed down, I might have a better shot at talking to him. Or I guess what I was really hoping for was a shot at having him actually listen to me when I *did* talk.

Despite my exhaustion, both mentally and physically, I threw on my running shoes and headed out to get some much-needed air. For the first time in a while, I just ran. I didn't think of anything. I let every thought that came into my mind escape with my next exhalation. I didn't even listen to music. I couldn't risk hearing a song that reminded me of either of the two men. These two men whom I had broken through my selfishness and my lies.

And I knew how they felt. My selfishness and lies had broken me, too.

I just let myself breathe. I listened to the trees brush their leaves together, and I felt my feet hit the pavement with a pace that forced me to keep moving even when I thought I didn't have it in me to take another step. I didn't depend on my mind to motivate me because I knew my mind would inevitably let me down. Instead, I relied on my legs to propel me, remembering my mom's inspirational words again: "Action comes before motivation."

*Just keep your legs moving, Lily. You'll have no choice but to follow them.*

♥

When I got to work the next day, I tried to give teaching my all, though I didn't really have it in me. I sat in the back of the room, feigning interest in student presentations on influential people. Most picked athletes or musicians. Some picked a coach they'd had. A few even picked a family member. But the only one that truly captivated me was Eva's presentation.

"The most influential person to me is my dad," she began as she displayed a picture on the screen of her and Adam at the beach. She looked to be about seven or eight when the picture was taken. She was in a purple bathing suit, her light-brown hair blowing in the wind as she tried to build a sandcastle. Adam was sitting beside her, the corners of his eyes crinkling with a smile. He wasn't looking at the camera; his attention was focused solely on Eva and the castle as he showed her how to dump the packed sand out of the bucket without having it crumble.

"He's an architect. I guess this is when he showed me how to make a home out of sand," she said with a nervous laugh.

Eva flashed some more pictures on the screen as she described why her dad had been so influential to her. I envied her ability to reveal these personal experiences with such strength as she talked about how Adam had raised her alone. He'd always gone to her basketball games, even if he had to leave work early. He helped her with her homework, and he took her sledding on snow days. Even at this young age, she appreciated how difficult that must have been for him.

"And here is when he tried to make cupcakes for my tenth birthday party," she said as she clicked to the next slide and displayed a picture she had clearly taken herself. It was angled up toward Adam. His counter was covered in cake mix, and he was licking pink icing from his fingers as he smiled.

The conclusion of the presentations required that the students choose a song that reminded them of their influential person. Eva chose the song "That is Why We Fight" by a band I had never heard of. I couldn't help but be amazed at the coincidence of the title. But as she passed out the lyrics and we listened to the music, I wondered why she had chosen a song about war and politics to represent her father.

"My dad loves this song," she said after it finished playing. "He says most things aren't really what they appear to be. You have to look deeper. Like songs, poems, stories. Even people. There is more to them than what's on the surface." She projected a few lyrics from the song on the screen. "Like these lines," she continued and then read them aloud.

*People quiet*
*Some are not so quiet, though*
*Some are silent*
*Some loud*

"He says there are three types of people. The quiet people represent those who don't really open themselves up. They stay hidden, and people don't really get to know who they are," she said as she flipped to her next note card. "Then there are outspoken ones. These people are themselves—take 'em or leave 'em." She looked up and made eye contact with me and some of her classmates, who seemed to be equally as impressed with her presentation.

"Then there is the third type: the type my dad tries to teach me to be. He says no one should really just be one extreme or the other with anything. Instead, you should try to take pieces of both. He's always reminding me not to complain about small things but also to speak up when I need to."

I sat mesmerized by the poise that a thirteen-year-old could possess when talking about such a mature topic. And something so close to her heart. It was in stark contrast to the emotional mess I had been lately.

"But the *title* is really my favorite part," she said, "because it's what really reminds me of my dad. He always fights to make things better. He fights for me. He fights for *everyone* he loves," she concluded as the class clapped. Eva closed out of her presentation on the computer and returned to her seat, completely unaware of the effect she had just had on me.

With that simple assignment, a thirteen-year-old had given me all the strength I needed at the time when I'd needed it the most. I knew I had to be a hundred percent honest with Adam, even though it would probably be one of the most difficult things I've ever had to do. I think that's where my fight comes from. Or anyone's fight, for that matter. It comes from knowing that what you're about to do is the right thing. And even though it isn't easy, you force yourself to do it anyway.

I guess sometimes it was good to have nothing. Then you knew you had nothing to lose.

*That is why we fight.*

# chapter thirty-eight

In the parking lot after school, I pulled Eva's parent contact form from my purse and plugged in Adam's address into my GPS. I didn't know what I planned to do once I got there, but I knew I had to go. It was finally *my* turn to fight. I spent the ten-minute drive to Adam's trying to regain my composure— and what was left of my dignity. I had no idea if Adam would even talk to me. I certainly didn't deserve a conversation. I had betrayed him, and I knew it.

As I pulled up to Adam's house, the reality of the fact that I had never been here before sank in. The two story brick home was modest, despite Adam's income. There were flowers planted recently in his front yard just in time for the start of spring. The driveway had a basketball net on the side. I could imagine him playing with Eva there on a summer evening. A few of the windows were up to let in the breeze, and the dark-red wooden door was left ajar. It had a welcoming charm to it, in spite of the fact that I might never actually be welcome inside. I couldn't help but think all that was missing was a white picket fence.

Parked outside, I decided to text him.

*I'm outside. I know you don't want to talk*

*to me. But if you don't come*
*out, I'm coming in.*

I felt confident in my assertiveness. Several minutes passed, and Adam finally emerged. I rolled down the passenger's window, and he leaned down reluctantly.

"What?" His tone was deliberately harsh.

"Please talk to me. I know I don't deserve it. But you do. I owe you an explanation."

He exhaled a sharp breath through his nose and shook his head, his eyes avoiding mine. "There's no explanation for what you did. You lied to me, Lily."

"I'm so sorry. I don't even know what to say to convey just how sorry I am." I swallowed a lump that had been building in my throat since I'd left work as I concentrated on blinking back tears.

"How about the truth," he sighed, finally bringing his gaze up to meet mine. "For once." It wasn't a demand. More of a plea, really.

He had asked me for the truth so many times, but until now, I hadn't been able to give it to him. "I can do that," I finally assured him, raising the corners of my mouth to force an apologetic smile as I unlocked the door. "Get in. We'll go for a ride. I know Eva's probably inside."

After some hesitation, Adam nodded. Then he went inside briefly to tell Eva he'd be right back.

The tension between us was palpable when Adam entered the car. In silence, we drove to the park at the end of the street, and I pulled into a space at the edge of the lot. I shut the ignition off after rolling down the window, desperately needing some fresh air.

"I'll tell you whatever you want to know." I knew I had to be direct. My only shot at reconciliation would be to tell him the complete truth. And even if Adam didn't take me back, he still deserved to hear it.

"Tell me everything. I wanna know all of it. Did he know about me the whole time we were together? Were you fucking both of us the entire time? When was the last time you were with him?" The words spilled from his lips rapidly and with no filter. "Why did you do this? Did you ever even *love* me?"

I just listened, letting him expel all of what he wanted to say before answering.

He finally turned to face me, and I closed my eyes before breathing in deeply. *Complete honesty, Lily. Remember, it's your only chance.* "I love you, Adam. That's the truth. But I told you I loved you before I actually meant it. I was scared I would lose you if I didn't." I couldn't avoid the tear that ran down my cheek, and I knew that even though I wiped it away, there would just be more to take its place. "That's what I'm most ashamed of."

I reached out to Adam's hand that was resting tensely against his thigh, but he pulled it away. The gesture was subtle enough not to seem harsh, but it stung just the same. And I felt the absence of his touch through my whole body.

"You shouldn't be crying." He said it unsympathetically and without concern for how it might make me feel. He said it because it was the truth. "I should be. I *have* been. Do you know how much you meant to me?" He rubbed his eyes with his fingers before answering his own question. "No, of course you don't. Because if you did... you wouldn't have been so fucking selfish."

I sniffled back the tears, forcing myself to find strength

where there was none.

"Why?" he asked, his glassy eyes begging silently for the truth. "What did he have that I couldn't give you? Tell me how this happened. Please, Lily."

I began with how we'd met in the airport—our immediate sexual attraction. I struggled to keep my voice steady as I told him of Atlantic City and how I had tried to say goodbye to Max, but I'd needed closure. Embarrassment coursed through me, and I felt my face redden with each indiscretion I revealed. My dinner with Max's parents and our night at the fundraiser seemed to hit Adam the hardest. And I knew why. I had felt something for Max.

And for the first time, I saw Adam actually cry. It wasn't a sobbing cry. He didn't even make a sound. He just turned away, and I saw a tear fall from his right eye through the reflection of the window.

"I'm sorry," I said because I didn't know what else I *could* say. "I love you. You have to believe me."

When he turned back to face me, there was an unmistakable emptiness in his eyes. I felt like I was a third party, viewing the scene from the outside. Like when you watch a movie and you already know the ending, but for some reason you still pray it'll turn it differently this time. "You've told me so many lies. I don't *have* to believe *anything* you say."

The tears flowed freely from me now as I begged this man to take me back. "Adam, please. Please don't do this. It was a mistake. *He* was a mistake. We're done, I promise. I just couldn't resist him." The last sentence fell from my mouth before I could censor it.

"Yeah," he said, taking my hand gently in his as he closed his eyes for a moment before continuing. "Well, now you don't have to." Then he let my hand drop from his. Without so much as another word, he got out of the car and closed the door gently behind him without turning around.

I watched him through blurred eyes stinging with tears until he vanished from sight. Adam Carter was gone.

Max once told me that sometimes in our quest to have everything, we sometimes find ourselves left with nothing. There was no truer statement in this moment. A few days ago, I'd woken up with everything. And now here I was, left with nothing.

And the worst part was it hadn't been taken from me. I had given it away. And in my path of destruction, I'd left two men who had truly cared for me with nothing too. I guess fighting for what you want isn't always enough. Sometimes you actually have to deserve it.

# chapter thirty-nine

I spent the weekend locked in my room, shifting back and forth between sleeping and crying. Amanda attempted to get me to open the door a few times, but I ignored her. I wasn't ready for someone to try to cheer me up. I hadn't suffered enough yet.

I knew that I had caused all of this. That was actually what hurt the most. I could deflect it onto Max all I wanted. But that wouldn't change the facts. I had lied. Deeply, thoroughly, repeatedly. I had gambled with my happiness, with Adam's trust, and with Max's hope. And I'd lost it all with the reckless abandon of a teenager. I had had so many opportunities to make things right. To take what chips were left and move forward from there. But I was too busy riding the wave to see that I was on a collision course. *God, I was really fucking stupid.*

Max had warned me, but I hadn't listened. Instead, I'd called him horrible and blamed him for my life's collapse. None of that had been fair. I could see now that while a part of me did love Max, a part of me had used him too. He'd satisfied a craving, a need I couldn't explain. I just wished I had realized this sooner, or at least before he had. I think that was the worst part about how things ended between us. He saw just how inconsequential he was in the grand scheme of my future. Max had always thought I'd been myself with him. I had thought so too. I guess we were both wrong.

But it was thoughts of Adam that elicited the deepest sobs. Max and I weren't innocents in this. We both knew the score. But Adam hadn't even known we were playing the game. He had given me so much of himself, and I had stomped all over it. I told myself that the things I did, I did to keep him. But all they really did was drive him away.

I remembered back to all of the times when I thought that I deserved better than Max or that I deserved less than Adam. And finally, I found myself face-to-face with what I really deserved. Nothing. Life wasn't meant to be lived by keeping score and tallying points. You get what you get. It's as simple as that.

So, by Sunday night, I had begun to deal with my fate. I'd started sorting through all of the errors I'd made, all the missteps, and all of the bullshit that had led me here. And as I unlocked my bedroom door and walked down the hallway to the living room, I realized that what I really needed was to grow the fuck up.

"Interested in takeout for dinner?" I asked Amanda, who had stationed herself on the couch in case I made an appearance.

"Sure," she replied, looking over at me as she sat up and made room for me next to her.

I sat down and pulled my knees up into my chest, resting my chin on them.

"What are you in the mood for?" she asked.

I thought for a moment. "Something different," I said, turning my head to look at her.

"I'm up for that." Her eyes stayed on mine, holding my gaze, letting me know that she understood.

And I really hoped that she did.

♥

Eventually my tears dried and I was able to get back to being myself. Not the *myself* of the past four months, but the real me. The one who had learned and grown from my experiences. I was now decidedly different than I was when this whole mess started.

Started.

That was a loaded term for me now. I had started so many things in the recent months, and for better or worse, I had seen them all through. But I don't think that gets me any congratulations or standing ovations. What I had started brought a lot of pain to people I cared about tremendously. There's no pride to be taken in that.

I'd started a relationship built on sex, need, and brutal honesty. The journey that relationship took me on was profound. I had been shaped more by Max Samson than by any other person on this earth. He'd taught me that it was okay to have desires and primal urges. It was okay to make your own rules, as long as you could bear the consequences. He'd taught me that it was okay to just be Lily. I would be forever thankful to him for that.

I'd also started down another path, laden with love, trust, and respect. I'd wanted so badly to be ready for all things Adam Carter. But I wasn't. I was so focused on my happily ever after that I didn't stop and look at the twisted paths I was taking in order to get to the castle. Or if I looked at them, I certainly didn't take them for what they were: a warning. I didn't need a prince to show me my way. I had needed a knight. It was the adventure that had shaped me, not the destination. There were lessons I had needed to learn, and Adam couldn't teach them to me.

But I was on firmer ground now, no longer treading on quicksand and waiting to be consumed by sadness. I had endured the journey. I had withstood the adventure. I had learned that perfect doesn't exist. That, in reality, you're lucky to just get pieces of it. And that's exactly what I had, though I didn't appreciate it at the time. Now, I knew better.

I didn't need a guide to show me the path anymore. I needed someone willing to stand beside me so we could discover it together. I was finally ready for my prince. But the bitch of it is, he doesn't want me anymore. And this was a destiny that I didn't know how to change.

After a few weeks, I started going back to the coffeehouse, a place where something magical had started. I hoped that I would see Adam there. This hope was what drew me back every morning for the rest of the school year. But I never saw him.

I hadn't seen Max either. He never returned to Swift after I had said goodbye to him at his house that day. He had told the school that a job offer had come in and he couldn't pass it up. He'd found a man to replace him as coach of the hockey team, a tough-as-nails older gentleman named Will. I heard Will had coached Max when he was young.

The rest of the school year passed without any drama. Teaching Eva was more than a little awkward, but I was her teacher, so I just had to deal. I threw myself back into teaching, putting my focus where it should be. When the last day arrived, I was actually sad to see my students go. We had been through a lot together, even though they didn't realize nearly how much.

So, with no prince and no knight, I decided that I should go on an adventure by myself. See if I could start my own journey toward happily ever after. With some financial help from my parents, I was spending my summer break overseas. I was going to troll around Europe and see if, for once, I could keep myself *out* of trouble. Which I should be able to do as long as I stayed away from France. There was something about a French accent coming out of a hot guy's mouth that I didn't think I'd be able to resist.

Now, as I sat in the airport bar, sipping on a tequila sunrise, I did the only thing I could do. Something that, at one point, I felt that I may never do again. I smiled. I smiled and remembered where I'd been. And hope to hell it no longer affects where I was going.

It had started on a plane. And now, hopefully, it would end on one, allowing me to start something new that was all my own. I was finally ready to fight for something I deserved: myself.

also in the

*love lessons series*

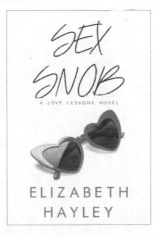

# also by
# elizabeth hayley

**Love Lessons:**
*Pieces of Perfect*
*Picking Up the Pieces*
*Perfectly Ever After*

❤

*Sex Snob*
(A Love Lessons Novel)

**Misadventures:**
*Misadventures with My Roommate*
*Misadventures with a Country Boy*
*Misadventures in a Threesome*
*Misadventures with a Twin*
*Misadventures with a Sexpert*

# acknowledgments

We need to first thank our husbands, who were entirely supportive during this whole process. You let us write, and write, and write. And text each other...a lot. You are both pieces of Max and Adam. You are our pieces of perfect.

To Amanda: Thank you for so eagerly reading our first draft. Over and over. And over. Thank you for using your "Wet-O-Meter" to evaluate all of the hot scenes, and for giving us encouragement and some well-deserved criticism. "Gall" is definitely a word.

To Trish: Thank you for reading our book cover to cover in one night—even the part that wasn't done and we told you not to read—because you couldn't put it down. If anyone is a master of reading this genre, it's you!

Most of all, we'd like to thank our readers! We hope you enjoyed reading this book as much as we've enjoyed writing it. And we hope you never go on a flight again without wishing for it to have a "happy ending."

Lastly, we'd like to thank each other! What started as a crazy idea has quickly turned into a reality, and we couldn't have done it without the other one pushing us to keep going.

To "Hayley": I can't believe we wrote a friggin' book!

There are no words to properly convey how thankful I am to have gone on this journey with you. I can't think of anyone else I'd rather have done it with. Here's to many more adventures together.

P.S. Is it bad that I keep looking at "done it with" and thinking that it's inappropriate? lol


To "Elizabeth": We actually did it! Thank you for looking at all of my "first drafts" a million times until they finally made sense. And thank you for always writing late at night so I could read about orgasms first thing in the morning. It made me want to get up each day! This has been so insane and so fun. I can't wait to keep writing with you!

P.S. No! My mind is perpetually in the gutter, especially now. That's what makes me think we found our calling.

# *about*

## e l i z a b e t h   h a y l e y

Elizabeth Hayley is actually "Elizabeth" and "Hayley," two friends who love reading romance novels to obsessive levels. This mutual love prompted them to put their English degrees to good use by penning their own. The product is *Pieces of Perfect*, their debut novel. They learned a ton about one another through the process, like how they clearly share a brain and have a persistent need to text each other constantly (much to their husbands' chagrin).

They live with their husbands and kids in a Philadelphia suburb. Thankfully, their children are still too young to read.

Visit them at AuthorElizabethHayley.com